Murder
on
Parade

A *Murder, She Wrote* MYSTERY

OTHER BOOKS IN THE *Murder, She Wrote* series

Manhattans & Murder
Rum & Razors
Brandy & Bullets
Martinis & Mayhem
A Deadly Judgment
A Palette for Murder
The Highland Fling Murders
Murder on the QE2
Murder in Moscow
A Little Yuletide Murder
Murder at the Powderhorn Ranch
Knock 'Em Dead
Gin & Daggers
Trick or Treachery
Blood on the Vine
Murder in a Minor Key
Provence—To Die For
You Bet Your Life
Majoring in Murder
Destination Murder
Dying to Retire
A Vote for Murder
The Maine Mutiny
Margaritas & Murder
A Question of Murder
Coffee, Tea, or Murder?
Three Strikes and You're Dead
Panning for Murder

Murder
on
Parade

A *Murder, She Wrote* MYSTERY

A NOVEL BY
JESSICA FLETCHER & DONALD BAIN

Based on the Universal television series created by
Peter S. Fischer, Richard Levinson & William Link

Doubleday Large Print
Home Library Edition

AN OBSIDIAN MYSTERY

This Large Print Edition, prepared especially for Doubleday Large Print Home Library, contains the complete, unabridged text of the original Publisher's Edition.

Obsidian
Published by New American Library, a division of
Penguin Group (USA) Inc., 375 Hudson Street, New York,
New York 10014, USA
Penguin Group (Canada), 90 Eglinton Avenue East, Suite
700, Toronto,
Ontario M4P 2Y3, Canada (a division of Pearson Penguin
Canada Inc.)
Penguin Books Ltd., 80 Strand, London WC2R 0RL,
England
Penguin Ireland, 25 St. Stephen's Green, Dublin 2,
Ireland (a division of Penguin Books Ltd.)
Penguin Group (Australia), 250 Camberwell Road,
Camberwell, Victoria 3124,
Australia (a division of Pearson Australia Group Pty. Ltd.)
Penguin Books India Pvt. Ltd., 11 Community Centre,
Panchsheel Park, New Delhi – 110 017, India
Penguin Group (NZ), 67 Apollo Drive, Rosedale,
North Shore 0632,
New Zealand (a division of Pearson New Zealand Ltd.)
Penguin Books (South Africa) (Pty.) Ltd., 24 Sturdee
Avenue, Rosebank, Johannesburg 2196, South Africa

Penguin Books Ltd., Registered Offices:
80 Strand, London WC2R 0RL, England

First published by Obsidian, an imprint of New American Library, a division of Penguin Group (USA) Inc.

ISBN: 978-0-7394-9213-0

Printed in the United States of America

PUBLISHER'S NOTE
This is a work of fiction. Names, characters, places, and incidents either are the product of the author's imagination or are used fictitiously, and any resemblance to actual persons, living or dead, business establishments, events, or locales is entirely coincidental.

The publisher does not have any control over and does not assume any responsibility for author or third-party Web sites or their content.

For Anne Mann and her wonderful Research Fund for Waldenström's (RFW). In concert with her husband, Dick Mann, over the years, she has elevated awareness levels in the medical community and raised more than a million dollars for research into and one day, we hope, a cure for Waldenström's macroglobulinemia, a rare type of blood cancer.

Chapter One

"By the Old Lord Harry, it seems to get hotter every day, and no relief in sight."

Seth Hazlitt wasn't exaggerating. A front had stalled just off the coast, trapping a flow of hot, humid air coming from the southwest and turning Cabot Cove into a sticky, steamy mess. The temperature had broken records for as far back as they'd been kept, and the forecast for the next several days was more of the same. You couldn't help but notice a discernible rise in tempers as people slowly moved through their days, perspiration dripping down their necks, eyes stinging from the polluted, stagnant, greenish air, seeking out any place that had a high-efficiency air conditioner. Fortunately, Mara's Luncheonette, where I sat with Seth and Sheriff Mort Metzger, had an AC that kept up with the heat.

I'd met them for breakfast that morning to discuss the upcoming Fourth of July weekend celebration. As a physician, Seth was concerned with the well-being of citizens who might overdo things in the heat. "Folks don't realize how heatstroke can sneak up on you," he said, motioning for Mara to refill his coffee cup. "Too many damn fools go runnin' around in this weather and before they know it, they're in the emergency room bein' treated."

Mort agreed. "The mayor's got us putting up notices around town warning people to take it easy until this heat wave breaks, but it doesn't look like it will until after the Fourth."

"I've heard people suggest we cancel some of the events," I offered.

"Hard to do that, Mrs. F," said Mort. "You know how folks around here feel about Independence Day. They take it real serious."

"Like the rest of the nation," I said, "and rightly so."

Mara brought a pot of coffee to the table and filled Mort's and Seth's cups. "More tea, Jessica?" she asked me.

"I don't have time," I said, "but thanks, anyway."

"What's your rush, Mrs. F?" Mort asked.

"Errands, and some correspondence to catch up on. I've been like everyone else these past few days, moving in slow motion."

"Best way to be," Seth advised.

"But not much gets done," I said.

I reached for my purse, but Seth waved me off. "My treat, Jessica," he said.

"Well, thank you, sir," I said, and prepared to leave. But Mort stopped me with, "Look who's here."

Coming through the door was Amos Tupper, Cabot Cove's former sheriff. After Amos retired, he moved to Kentucky to be near family. Mort, who'd been a police officer in New York City, replaced Amos and took up residence in Cabot Cove with his wife. I loved Amos, and still do, but I had to admit—not for public consumption, though—that the efficiency of our police department had improved since Mort arrived, bringing with him his New York street smarts. Cabot Cove had grown considerably, and with that growth had come a predictable increase in crime. Nothing major for the most part, thank goodness, but challenging enough to warrant a more—how shall I say it?—a more energetic approach to the job of keeping the town's citizens safe and happy.

"Hello, there, Amos," Seth said, struggling to get up from his chair, which was wedged against the wall.

"No need to get up for me," Amos said, coming to our table and shaking everyone's hand. He plopped down in the vacant seat next to me.

"We heard you were coming," said Seth. "Just wish you'd brought better weather with you."

"It is hot," Amos confirmed, wiping his brow with a handkerchief. "You must be breaking all sorts a' records."

"Ayuh," Seth said. "That we are."

"How are things with you, Mort?" Amos asked.

"Not bad, Amos. Got things pretty much

under control. Getting ready for the Fourth."

Amos ordered a short stack of Mara's signature blueberry pancakes and coffee. "I had trouble finding a place to stay," he said to no one in particular. "Looks like Cabot Cove's Fourth of July celebration is attracting more people than ever."

Seth, Mort, and I looked at each other.

Amos was right. While our annual Fourth of July weekend was always a major event in Cabot Cove, this year promised to be the biggest yet. But not everyone was pleased with that. Past celebrations had always been festive but manageable in size and scope. This year was decidedly different, thanks to Joseph Lennon and his corporation, Lennon-Diversified, Ltd.

Lennon had moved his corporate head-quarters from Massachusetts to Cabot Cove a year ago, wooed in part by a generous tax incentive designed to entice companies to relocate to Maine. He'd purchased the area's biggest building in our largest industrial park and expanded it to a size that had become a source of consternation for many citizens. The park itself was situated on a prime parcel of waterfront land. Originally, the property was to be turned into a multiuse area, with light industry and residential units coexisting side by side. But Lennon and his battery of lawyers managed to get the zoning law changed, allowing Lennon to conscript a large portion of the land directly on the water for his expansion plans. The rear of his building sloped down to the water's edge, where he added a promenade and dock for his employees' enjoyment. It was off-limits to others. Next to the building was a spacious grassy area that also went down to the water. Lennon designated it as a public park, which took the edge off his land grab at the rear of his building.

He hadn't created as many new jobs as had been expected. That was bad. On the other hand, he'd lowered the tax base. That was good. And he was a generous contributor to the town's various social and civic organizations, another plus for him and his company.

But there was a cost for his generosity. He'd injected himself into every aspect of our lives, using his clout as a major taxpayer, and his wealth, to influence countless decisions that otherwise would have been made by town leaders. Our Fourth of July celebration was a prime example of Lennon's looming presence and overbearing personality and tactics.

In previous years, we'd been perfectly content to have a small fireworks display, provided by a company in Bangor. Nothing special, but just right for a town the size of Cabot Cove. This year Lennon had persuaded our town leaders that we should set an example for the rest of Maine by presenting a pyrotechnics display to rival the famed New York and Washington spectaculars. Any arguments against it fell by the wayside when Lennon agreed to foot the bill and to make all the arrangements. He contacted Grucci, the world's most famous fireworks display company, and booked a twenty-five-minute show that cost seventy-five thousand dollars. Grucci had provided fireworks displays for many presidential inaugurations and for myriad Olympics. "Grucci is the best," Lennon announced in a press release after the deal had been made. "It's time Cabot Cove awoke from its slumber and joined the big time."

Lennon hadn't stopped with the elaborate fireworks display. Because he was the major tenant in the industrial park, he'd co-opted it for the Fourth as a site for a rock-and-roll concert to take place before the fireworks. And he'd used his influence with state officials to arrange for a flyover of F-16s from the Maine Air National Guard base. No doubt about it. The man thought big.

But Cabot Cove in "the big time"?

That didn't sit well with a number of people in town, although there was another contingent that welcomed this infusion of energy backed by big money. Seth Hazlitt was firmly in the camp taking the position that Cabot Cove should preserve its roots as a smaller community whose growth was steady and controlled. Mort seemed ambivalent, which reflected his position as the sheriff, who wasn't supposed to take sides in such debates. As for me, I accepted Mr. Lennon's right to spend his money any way he wished, as long as it wasn't used for negative purposes. What *did* bother me was a series of rumors about the man's personal life and business activities that were less than complimentary. But I kept in mind that they were, after all, just rumors.

"How's the family?" Mort asked Amos.

"Doin' well, Mort. I like it down there. Got a bunch of hobbies. It's nice to come back to Cabot Cove, though. Can't believe how much the town has grown." He waved to Barney Longshoot, who was sitting at the counter.

"Well," Seth said, "time for me to be going. I've got a full day of seein' patients."

After promising to catch up with Amos later in the day, Seth and I walked toward the door. We'd almost reached it when it opened and in walked Dr. Warren Boyle.

"Good morning, Doctor," Seth said as the handsome young physician stepped aside to allow us to leave.

"Good morning, Doc," Boyle said. "Mrs. Fletcher."

"Hello, Dr. Boyle."

"I think I lost a few pounds just walking over here," Boyle said, flashing a boyish grin. "I thought Maine wasn't supposed to ever get this hot."

"You shouldn't believe everything you read," Seth said, the edge to his voice telling me that he wasn't making small talk.

"Good advice, Doc," said Boyle. "You tell your patients that?"

"Most of them know it without me having to tell them. Have a good day, sir."

"You, too," Boyle replied. "Stay cool, Mrs. Fletcher."

Seth and I stepped outside into what felt like a sauna.

"Arrogant young fella, isn't he?" Seth muttered.

"More self-assured than arrogant," I suggested.

"All the same to me. Drive you someplace?"

"Home, if you don't mind."

Like many residents of Maine, I had never considered air-conditioning a necessity. Sure, there were bound to be some days during the summer that became uncomfortably hot, but strategically placed fans usually did the trick. We'd had an unusually warm summer a few years ago, though, which prompted me to purchase two window air conditioners for my home on Candlewood Lane, one for the kitchen, the other for my study, where I do my writing. I wouldn't have bothered had I not been a writer and someone who enjoys cooking. I function just fine in hot weather as long as what I'm doing doesn't involve thinking. But my kitchen and my writing room had become uncomfortable that summer, and I found myself focusing more on how hot I was than on the dishes I was creating or the words I was putting on the page.

As Seth drove up Main Street from the harbor, the air coming in the open windows of the car thickened. Away from the waterfront breezes, it gathered heat from the buildings and pavement and pressed down upon us like a flatiron. Seth switched on the air-conditioning and in tandem we closed our windows, eager to escape the blistering temperature. Cocooned in the cooling space, I thought about what had transpired at Mara's that morning.

It was good to see Amos Tupper again, and I was glad he would be in Cabot Cove through the Fourth of July weekend. He and Mort Metzger seemed to get along nicely, although there was bound to be some tension between them. I think Amos was envious of Mort's more modern approach to solving crimes, and Mort probably wished he was viewed as warmly as

Amos had always been. No matter. They were both good men, and I counted my friendship with them among my blessings.

The growth of Cabot Cove had taken many directions, including an influx of new physicians, some of them Maine natives looking to set up practice, others emigrating from larger cities in search of a less stressful lifestyle. It wasn't long ago that Cabot Cove's citizens had to travel to larger cities like Boston, Bangor, and New York when in need of a specialist. That certainly had changed. We now had a good representation of specialists in our area, and they were welcomed by everyone, including old-time doctors like Seth Hazlitt.

Dr. Warren Boyle's arrival was a little different. Besides relocating his company from Massachusetts to Cabot Cove, Joseph Lennon had also imported the young Dr. Boyle, and he made no secret that he'd financed the move. He'd spent a million dollars or more to set up Boyle's practice in a spacious wing of Lennon-Diversified's corporate headquarters, with a separate entrance and parking facility. I'd joined many who'd been invited to an open house at

Boyle's new facility, and couldn't help but be impressed with its sparkling exam rooms, the colorful art collection on the walls, nurses who looked as though they'd just stepped out of a photo shoot for a major fashion magazine, and the array of high-tech, state-of-the-art diagnostic equipment. Seth was with me on that visit. As we drove back into town, his silence spoke volumes.

"Quite a facility he has," I said on that day.

"Ayuh, that it is."

"He seems pleasant enough."

"He's got a nice way about him," Seth agreed.

"It must have cost a fortune for all that equipment," I said.

"Pocket change for Mr. Lennon," said Seth.

"But a worthwhile reason to spend some of his money," I said. "Supporting health care is always worthwhile."

Seth grunted and kept his eyes on the road. I knew when not to force conversation with my friend of so many years, and I dropped the subject.

*   *   *

It was obvious that Seth was not especially pleased that Dr. Boyle had set up shop in Cabot Cove, which surprised me. Seth himself had added a young physician to his practice, Dr. Jennifer Countryman—"Dr. Jenny" to their patients—and had discovered to his surprise that he was grateful to share some of the responsibilities and gain himself some well-deserved time off. He'd also been extremely welcoming to other new doctors who'd decided to practice in our area. He'd made himself available to show them around and to introduce them to our citizens, and had never uttered a negative word about any of them, at least not in my presence.

But Boyle's arrival was different. Maybe it was because of his link to Joseph Lennon and the elder man's bullying ways. Maybe it was because Boyle advertised his services on an almost daily basis in our local paper and in publications from nearby towns. He had flyers distributed throughout our business district. The headline on all his marketing materials read: 21ST-CENTURY MEDICINE COMES TO CABOT COVE. I suppose that by extension, one could take from the flyers and ads that he considered medicine as practiced prior to his arrival to be hopelessly old-fashioned and out-of-date. Obviously, that message didn't sit well with local physicians like Seth.

"Did you see his ad in the *Gazette*? You'd think he's set up a regular Mayo Clinic here in town." Seth had had little to say for the duration of the ride home from Mara's, but he'd obviously been brooding about Dr. Boyle. " 'Medicine for the Twenty-first Century' indeed! Makes it sound like we're still puttin' leeches on people to draw out the bad blood."

I laughed. "Aren't you?" I asked playfully. "It shouldn't affect you, though, Seth. The way Cabot Cove is growing, there'll never be a shortage of patients to keep every doctor in town busy."

He pulled up in front of my house, turned off the ignition, and faced me. "I'm not concerned about that, Jessica. It's time I cut down my schedule anyway. But I hate to see good people flocking to somebody like Dr. Boyle when they don't need to. Mrs. Carson informed me yesterday that she'll be seeing Boyle from now on for her bad back. The only thing she needs for that back is for her lazy husband to do some of the heavy lifting around the house. Of course, that didn't sit well with her. She says the good Dr. Boyle has scheduled a whole mess of scans to get to the bottom of her back problem. Imagine what that'll cost. Wasted money, I say."

"Well," I said, injecting lightness into my voice, "she'll probably be back in your office once she realizes that Dr. Boyle doesn't have the answer for her aches and pains." I patted his hand. "Thanks for the lift. Don't forget dinner at my house tonight."

"Wouldn't miss it, Jessica, not with lobster salad on the menu."

Seth turned his car around, and I waved as he drove away. I felt a certain sadness. Warren Boyle's arrival in town had obviously forced Seth to face the fact that he was aging and would one day have to take down the M.D. shingle that he displayed so proudly in front of his home. He was probably right in assuming that Boyle considered older physicians like himself to be medically behind the times, which certainly wasn't true in Seth's case. He was always off at some medical conference catching up on the latest research, and his library contained anything and everything new that was published in his field.

Oh, well, I thought as I pulled mail from my mailbox and carried it inside. The first piece I opened was a mailing from the Boyle Medical Center announcing that a dermatologist from Boston would soon be joining the practice, offering a full array of beauty treatments, including Botox injections and skin abrasion "for a lovelier you."

I sighed and tossed the mailing in a wastebasket. Yes, Cabot Cove was growing. No doubt about that. The question was whether everything connected with that growth was for the better.

I went into the bathroom and peered at myself in the mirror. Was I a candidate for Botox or skin abrasion? If so, I wasn't about to admit it. Not that I have anything against plastic surgery or other beauty treatments. If people feel better because they think they *look* better, good for them. For me at that moment, the face I'd arrived with on this earth was perfectly fine, thank you. But there *were* those lines around the eyes . . .

Chapter Two

I settled in to do what I'd planned to do, catch up on correspondence. Most of it was in the form of e-mails, which I find frustrating. After deleting dozens of unwanted messages from charlatans looking to sell something—or to inject a virus into my computer should I be foolish enough to open their attachments—I set about responding to legitimate messages. As a former English teacher, I admit to impatience with sloppy writing, and e-mails certainly encourage it. People dash off messages without having the opportunity to see what they've written on paper before sending it, and the mistakes in much of their writing testify to the problem with this. While I respond to e-mails with my own e-mails, I also try to send notes by "snail mail." Why? Because going to the mailbox, pulling out an envelope, opening it, and reading what's inside is infinitely more pleasurable than reading what comes up on a computer screen. At least it is for me and for a number of my friends.

After an hour of this, I closed the computer, made myself a light lunch, called Ron Silver, owner of Cabot Cove's biggest and best lobster pound, to tell him I'd be picking up my order in a few hours, and headed downtown to a series of meetings to which I'd committed. Because of the heat, I considered calling a taxi rather than riding my bicycle, but decided to brave the weather. By the time I reached the city hall, however, I wished I'd reconsidered. My blouse was stuck to my back, and my hair had collapsed in the humidity. After attempting to put myself back together in a ladies' room, I walked into Mayor Shevlin's conference room, where a committee comprising two dozen men and women had gathered to put the final touches on plans for our Independence Day festivities.

"Hello, Jessica," Kathy Copeland and her sister, Wilimena, said as I came through the double doors. Kathy and I had been Cabot Cove buddies for many years, but I really got to know her when we traveled together to Alaska. Wilimena, known to friends as Willie, had disappeared off a cruise ship there, and Kathy and I retraced Willie's steps in the hope of finding her. We were successful, but not until after a harrowing week. Willie had gone to Alaska in search of a stash of gold allegedly left her by a distant relative. She'd found it—and almost lost her life in the bargain.

Until that Alaskan adventure, Wilimena Copeland had defined the term "flighty." She'd been married multiple times, and had vanished for months on end when pursuing her latest paramour. To say that her near-death experience in Alaska had sobered her approach to life would be an understatement. She'd settled in Cabot Cove, used much of her gold money to refurbish our senior citizens' center, and was now a valued member of the community. Injuries suffered in Alaska had left her with a bad leg, and she used a cane most of the time. That Alaskan escapade had also had a profound impact on me; in fact, it became the basis of the plot in the last novel I'd written, *Panning for Murder*. As writers are fond of saying, "Everything gets used."

Our mayor, Jim Shevlin, called the meeting to order, and we took seats around the large conference table. After thanking everyone for coming out in the heat to attend, he turned the meeting over to Cynthia Welch, who held the title at Lennon-Diversified of vice president of strategic planning and marketing. "As you all know," our youthful mayor said, "Ms. Welch has been the point man—oops, point woman—for Mr. Lennon and his generous support of this year's celebration of the Fourth. I'm also sure you realize that we're in very capable hands. Cynthia, the floor is yours."

I judged Ms. Welch to be in her late thirties or early forties. She was strikingly beautiful by any definition, slender and statuesque with long, coal black hair that cascaded down her back, and a classically chiseled face that was a palette for expertly applied makeup. She wore diamond earrings, a pale yellow linen suit and white blouse, and heels so high I marveled that she could walk upright. I'd been introduced to her on a few occasions, and came away each time realizing that she was, indeed, a formidable woman. Any glass ceilings in her future were sure to be shattered.

"Thank you for being here," she said from a podium that had been wheeled in, "and for your hard work to make the weekend a success." A screen behind her promised an audiovisual presentation. "We're getting down to the wire now," she said, "and there are lots of loose ends to be tied up. The black binder in front of each of you is the battle plan we've come up with to—"

"Battle plan?" Chester Carlisle growled. "What the hell is that?"

Chester, a large, imposing, crusty seventy-three-year-old member of the town council, had been one of the few on the board who'd voiced his displeasure with Lennon-Diversified taking over our Fourth of July celebration. Chester seemed always to find something wrong with decisions made by the council. Seth Hazlitt was known in town as a bit of a curmudgeon—Cabot Cove's resident Andy

Rooney—but Chester made Seth look like a mild-mannered pussycat.

Cynthia smiled. "Just a term we use in business to choreograph major events, Mr. Carlisle. I'm sure you'll agree that this Fourth of July in Cabot Cove certainly ranks as one of them."

Chester started to argue the point, but a young man in a gray suit, who remained glued to Welch's side wherever she appeared, said sternly to Chester, "Please give Cynthia the courtesy of your quiet attention, sir!"

Chester grumbled something under his breath, but fell silent as Ms. Welch continued.

"The entire day and night are laid out in those binders, minute by minute," she said proudly. "In addition, I've prepared a Power-Point presentation that will give you a visual sense of how things will proceed—the downtown parade, the musical groups, the high school theatrical troupe with its reenactment of events of this special day many years ago, the rock concert, fireworks—all of it. Joe Lennon wants things to go off without a hitch, and since he's financing this entire event, I'm sure you all agree that we owe him that."

I glanced at Kathy, who raised her eyebrows. Ms. Welch's comment about Lennon-Diversified financing our Fourth of July weekend was heavy-handed at best, if not offensive. I looked around the room. Most people didn't seem to react the way Kathy and I had, although Jim Shevlin had an expression on his face that was a cross between boredom and resignation. I'd had a conversation with Jim soon after the council had voted to accept Lennon's offer to bankroll the holiday, and he'd expressed his reaction to the vote. "I'm not sure this is the way to go, Jessica," he told me. "It's as though Lennon and his people—and his money—want to take over Cabot Cove. Next thing you know, he'll be financing a move to impeach me and put himself in the mayor's office."

I had laughed and said, "If he did that, Jim, the town would be up in arms. Let's give Mr. Lennon the benefit of the doubt and take him for what he claims to be, a wealthy man who wants to contribute to his community."

That seemed to salve Jim's concerns.

But as the weeks went by, I wasn't sure that I believed what I'd told him anymore.

Now Ms. Welch forged ahead with her talk, augmented by an elaborate slide show that filled the screen with graphs, maps, and bulleted points, all accompanied by Lennon-Diversified's logo. When she wrapped it up twenty minutes later, she asked, "Any questions?"

"I've got one," Chester said. "What in hell are we having a rock-and-roll concert for? That's not the sort of music people around here enjoy."

"I'll answer that," said the young executive who'd quieted Chester the first time. "Mr. Lennon believes in bringing together all age groups in the community and feels that to just continue doing what was done before creates a chasm between young and old. It's no secret that too many talented young people leave Cabot Cove for more exciting venues. Mr. Lennon is committed to correcting this."

Chester, who didn't always hear well, turned to the person next to him and asked, "What'd he say?"

"He said that— It doesn't matter, Chester. I'll explain later."

Ms. Welch and her male colleague presented such a formidable presence that questions were few. There was one about how traffic would be handled; the reply was that Sheriff Metzger and his officers had everything under control, and traffic would move smoothly. Another question had to do with plans in the event it rained. That query was dismissed by Ms. Welch with a wave of her hand. "It won't rain," she said. "And if it does, procedures are spelled out in your battle plan." She checked her watch. "Thank you for coming today, and for your attention. Let's make this Fourth of July a day of national pride for all Cabot Cove citizens." With that, she walked out of the room, leaving her compatriot behind to pack up the audiovisual equipment.

"What do you think, Jessica?" Kathy asked me as people stood, milled about, and exchanged reactions to the meeting. When I didn't respond immediately, she said, "It's all so cold and impersonal, not like planning town events used to be."

I had to agree with her. While meetings of previous planning committees had been much more raucous, with lively disagreements occasionally spilling over into arguments, at least they had involved the participation of a large cross-section of the Cabot Cove populace. And no one was ever denied the opportunity to express his or her opinion. Suggestions may not have been accepted, or even warmly received, but they all had a fair airing.

"It's like something George Orwell might have written," said Wilimena. "Lennon sounds like the original Big Brother."

"I was thinking precisely the same thing," Kathy said.

"He's managed to take over the town, and no one seems interested in stopping him," Wilimena continued.

"Chester certainly would if he could," Kathy said.

I looked to where Chester was engaged in a heated discussion with Mayor Shevlin and other council members. While I agreed with Chester's response to the takeover of Cabot Cove's Independence Day by Joseph Lennon and his people, there was little that could be done about it at this late date, and I wished he would tone down his displeasure. There were those in town who felt Chester was "losing it," a stance with which I didn't agree. He was irascible and loud, and tended to swear too much for my taste. But he meant well and was passionate in his love for Cabot Cove and its traditions.

Chester Carlisle had been born and raised in Cabot Cove. He'd gone off to college in New Hampshire, but he returned to his birthplace immediately after graduating and took over the management of his family's auto parts dealership. He'd been involved in civic affairs for as long as I'd lived there and had once run for mayor, losing a close election to his competitor. He'd been encouraged to run again by friends and family, but his initial foray into politics had soured him on seeking elected office—at least temporarily. He'd been content to manage the business and volunteer for myriad town committees. Now a widower and retired, with his son in charge of the auto parts company, Chester was freer than ever to get more deeply involved in the town. The problem was that over the years Chester had become steadily more entrenched in his views, rarely allowing a dissenting opinion to sway him. Rumor had it that he'd also become a heavy drinker, which, if true, would only serve to fuel his naturally combative nature. But, as anyone who's ever lived in a small town knows, rumors often circulate even though they may have no basis in fact. I'd witnessed plenty of tantrums on the part of Chester Carlisle, but I couldn't say that he appeared inebriated at any time, at least not in my personal experience with him.

There were those who felt that Chester's presence on the town council had become detrimental. Others wondered why he'd been reelected the last time out. But Chester had his followers, too, who agreed with his view of things and liked having an irritant on the board. "No point in being a rubber stamp," Chester had said on many occasions.

"Oh, my goodness," Kathy said in response to Chester's rising voice.

He was now yelling at the mayor and his fellow council members: "I'm telling you, there isn't one of you with the backbone to tell Mr. Joseph Lennon and his accomplices to get lost, to butt the hell out of our business and let Cabot Cove be what it's always been, a damned decent town that doesn't need Lennon's money or anything else from him."

"Calm down, Chester," Jim Shevlin said, placing his hand on Chester's back and trying to steer him out of the room. I looked to where the executive from Lennon-Diversified had finished packing up and now stood alone in a corner, his attention focused on the scene playing out in front of him.

The mayor managed to get Chester halfway to the door, but the irate senior citizen spun away and approached the Lennon-Diversified man.

"What's your name?" Chester demanded.

"Dante."

"Dante what?"

"Why don't you go home, sir, and take a nap?" Dante said.

"Don't tell me what to do," Chester shouted. He was now only a few feet from the younger man, and his imposing physique caused Dante to take a few steps back. "And you tell that boss of yours, Mr. Joseph Lennon, that we don't need his money or his business here in Cabot Cove."

"What did you do, forget to take your

medicine this morning, old man?" Dante said, grabbing the overhead projector by its handle and moving in the direction of the door.

Chester lunged at him, but two men who'd gotten close grabbed his arms and kept him from physically attacking. "The whole damn bunch of you ought to be shot," Chester bellowed as he was led from the room.

"Poor Mr. Carlisle," said Wilimena. "I wonder if he *is* losing it."

"I don't think so," Kathy replied as the three of us left the delightfully air-conditioned building and stepped out into the baking sunshine. "He's always been emotional about things. I like that in a man. That's why I voted for him."

"He cares deeply," I offered, "but it would be better if he could rein in his emotions. So little gets accomplished by shouting."

We walked slowly to the corner— Wilimena's gimpy leg and the heat assured a leisurely pace.

"Where are you off to next?" Kathy asked me.

"Another meeting. I volunteered to work with the youngsters putting on the pageant."

I laughed. "They are so adorable, proudly dressed up to resemble our forefathers and speaking their historic words."

"Did you see the rock-and-roll band?" Willie asked.

"No," Kathy and I said. "Are they here already?"

"They sure are," Willie confirmed. "Lots of hair and strange clothes. I was down near the depot when their bus pulled in. They have enough electronic amplification to broadcast to the entire state of Maine."

"Where are they staying?" I asked.

"The Holiday Inn, I think," Wilimena said. "I'm heading home," she continued, and said good-bye to us, limping off.

"Can I drop you somewhere, Jessica?" Kathy asked.

"You know, I think you might. I left my bike parked back at the town hall, and after this next meeting I'm picking up live lobsters from Ron Silver. Carrying them home on the bike in this heat is guaranteed to steam them before I even get there."

"Where's your meeting?"

"The middle school."

"And how long will it go?"

"Should be over by four."

"I'll pick you up," Kathy said. "Don't worry if it runs late. I'll come in and watch."

None of our schools in Cabot Cove are air-conditioned. The middle school had been closed since the end of the school year in June, and the maintenance crews had gone to work to spruce things up for the upcoming year. Even with the windows wide open, it was stifling inside as I entered and went to the gymnasium. A rehearsal for the Independence Day pageant was under way, directed by Robin Stockdale, a drama teacher at the high school. She saw me arrive and came to where I'd taken a seat on the lower tier of the bleachers.

"Hi, Robin."

She plopped down next to me. "Got some patience to lend me?" she asked. "I'm about tapped out."

"Oh? Some of your little thespians forgetting their lines?"

"I wish that's all it was," she said, directing a stream of air at a wayward lock of hair that had limply fallen down over her forehead. "It's her."

I followed her gaze to where a young woman was talking with some of the young actors and actresses.

"Who is she?" I asked.

"Josie Lennon."

"The Lennon family."

"Yup. Joe Lennon's daughter. Twenty-four years old and a legend in her own mind."

I laughed. "Hard to achieve legendary status at twenty-four."

"Not if you have a daddy who tells you you're the best actress in the world."

"She's an actress? Professional?"

"So she says. Her father insisted that she codirect the pageant with me."

"When did that happen?"

"A few days ago. She showed up here, introduced herself, handed me a printed bio and a bunch of headshots, and said she had some way-out ideas about how to spice up the performance."

"And?"

"She doesn't have any ideas that make any sense, at least not as far as I'm concerned. She wants to have recorded rock music accompany the play. You know how Elsie Fricket usually accompanies the pageant on the piano. Well, Ms. Lennon decided that 'old-timey' music wasn't appropriate for

Independence Day. Rock is what was called for. Needless to say, Elsie left in a huff."

"That's—that's—"

"That's lots of things, Jessica, none of them making me happy. Heavy metal accompanying the words of Jefferson, Hancock, and Davis. Oh, boy! Come on, I'll introduce you. I told her you'd volunteered to help out and would be coming this afternoon."

"Nice meeting you," I said after Robin had made the introductions.

"Me, too," Josie said.

Her looks were unusual, not beautiful but attractive in the way women with unusual features are often attractive. "Exotic" might be a better word to describe her. I'd not met her mother, who was spending the summer at one of the Lennons' multiple homes, this one in British Columbia. But I had met her father on more than one occasion, and he looked nothing like her. She was no taller than five feet, two inches, and had a slender body, a dancer's body. She was blond, but my height advantage allowed me to see black roots testifying that it wasn't natural. Her facial features had a hint of what might have been Asian, or Arabic, ancestry, although I knew that her father was neither of those.

"I hear that you're helping Robin out with the production," I said.

"Trying to," she said, her tone indicating she wasn't especially pleased at the way it was going.

"Robin says you're an actress."

"That's right. In New York. I came home for the summer."

"Theater?"

"Uh-huh. I was in an Off-Broadway play last season."

"That's wonderful," I said. "Some of the best theater these days is being staged Off-Broadway. Do I know the play?"

"Probably not. I'm doing a one-woman show in New York next season."

"Oh? That's impressive."

She returned her attention to a young man who'd been reciting something when I arrived. "Let's try it again, Adam," Josie said. "And this time say it like you mean it."

The youngster cleared his throat. Sweat trickled down his cheek. I wasn't sure if it was the heat or his fear of Josie Lennon that caused him to perspire. He straightened his shoulders and said in his pre-puberty voice, "Thus may the Fourth of July, that glorious and ever memorable day, be celebrated through America, by the sons and daughters of freedom, from age to age till the time shall be no more."

"That was wonderful," Robin said.

"It's too flat," Josie countered. "That's why I want music playing behind him."

Robin's face tightened.

"Who wrote that?" I asked, more to change the subject than out of real curiosity.

"It was in a newspaper, the *Virginia Gazette*," Robin answered. "July 1777. We adapted it for our play."

"Let's try it again, this time with music," Josie Lennon said. A large boom box sat on a chair near her. She turned it on and adjusted the volume. It was the sort of music about which I know absolutely nothing, with whining guitars and a heavy backbeat from the drums. "Okay," she said to the young man, "try it again but with more feeling this time."

I stifled a smile and walked away with Robin.

"Can you believe it?" Robin said.

"Ah—well, it is *different*," I said.

"She's come in here and taken over, Jessica. I mean, really taken over. That one-woman show she mentioned? Her rich daddy is bankrolling it. At least that's what I hear. Paying for the theater, everything."

"She's fortunate to have a father with the wherewithal to help her launch an acting career. I know so many struggling actors and actresses in Manhattan who'll never have that sort of support."

"I'll say this, Jessica—I am fed up with Joseph Lennon and his taking over of our celebration. I wish he'd never come here."

"Too late," I said. "What's done is done. Maybe next year the council will make a different decision based upon what it learns from this experience. Now, what do you want me to do?"

I spent the better part of the next hour mopping my brow and working with a female student who was to act as the narrator for the pageant. She was a charming, energetic youngster who took her role very seriously. The problem was I kept looking over my shoulder to see if Josie Lennon would decide to inject herself into what we were doing. Fortunately she didn't, although the music from her CD player was consistently annoying. I considered asking her to turn it off, or at least to lower the volume. But I resisted the temptation and concentrated on my task of the moment. Before I knew it, it was a few minutes past four, and I saw Kathy Copeland sitting in the bleachers.

"Ready?" she asked after I'd complimented the young narrator on her performance and wished her well on the Fourth.

"Yes," I said. "Tell me your car is air-conditioned."

Kathy laughed.

Ron Silver's lobster pound was on the dock from which Cabot Cove's active fishing fleet, including a number of lobster fishermen, operated. Ron, a delightfully funny man, smiled as Kathy and I entered his facility. "Lobster on the menu tonight," he said in an approving voice. "How come I wasn't invited?"

"Well," I said, "you are now."

"Just kidding, Mrs. Fletcher," he said. "I've got them ready to go for you." He handed me the sack containing my lobsters and said, as he always did, "The thanks is in the bag."

I paid, and Kathy and I got in her car,

then swung by the city hall to pick up my bicycle, which fit nicely in her trunk, and drove to my house.

"I'd invite you in for tea," I said, "but I'm afraid I'm running late. I've got to get these lobsters steamed and cut up. I'm serving lobster salad tonight."

"Sounds yummy. I'm sorry Willie and I couldn't make it."

"Me, too, but I'll invite you again."

"Who's coming?"

"Seth Hazlitt, Jim and Susan Shevlin, and Tim and Ellen Purdy." Tim was Cabot Cove's resident historian, and his wife, Ellen, won the annual quilting bee prize every year, or so it seemed.

"Say hello for me," Kathy said as she helped me remove my bike from the trunk.

"I sure will. And thanks for the ride. I didn't look forward to pedaling home in this heat."

"Wonderful dinner, Jess," Ellen Purdy said as we left the table and moved to a screened porch at the rear of my house. Ordinarily, we would have had dessert in the living room, but it was too warm there. I'd hoped that with the AC units in the kitchen and study blowing full blast, enough cool air would make its way to the rest of the house, but it hadn't happened. As it turned out, a breeze had come up, sending somewhat refreshing air onto the porch, aided by a large floor fan I'd set up in a corner. I brought out the pecan pie I'd purchased at Charlene Sassi's bakery, along with plates, mugs, silverware, and a carafe filled with iced black coffee. There were no tea drinkers that night.

"Too bad you missed the dinner at Joe Lennon's house," Tim Purdy said to me.

"I was sorry to have missed it, too," I said. "I was in New York to see my agent and my publisher. You had a good time?"

"Very nice," Susan Shevlin replied. "He knows how to entertain."

"Quite a house he has," Ellen said, "although I could have done without his hunting trophies hanging on the wall."

"He goes to Africa every year big-game hunting," Tim filled in.

"Big-game slaughter," Ellen said.

There were nods all around.

"His wife was away?" I asked.

"She's always away somewhere," Tim said. "He had his vice president, Cynthia, there as the hostess in her absence, and her assistant, Dante. Impressive guy. Told me he was in the military—ordnance, I think—before he came to work for Lennon."

"What's ordnance?" Ellen asked.

"Arms, ammunition, artillery," her husband replied.

"Was his daughter, Josie, there, too?" I asked them.

"Yes," said Tim. "You know her?"

"I met her today. She's helping Robin Stockdale with the pageant."

"Have you met Lennon's son?" Jim Shevlin asked.

"No."

"Nice enough young man," Susan said. "He works with his father."

"He came off more like a servant than a son," Jim said. "The old man says jump, the son asks, 'How high?' "

Susan raised an eyebrow at her husband. "It wasn't that bad," she said.

"Made me uncomfortable," was Jim's response.

"What do you think of plans for the Independence Day weekend?" Tim asked.

"They're elaborate," I said.

"Puts us right up there with Washington and New York," Susan said.

"And Lititz, Pennsylvania," Tim said.

"Where?" It was a chorus.

"Lititz," Tim said. "They have a candle festival every Fourth, thousands of candles floated in water by the kids. They even choose a Candle Queen."

"Flagstaff, Arizona, has an interesting celebration," Jim said. "A three-day American Indian rodeo. Seems fitting considering they were here before us."

"Anybody know why our signatures are called our 'John Hancocks'?" Tim asked.

"Because he signed the Declaration of Independence," the mayor answered.

"More than that." Tim was in his element—history was his passion. "John Hancock's signature was big and ornate. You can't miss it on the document. By the way, he was the first to sign the Declaration of Independence."

"More pie?" I asked Seth, who'd been strangely quiet throughout dinner and ever since.

"No, thank you. I've had my fill."

"How are things in the medical biz, Doc?" Jim asked.

"Gettin' worse every day," was Seth's reply. "If the government has its way, we'll spend more time in medical school learning how to fill out forms than being taught how to cure people."

"Is it that awful?" Ellen asked.

"Ayuh, it certainly is."

"What do you think of the new physician, Dr. Boyle?"

Seth shrugged. "Maybe I will have just a dite more of that pie, Jessica," he said, his lack of response to the question speaking volumes.

Ellen cocked her head. "Molly Wynn says you refused to give her a prescription she wanted," she said, keeping the subject of medicine on the table. "She said she was switching to Dr. Boyle."

Tim frowned at his wife, but she ignored him. Everyone waited for Seth's reply.

"That she did," Seth said. "She came in after seeing one of those infernal TV commercials from a pharmaceutical company and told me she wanted to try the drug they were pushing. I told her she didn't need it. Got herself all in a huff and left the office. She's not the only one. I've got people comin' in all the time wanting me to prescribe some drug they've seen on TV, whether it's good for them or not. In some cases it'd even be dangerous for them to take it."

There was general agreement with what he'd said.

"What do you think of the scans Dr. Boyle is offering?" Ellen asked. "Tim and I are considering having them. He's offering a special this month."

"See what I mean?" Seth grumbled. "Either you or Tim have some symptoms requiring a scan?"

Tim and Ellen looked at each other.

"No," Tim said.

"The pie is especially good, Jessica," Seth said, ending the discussion and downing his final forkful.

"I'll tell Charlene Sassi you liked it."

The night concluded with a discussion of the meeting that had been held that afternoon, and Chester Carlisle's behavior at it.

"He's so volatile," our mayor said. "I thought he was going to physically attack that young exec from Lennon-Diversified."

"I've been telling Chester for years that he's got to curb his anger," Seth said. "Even suggested he see a shrink. He didn't take too kindly to that bit of medical advice."

Seth chortled. "Thought he might take a swing at me right there in the office."

After everyone had left and I'd restored order to the kitchen, I settled in my air-conditioned study and turned on the TV news. After a succession of national stories, the anchor team turned to local Maine coverage. At the end of a report about a heated debate in the state's legislature over a proposed bill, Joseph Lennon's face filled the screen. A team from the Bangor station had come to Cabot Cove to cover the upcoming Independence Day weekend, and the female reporter asked Lennon why he had chosen to turn what had always been a modest celebration into one rivaling those of big cities.

"I've put together a more ambitious celebration because Cabot Cove is now my home, and home to my corporation. This is the twenty-first century, and Cabot Cove should recognize and embrace that reality. We're going to be doing everything in a big way, and the Fourth of July fest is just the beginning."

"How have the town's old-timers responded to your efforts?" Lennon was asked.

"They love it!" he said, flashing a radiant smile. "Wouldn't you?"

The announcer's face filled the screen. "More coming up on the Red Sox road trip after these messages." The newscast gave way to commercials, and I turned off the set. As much as I embrace progress, provided it's achieved in an orderly and reasonable way, I did not agree with Lennon's characterization of what Cabot Cove had been and was, nor did his bravado proclamation please me. I couldn't help but think of that wonderful old tune written by someone I'd had the pleasure of meeting long ago, Sy Oliver, who'd created so many great arrangements for the big bands of Jimmie Lunceford and Tommy Dorsey. He'd written, "Tain't What You Do (It's the Way That You Do It)."

Not only an infectious tune, but a sage bit of advice from which Mr. Joseph Lennon could learn a thing or two.

Chapter Three

I awoke on Thursday morning with a hangover—not the alcoholic variety, but one from a sweaty, uncomfortable night's sleep. I've never enjoyed sleeping in air-conditioning and had resisted adding a third window unit for my bedroom. A portable fan, as well as an attic unit, drew in fresh, albeit warm, air from outside, but nothing did the trick in this heat wave. All the fans seemed to do was to circulate hot air around me as I tried to sleep.

The sun was creeping over the horizon when I got out of bed, put on the kettle for tea, and retrieved the local newspaper from the front steps, along with the *New York Times* and the *Boston Herald*.

The large front-page story in the *Cabot Cove Gazette* was, of course, the upcoming Fourth of July weekend (no major crimes had occurred the night before to preempt the space). The Fourth was on a Saturday, two days away. Joseph Lennon's picture was there—no surprise—along with a piece about how plans for the event were progressing smoothly. I studied Lennon's photograph closely. It was obviously a professional portrait, the lighting dramatic, his expression one of serious concern for all living things. The times that I'd met him, I hadn't taken particular notice of his eyes, but had been content with a more overall impression. He was a good-looking man with prominent cheekbones and a full head of heavily gelled black hair. He wasn't tall, probably five feet, seven or eight inches, but he carried himself taller. His tan was perpetual, undoubtedly the result of artificial means. I'd noticed in one of Dr. Boyle's mail pieces that he had established as part of his growing medical practice a tanning salon and massage therapy facility. I found it strange that a physician would promote tanning by machine, given all the negative things written about such procedures. Maybe he'd established the tanning salon to provide his benefactor, Joe Lennon, with easy access to a healthy-seeming, year-round glow.

Now I peered into his eyes. They were dark, bordering on black, and narrow. Mean eyes? I hated to make such a judgment on the basis of a photo in a newspaper, but it was the first thought that came to me.

I read the rest of the paper, pausing at a full-page advertisement run by Dr. Boyle in which he endorsed the scans Ellen Purdy had mentioned: a carotid artery scan, an abdominal aortic aneurysm scan, and a peripheral arterial disease scan. You could order them separately, but if you opted for all three, you saved twenty-five dollars. I had no idea whether such scans were beneficial or whether they would save lives. I had to assume they would. But it wasn't long ago that doctors and lawyers were prohibited from advertising their services by their sanctioning bodies, the American Medical Association and the American

Bar Association. Ads like this one were another example of things changing before our very eyes. Change for the better? Maybe. Maybe not.

After showering and dressing in loose-fitting clothing and sandals, I called Jim at Charles Department Store, a small but remarkable establishment that seemed to carry everything you could possibly want or need, as well as things you'd never thought of.

"Good morning, Jim. Jessica Fletcher."

"Good morning, Jessica. Managing to stay cool?"

"No, and that's why I'm calling. You don't happen to have in stock a small air conditioner that will cool my bedroom, do you?"

"Oh, Jessica, I wish I did. We're sold out. I do expect a shipment next week, but this heat wave will probably break by then."

"Let's hope so," I said. "But put one aside for me anyway. I might as well be ready for the next one."

"Shall do, Jessica. Have a great day."

I'd no sooner hung up than the phone rang.

"Morning, Mrs. F," Sheriff Metzger said. "Sleep well?"

"As a matter of fact, I didn't, Mort."

"Too hot, huh? I know just what you mean. Makes you sleepy in the day, and keeps you up all night."

"Exactly."

"You should get an AC for your bedroom. That's the most important place for AC. Got to have a good night's sleep."

"You'll get no argument from me. I just ordered one from Charles. What's up?"

"I thought you might enjoy seeing how fireworks are done. Joe Lennon has arranged a demonstration by the fellas from Grucci out at the industrial park."

"Sounds interesting. What time?"

"Eleven."

"I'm free until one. I'll be there."

After turning the air-conditioning unit in my study up full blast, I called a local cab company to arrange to be picked up at ten forty-five, then went back to work on an outline for my next murder mystery that was due the following week. Coming up with compelling outlines is like pulling teeth for me. Writing the entire book is so much easier than sketching out a plot. I'd been working on this particular outline for two weeks, and knew I had at least another week's work ahead of me. Maybe it was the blessed cool of the room, but this morning's efforts seemed to go smoother than on previous days. I glanced up at my bird clock. A gift from a friend, it featured different, authentic birdcalls sounding on the hour. The big hand was almost on the white-breasted nuthatch; time to get ready to leave, but the thought of vacating the comfortable room wasn't appealing. I mustered my courage and exited my house.

"Where to, Mrs. Fletcher?" Nick asked.

"The industrial park on the north."

"Going for the fireworks display?" Nick had been driving a taxi in Cabot Cove for at least ten years and seemed to know everything that was going on in town. His cousin Dimitri, who owned the cab company, now served as dispatcher for his growing business, rarely taking the wheel of one of his vehicles himself.

"Yes."

"I thought I might hang around myself and learn something," he said, "although with this heat wave, lots of people who ordinarily wouldn't be calling for a taxi are doing just that."

"I can imagine."

"I'll be fine just as long as I don't get caught up in a traffic jam and overheat," he said.

Yes, Cabot Cove certainly had grown. The notion of traffic jams was a fairly recent phenomenon, caused in part by industrial parks like the one in which Lennon-Diversified was located. A number of such parks had also sprung up outside of town, and many Cabot Covers had found employment at them, meaning a commute that, at times, caused congestion during our version of rush hour—nothing like what New York or Los Angeles experienced, but something to which we'd not yet grown accustomed.

Nick pulled into the industrial complex, where a large stage had been set up in front of Lennon-Diversified's impressive marble building. The stage was just as it had been depicted on Cynthia Welch's PowerPoint audiovisual presentation the previous day. What hadn't been on the screen was the beehive of activity going on around the stage. A bus had pulled up close to it, and young men were busy hauling out what appeared to be massive pieces of amplification equipment and toting them up onto the stage. It must be the band, I thought, as Nick maneuvered to where a group of perhaps thirty people stood.

"This is fine," I said.

I signed the chit—I have an account with the taxi company and am billed monthly—and got out. Nick laughed. "Sure you don't just want to go home, Mrs. Fletcher, and stay cool? Must be fifteen degrees hotter here in the park. It's all the asphalt. It retains the heat."

"No, as long as I'm here I might as well stay. Thanks, Nick."

"Pick you up?"

"I'm sure I'll get a lift from someone. Are you staying?"

If he was considering it, his ringing cell phone changed his mind. "Got to go," he said. "Mrs. Kalisch needs a ride out here to Dr. Boyle's office."

Dr. Boyle, I thought, and Seth Hazlitt immediately came to mind.

Agnes Kalisch had been a patient of Seth's for as long as I'd known her. Had he sent her to Dr. Boyle for a second opinion or for some sort of specialized testing? As far as I knew, Boyle was a general practitioner like Seth—a primary-care physician, in today's parlance. Was Seth's practice about to go the way of small businesses in towns and cities across America, falling victim to large discount chain stores and fancy new approaches to doing business—or practicing medicine? I hoped not.

"Hey, Mrs. F," Mort Metzger called. Kathy Copeland was with him, and they came to where Nick had dropped me off.

"Hot enough for you?" Mort asked, removing his Stetson and wiping his brow with a handkerchief.

"More than hot enough," I replied. I asked Kathy where her sister, Willie, was.

"Smarter than I am," she responded. "She says she's staying in the condo for the duration of the heat wave."

"She'll miss the fireworks and the concert," Mort said.

"I don't think she meant it," said Kathy. "You know Willie, always overstating things."

We joined the rest of the crowd that had gathered in front of the stage. Mort had assigned uniformed officers to various positions for crowd control, although the heat had obviously dampened the spirits of many who would otherwise have shown up. There wasn't much of a crowd to control.

"When is it going to start?" Kathy asked. "I'm wilting."

"Seems it's about to," Mort said. "Excuse me. Looks like somebody passed out over there."

He was right. A woman was prone on the ground, surrounded by concerned onlookers. Someone had had the foresight to arrange for an ambulance to be on hand, and its EMTs immediately went to work reviving the woman. Kathy and I watched as Mort took charge of the situation, but our attention was soon drawn back to the stage. Joseph Lennon had just come out of his building and now stood at a microphone. He was dressed immaculately in a tan suit, blue shirt, and green tie. What I especially noticed was that he seemed as cool as though it were an early fall day. There didn't seem to be a drop of perspiration on him, and I thought of the character, played by E. G. Marshall in that wonderful film *Twelve Angry Men*, who never perspired in a sweltering jury room, even when tempers heated up.

"It looks like we've got a bunch of brave souls here this morning," he said, adding a laugh. "Never say that Cabot Covers are weak." Another well-placed laugh, just long enough to make its point. "Actually, this demonstration was a last-minute decision I made. I thought that as long as the famous Gruccis were going to be here showing off their spectacular fireworks, you might enjoy seeing how they do it— although I'm sure they won't share *all* their secrets."

Two young men in jeans and T-shirts carrying a variety of items joined Lennon on the stage. Immediately following them was a middle-aged man wearing a shirt on which GRUCCI was emblazoned.

"It's hot," Lennon said, "so I won't take any more of your time. "My son, Paul, whom many of you know, will take over from here. Let me finish by saying that this Fourth of July in Cabot Cove will make the nation sit up and take notice." He turned as a young man in a three-piece suit whom I assumed was his son came out of the building and walked to the microphone. His father never looked at him; he simply left the stage and disappeared.

Paul Lennon spoke into the microphone. "You heard what Joe said, so we'll get right to it." He beckoned the oldest of the three men from Grucci to join him, and played the role of a talk show host, asking questions he read from a clipboard. He started by asking about the history of fireworks.

"Well, actually they go back to the second century BC, in China," the man replied. "They were originally used in religious celebrations, but were eventually adopted by the military for warfare in the Middle Ages. They called them 'flaming arrows.' Around the tenth century, the Arabs came up with gunpowder, which spawned the invention of cannons and guns. But rockets were also used to deliver explosive charges against enemies. Every time we sing 'The Star-Spangled Banner' and the famous line 'and the rockets' red glare,' we're singing about rocket warfare."

"How do fireworks work?" Paul Lennon read from the paper on the clipboard and wiped his brow with a white handkerchief.

"It's pretty complicated," the Grucci representative said. "I'll be taking you over to our launch area to show you how things are constructed and carried out. Let me just say that the shells have more than one chamber, each one separated from the others by cardboard disks and ignited by timed fuses. Packed into each chamber are the effects we want to achieve from each rocket—stars, streamers, special effects like whistles and loud explosions. Each shell has to burst open with a lot of force once it reaches its desired altitude. The longer the cardboard shells resist the explosion, the bigger the display will be."

He went on in response to Paul's questions. Much of what he said was highly technical and, frankly, uninteresting. Someone from the audience shouted a question: "How high do fireworks go?"

"Good question," said the Grucci rep. "Ten-inch and twelve-inch shells can go up to as high as thirteen hundred feet. They're the ones whose displays are pretty much symmetrical. Eight-inch shells are really popular because they produce patterns in the sky, like butterflies, five-pointed stars, and the like. Five- and six-inch shells get up to about six hundred feet. Those displays in the finale that are loud and colorful are generally made from three- and four-inch shells. Adding some titanium to the mix produces those brilliant white flashes that bring about all the 'oohs' and 'aahs.'"

After a few more questions from people

in the audience—the number had thinned considerably, and only sheer determination kept me from bolting—we were led to where the experts from Grucci would launch their fireworks display as the culmination of Saturday's celebration. Ms. Welch's assistant, Dante, was there, talking to one of the crew. Paul had disappeared, probably desperate to get out of the heat.

I'd had no idea that it took so many people to put on such an event. There must have been a dozen people from Grucci working steadily to get things ready, including large trays filled with sand into which steel pipes were sunk.

"This is where it all happens," our guide said. "The shells are placed in these steel casings and are attached to wires that provide electrical connections to fire a lift charge that sends the shells up into the air. That charge also lights a time fuse at the base of the shells that controls when during its flight it will explode."

He ended his talk with, "I want you all to know that our most important priority is safety, for our own people and for the residents of wherever it is we're putting on shows. We've worked closely with every government agency in Cabot Cove and the state of Maine to make sure that everything goes off without a hitch. I see Sheriff Metzger is here, and I want to personally thank him for his cooperation and that of his fine police force. And let me not forget Cabot Cove's excellent fire department. It's been a joy to work with them, and everything is right on schedule for a great show Saturday night. Our thanks to Joseph Lennon of Lennon-Diversified, and his very knowledgeable staff. Now, go home and cool off."

A wonderful suggestion, I thought.

"Need a ride home?" Kathy asked.

"If you don't mind."

"I've got to get out of this heat. It's killing me."

We were walking to her car when a commotion caught our attention. A group of four people were approaching the stage carrying crude homemade signs protesting the fireworks display.

"Oh, my," I said when I saw that the small contingent was led by Chester Carlisle.

Mort Metzger left where he'd been conferring with the two EMTs and stopped

Chester and his friends. The woman who'd passed out now sat on the ambulance's gurney and appeared to have recovered, aided by bags of ice pressed to her forehead and neck. Kathy and I turned to watch the sheriff.

"Now, just what in the devil do you think you're doing, Chester?" Mort asked.

"Protesting this fiasco," Chester said.

"Why would you want to protest something positive like a fireworks display on the Fourth of July?" Mort asked.

"I'm not against fireworks," said Chester, "but I am against one man taking over the town and calling all the shots."

"Mr. Lennon is being generous, that's all," Mort answered. "Let's not stir up trouble, Chester. The town's excited about this Fourth and doesn't need you throwing a wet blanket over it."

"The Fourth of July celebrates our freedoms," a woman with Chester said, "including freedom of speech." I didn't know her name, but I had seen her around town now and then, in the supermarket or at Weinstein's Pharmacy.

"That may be true," said Mort, "but it doesn't mean you can disrupt things. Now, why don't you good folks go on home with those signs and just enjoy the weekend that's coming up." He gestured to Kathy and me. "Like Mrs. Fletcher and Ms. Copeland are doing."

Chester said to me, "I've heard you talk about how you like Cabot Cove's small-town character, Jessica. The town's growing too damn fast, and that's a fact. People like Lennon and all his money are ruining it."

"That's up for debate, Chester," I said. "I do like Cabot Cove's atmosphere. That's why I choose to live here. And I'm not pleased with some of the growth that's taken place. But it's the sort of thing that's best considered in a structured forum, not out here in this—in this—in this dreadful heat." I smiled. "Mort is right," I said. "Let's just enjoy the upcoming weekend and take a look at the town's growth once it's over."

"She makes sense," Mort told Chester.

Chester looked to where the young "roadies" were setting up their equipment onstage under an immense canvas top. "Bunch a' hippies," he growled. "We don't need their kind comin' in here and causin' trouble."

Mort turned to look at the activity on the

stage. "Doesn't seem to me that they're making any trouble. Just because their hair is long and—"

Chester cut him off. "We'll leave, Sheriff," he said, "but you mark my words. Before this weekend is over, you'll have your hands full—and a full jail." He and his friends turned and walked away.

"I worry about the man," Mort told us. "He gets more irrational every day."

Kathy and I didn't reply.

"You okay, Ms. Copeland? You look a bit flushed."

"I'm just hot, Sheriff. I'll be fine as soon as I get in my air-conditioned car."

"Well, I'd better be going, then," Mort said, touching the brim of his Stetson. "You ladies have a good day."

I took a few steps in the direction of the parking lot, but Kathy stopped me with, "Wait a minute, Jessica. I really don't feel well. I'm a bit dizzy."

I came back to her and saw that her face had reddened, and sweat ran down her cheeks. "It's this heat," I said. "Come on. Let's go into the Lennon building. It'll be cool in there."

We climbed a short set of wooden steps

to the stage, crossed it, and walked through the doors into the building, where a blast of frigid air hit us, causing us both to let out sighs of relief and pleasure.

"Heavenly," I said. "Feeling better?"

"Instantly," Kathy said. "I thought I was going to faint out there."

I took in the vast lobby with its gleaming marble floors and walls. It was an atrium, with a stained-glass window high above creating a crazy-quilt pattern of multicolored lights on the white floor. At the far end was a long marble desk, behind which sat a woman. I could see her blond hair but not her face. I thought about going over and starting a conversation, but I never had the chance.

"Something I can do for you?" a gruff male voice asked us. It belonged to a gentleman in a gray uniform. A patch on his chest read, SECURITY: LENNON-DIVERSIFIED.

"Yes, thank you," I said. "My friend was feeling faint from the heat and we came in to get cool. Is there some place to sit for a minute?"

"No, ma'am. And unless you have official business, you'll have to leave."

Official business? I thought. You'd think

we'd wandered into a top-security government facility.

"It sounds like we're in the Pentagon," Kathy said, echoing my thought.

"Really, sir," I said. "You can't grant us a minute to cool down?"

"Afraid not," said the guard, indicating the doors leading outside.

"It's all right, Jessica," Kathy said, tugging on my arm. "I don't want to stay."

I nodded at the guard and wished him a pleasant day.

As we crossed the marble floor, I looked to a far wall and saw two sturdy closed doors beneath a large red sign: NO ENTRY—SECURED AREA.

"What's behind those doors?" I asked.

"Have a good day, ladies," was his only response.

At that moment, the doors flew open, banging back against the marble walls. Joseph Lennon came striding out, Cynthia Welch close on his heels. "Joe, you promised me. You can't renege now, not after all I've done for Lennon-Diversified, for you. I've put fifteen years into this company, turned down other opportunities."

"I told you I have no choice in the matter."

"Of course you have a choice. It's your company, isn't it?"

"Cynthia, you're a lovely lady, but—"

"Don't patronize me, Joe. I'm not one of the little chippies you keep to amuse yourself. We're far beyond that, you and I."

"Cynthia, this is a corporate matter. I have a board to report to."

"You handpicked everyone on that board. Make them listen to you. Make them— It's her, isn't it? She's muscling me out."

"She has nothing to do with this."

"You're lying. I can always tell when you're lying."

Paul Lennon ran after the pair. "Hey, I'm part of this conversation. I have a say in this, too. I've been working my butt off for you."

Lennon whirled on his son. "You have no say, do you understand? None whatsoever. Your opinion is worth nothing. You've bungled three deals in the last six months. You're an embarrassment. You have no talent, no brains, not even common sense. I can't afford your incompetence."

Paul seemed to shrink into his body. "Then why—"

"Shut up!" Lennon had caught sight of

Kathy and me. Even from the far side of the hall, I could see him smooth out the tension in his face and put on a polished smile. He waved Cynthia and Paul away, saying, "Get out of here. We'll deal with this later," and walked toward us.

"Ladies, is there something I can help you with? Roger? What is going on here?" Lennon's eyes hardened as they fell on the security guard.

"I was just escorting them out, Mr. Lennon."

"And why were they here?"

I spoke up. "Hello, Mr. Lennon. We just came in to cool off. My friend Kathy here was feeling faint, and we took advantage of your lovely lobby to escape from the heat."

"It's Mrs. Fletcher, isn't it? I believe we've met before."

"Yes. This is my friend Kathy Copeland."

"Ms. Copeland, are you feeling better now?"

I knew he was trying to be gracious, but he couldn't quite control the edge in his voice.

"Much better, thank you. Your . . .

um . . . Roger was just . . . um." She threw a quick smile at the guard.

"I'm so glad to hear he was helpful."

"Yes," Kathy said.

"We were just on our way out," I said, taking Kathy's arm. "Thank you, Roger. No need to walk us out, Mr. Lennon."

But he put a hand on my elbow and guided Kathy and me to the door. Roger trailed behind him, nervously gnawing on his thumb. Kathy and I stepped out onto the stage, momentarily blinded by the harsh sun.

"Not a very friendly way to run a business, is it?" Kathy said to me as the door closed with a whoosh.

"Not at all."

"That was some fight. I wonder what it was about. Ms. Welch is always so calm and collected. I thought she was going to go for his throat."

"They obviously didn't see us," I said absently. "What was it again that Lennon-Diversified produces?"

"I have no idea."

"I read about the company when it moved to Cabot Cove, but I can't quite remember. Something to do with investing in companies—biomedical research, perhaps. Was it pharmaceuticals? I'll have to look it up when I get home."

"Whatever it is," Kathy said, "it's not customer-friendly. What's so secret that we couldn't stand in the lobby to cool off?"

"I suppose Roger was just doing his job," I said. "Sometimes a little power goes to a person's head. How are you feeling?"

"Much better. Come on, let's go before I feel faint again."

We got in Kathy's car, and as we started to pull out of the parking lot I looked back at what was happening on the stage. The technicians from Grucci had left, but the young men with the band were busy stringing cables and securing huge speakers on stands. The air-conditioning in the car hadn't started to work yet, but I felt a sudden chill. What was intended to be a joyous celebration of our nation's freedom—and that day in 1776 in Philadelphia when members of the Second Continental Congress adopted the final draft of the Declaration of Independence—had suddenly become for me an ominous occasion. Previous Fourth of July celebrations in Cabot Cove had been spirited, yet carefree days,

filled with a sense of patriotism and grati-
tude for having been born in our wonderful
country. That feeling would always be present, of course. Nothing could ever take it
away. But something was distinctly different this year. Maybe it was the scope of
the celebration that tainted it. Maybe Chester's protest had taken away some of the
joy of anticipation. Maybe seeing the true
colors of Joseph Lennon emerge had done
it. I didn't know what it was, couldn't pin-
point it at that moment as Kathy drove me
home, but I felt it nonetheless.

And I didn't like it one bit.

Chapter Four

"Jessica Fletcher?"

"Yes."

"I hope you'll remember me. Rick All-cott? Washington, D.C.?"

"Of course I remember you, Special Agent Allcott," I said.

I'd met him while in Washington two years earlier. I was there to attend a series of lectures given by the Federal Bureau of Investigation on new forensic and investigative techniques that the bureau had developed. The series had been mounted as part of a continuing campaign to encourage writers of murder mysteries and thrillers to present the FBI in a favorable light, highlighting the advances it had made in the use of technology to solve crimes. Special Agent Allcott had helped host the confab for the twenty writers in attendance, and we'd struck up a long and pleasant conversation at a reception at the conclusion of the program.

"*Former* special agent," he said with a laugh. "Now happily retired."

I, too, laughed. "You looked far too young to be nearing retirement age," I said. "I'm delighted to hear from you. Are you still living in Washington?"

"The Eastern Shore. More peaceful there. But I'm calling from Cabot Cove."

"You are? What brings you here?"

"Well, let's see. You might remember from our conversations that I'm a baseball fan. No, make that fanatic."

"I do recall that, and if I remember correctly, you were determined to attend a game at every major-league stadium in the country."

"Right you are. I haven't achieved that yet, but I'm working on it. I just left Boston. Saw a terrific game yesterday. What a

great stadium Fenway Park is. A real throw-
back to another era. Anyway, you had told
me about your idyllic Cabot Cove and the
wonderful Fourth of July celebrations you
enjoy, so I figured that as long as I was in
New England, I'd stop by and see for myself."

"That's splendid," I said. "You'll be here
through the weekend?"

"Right. It wasn't easy finding a place to
stay, but I managed. Nice little bed-and-
breakfast a few miles outside of town. Blueberry Hill. You know it?"

"Yes, I do. The owners, Craig and Jill
Thomas, are friends. Lovely people."

"They certainly are. I have a terrific room
overlooking a stream at the rear of the property, and I've already put my name on one
of the rocking chairs on the porch. Charming, absolutely charming."

"Well, welcome to Cabot Cove," I said.
"I'd love to catch up with you in person."

"I insist upon it. Free for lunch?"

"Afraid not. Actually, I don't know where
I'll find time to eat at all today. I have a one
o'clock doctor's appointment and a series
of meetings and errands right after that."

"Maybe dinner, then?"

"Hmmm. Yes, that would be nice."

"Bring along any of your friends. Love to meet them."

"I may just do that."

"You'll have to recommend a place."

"Of course. How about Peppino's? It's right in the middle of town, the old railroad depot building. It has very good Italian food."

"Sounds fine with me. Time?"

"Six?"

"See you there."

It was good to hear from Richard All-cott out of the blue. I'd taken a liking to him while in Washington. A short, slim man with large horn-rimmed glasses, he had a gentle manner and an easy, sincere laugh. His wardrobe matched his low-key personality—gray or tan corduroy jackets, blue button-down shirts, muted ties, and loafers, which didn't match up with the stereotypical impression too many people have of federal law enforcement agents. Perhaps his assignment with the bureau didn't call for a more macho appearance. He'd spent most of his FBI career, he'd told me, pursuing white-collar criminals, fraud, embezzlement, violations of the postal code, and other nonviolent crimes. Whatever his law enforcement experience was, however, I'd found him to be a thoroughly likable, charming man. I hadn't noticed a wedding ring, which didn't mean he wasn't married. Was he traveling with a wife, or did his love of baseball and baseball stadiums preclude her accompanying him on his jaunts to different cities? I called my friend Joe DiScala, who owns Peppino's along with his son, Joe Jr., and reserved a prime table for four at six that evening. Might as well have extra seating in the event his wife was with him, and in case any of my Cabot Cove chums would enjoy meeting him.

I stepped out onto my rear porch to determine whether it felt as hot as my outdoor thermometer read: 96 degrees. *More like a hundred and ninety-six*, I thought as I retreated back into the house and puttered around the cool kitchen. I had a one o'clock appointment to see Seth Hazlitt, not a friendly visit but a medical one. I'd developed a sinus infection that he'd been treating. It was virtually gone, but he wanted a follow-up examination to be certain I didn't need another round of antibiotics. Call a taxi, or ride my bike? I decided I couldn't constantly succumb to the heat, so opted to ride my trusty bicycle to Seth's office at his house, a short trip but long enough to generate plenty of perspiration that pasted my shirt to my body and ran down into my eyes, stinging them.

"You look as though you just stepped out of a sauna," Seth's nurse, Harriet, said as I came through the door.

"It's hotter out there than a sauna," I replied. "Ah, the air in here feels wonderful." I plucked the front of my blouse.

"What did we ever do without AC?"

"I remember when there was no air-conditioning," I said, going to a mirror and trying to rearrange my limp hair into something vaguely resembling respectable style. "I used to go to the movies as a child when the theaters bragged about their 'air-cooled' system, nothing more than a fan blowing over blocks of ice. But it did feel good."

Harriet laughed and said, "Imagine what places like Miami and Houston would be like without air-conditioning. They certainly

wouldn't be the thriving cities they are today, that's for sure."

"Is he running late?" I asked. Seth always
tries not to keep patients waiting, but
sometimes it's unavoidable.

"No, he should be free in a few minutes."
She lowered her voice. "You know Doc as
well as anyone, Mrs. Fletcher—better than
most."

"We do go back a ways."

"Have you noticed anything strange
about him lately?"

"Strange? How so?"

"Oh, I don't know, he seems—he seems
sad these days, withdrawn."

I nodded. "Yes, I have observed that,
Harriet. It's probably nothing. Maybe the
heat. It makes everyone cranky."

Her expression said she didn't buy what
I'd said, and knew furthermore that I didn't
mean it. I smiled. "He isn't his old self," I
agreed.

"I worry about him," she said.

Harriet had been Seth's nurse for at
least thirty years. She ran the office with
all the precision of a Prussian officer, sometimes to Seth's chagrin when she chastised

him for his lack of external organization. Though he wasn't the most orderly of men, he possessed an internal sense of order that served him well enough. He needed someone like Harriet, and her impending retirement might well be contributing to his recent bouts of melancholy. She'd been encouraging him to start the process of hiring her replacement, but he'd dragged his feet, probably because he didn't want to face the reality of her leaving. Call it denial.

"We all worry about Seth," I said, taking a chair next to her desk.

She spoke even more softly now. "Dr. Jenny says she thinks he's concerned about losing some of his patients. And I think she's worried about that herself."

My eyebrows went up. "Has that been happening very much?" I asked.

She nodded, her expression serious. "Too much," she said for emphasis. "It's like people who've been patients for years have suddenly decided he's too—how shall I say it, Jessica?—that he's too old-fashioned, out of touch with what's new in medicine."

I came forward in my chair. "That's simply not true," I said. "Seth keeps up with medical advances as well as any other physician."

"You and I know that, Mrs. Fletcher, but try telling it to someone who's made up his or her mind. Patients can be so stubborn."

Doctors, too, I thought, *including Seth Hazlitt*. His stubbornness came to the fore more in his personal life than in his medical practice. But he could be hardheaded, too, at times, when challenged by a patient who was more interested in talking than listening.

"Like Mrs. Kalisch," Harriet continued, obviously eager to vent her feelings to someone with whom she felt comfortable. "She's been a patient of Dr. Hazlitt's for years. He's treated her entire family. She arrived for an appointment the other day and informed him that she was going to switch to Dr. Boyle out at the industrial park, and wanted us to transmit her entire medical file to his office."

"I saw her arrive there this morning. I was at the park for the fireworks demonstration."

"I felt so sorry for Doc," she said. "When

he told me to arrange to transfer her records to Dr. Boyle, I thought he might start crying."

I decided that Harriet was overstating things, but didn't voice my feeling. Instead, I said, "Well, people do change doctors now and then."

"For good reasons, I'm sure, Mrs. Fletcher, but Agnes Kalisch doesn't have a good reason. It's like she's infatuated with Dr. Boyle's high-tech equipment and his ads in the newspaper. I told Doc that maybe he should start advertising."

A laugh erupted from me. "I can just imagine his reaction to that suggestion."

She joined me with her own laugh. "He sputtered and complained about doctors advertising their services. I thought he might start swearing, but he never did. He never uses four-letter words."

"To his credit."

The door opened and Seth held it for the patient he'd just seen.

"Hello, Jessica," he said. "Feeling better?"

"I feel good," I said, "except for the heat. It bleeds some of the energy right out of you."

"Ayuh, that it does. Had a good chat with Harriet?"

"Yes."

"I suppose she's been tellin' you that I'm grumpy and grouchy these days."

"I would never say that to anyone," Harriet said, her hand to her bosom.

"Yes, you would. Come on in, Jess, and let me take a look at you."

He rolled down a fresh paper covering for the examining table in his treatment room, and I perched on the edge of the table.

"How was the fireworks demo this morning?" he asked.

"Interesting," I replied. "A little too technical for me, but interesting nonetheless. I'd never realized how much goes into putting on a fireworks show—the number of people, the equipment, and all the permissions and safety considerations."

"A dangerous business. Now, let me see those sinuses of yours."

After examining my nose, ears, and throat, and asking a series of questions, he said, "I'd say you're well over your infection, Jessica. Good thing, too. Sinus infections can turn into something a lot more serious if they're not treated properly."

"I'm sure that's true. Now, Doctor, tell me how *you're* feeling."

"Fair to middlin'."

"No better than that?"

"Too busy for a man my age. Time I started to slow down and pack it in."

"I thought Dr. Jenny was helping you cut back. Can she take over more of your patients for you?"

"She's very good, and a lot of the mothers with young children have really taken to her. But truth to tell, some of the old-timers haven't—" Seth hesitated. "Now I don't want you jumping down my throat, but I think some of 'em are not quite comfortable with a woman."

"Well, they'll just have to wait to see you if they don't want to see her," I said. "I don't have a lot of sympathy with that point of view. If a doctor is good, gender shouldn't matter. But I'm old enough to understand that what's right isn't always what's done."

"True." He fiddled with his stethoscope and looked suddenly embarrassed. "I've been talking to someone in Bangor who specializes in selling medical practices."

"About selling *your* practice?"

"Ayuh. I'm tired of all the paperwork for these infernal insurance companies. They've all got some clerks deciding what medical procedures they'll pay for. They love getting the premiums every month, but they fight like the dickens not to pay out any of it."

"Sure you want to do that, Seth? Somehow, I can't conceive of you not practicing medicine here in Cabot Cove. You'll have lots of very unhappy people if you go through with selling the practice."

"That may be, but the writing's on the wall. Time to face reality."

"How about if I change your reality, at least for one evening?" I said.

He looked at me quizzically.

I told him of my call from retired FBI special agent Allcott, and of our dinner plans that evening. "I want you to meet him, Seth. You'll like him, and it will do you good to enjoy some delicious Italian food, a glass of Chianti, and interesting conversation about something other than medicine."

"I don't know, Jess, I—"

"I insist. I'm meeting him at Peppino's at six. There will be a seat reserved for you."

"Well, all right. Now that your sinus infection is cleared up, your powers of persuasion are operating at full strength."

I laughed and patted his arm. "Bring your best appetite," I said on my way out the door. "There'll be no doggie bags tonight."

I rode into town despite the heat and stopped in Charlene Sassi's bakery to pick up one of her to-die-for cinnamon buns to have for breakfast the next day. The shop was busy. I took a number and got in line behind Agnes Kalisch.

"Hello, Jessica," Agnes said.

"Hello, Agnes. How are you?"

"Not well, I'm afraid."

I knew what was coming. Agnes Kalisch was one of those people who insist upon discussing their various physical ailments with anyone who will listen.

"I'm sorry to hear that," I said.

"I'm always so tired these days, no energy at all. I can barely get out of bed in the morning and get on with the day."

"Are you seeing the doctor?" I asked, knowing the answer.

"I'm seeing Dr. Boyle."

I couldn't resist. "Oh? I thought you were Seth Hazlitt's patient."

"I was until recently. He's—well, Seth is a fine man and all that, but I'm afraid he's fallen behind the times medically."

"Really? I've always found him to be very much on top of things."

She became conspiratorial. "Well, Jessica, that may be your experience, but it isn't mine. I told him about my chronic fatigue and all he did was draw blood and put me on iron pills. I'm anemic, you know."

"I didn't know, Agnes."

"Well, it's true. He sent me for a bunch of tests last year and this year, and the only answer he had was to put me on iron pills and vitamin C, which he says helps absorb the iron in my body. The pills didn't help one bit, and then—and *then* he wanted to poke a needle in my back to see if I had some rare disease he mentioned, something with a big fancy name, Walder Macro-something or other. That's when I decided to change to Dr. Boyle. He's got me on special nutrients he invented and sells right there at his offices. Have you been there, Jessica? State-of-the-art everything, and modern. Frankly, I don't think Seth Hazlitt knows what he's doing half the time." Her voice lowered even further. "I think he might be getting senile."

"Agnes! That's ridiculous," I said, louder than I'd intended, only to draw curious looks from the others in the shop. I brought down my voice level. "Seth Hazlitt is anything but senile. He's one of the brightest and most astute men I've ever known."

"You're entitled to your opinion, Jessica."

One of Charlene's counter help called Agnes's number, and she walked away, leaving me very upset. How many others had Agnes talked to about Seth's alleged senility? It wouldn't take much for that rumor to spread all over town, as far-fetched as it was. That's the trouble with rumors. It doesn't matter if they're true or not at the outset. Give them enough time to fester, and involve enough people, and it isn't long before they become what's construed as the truth, and all the denials in the world won't change it.

I bought my cinnamon bun, hot out of Charlene's oven, and swung by the library to put the final touches on a program to be held there on Saturday morning prior to our Independence Day Parade. Lee Walters, our head librarian, had come up with the idea to hold a discussion about the First Amendment geared to younger readers, and I'd agreed to be on the panel. Lee and I met for only fifteen minutes; everything was in order and there was little to discuss.

"Plans for the evening, Jessica?" Lee asked as I prepared to leave.

I told her about the unexpected arrival of my FBI friend from Washington and our dinner plans. "Seth Hazlitt is joining us," I added.

"How is Seth?" she asked, her brow furrowed in exaggerated concern.

"Fine. Why do you ask?" I knew the answer the moment I asked the question.

"I've heard he's having some—I don't know how to put this gently—I've heard that he's having some—well—some emotional problems."

"Lee, let me assure you that none of that is the least bit true." I shook my head. "I can't believe that well-meaning people in this town are willing to spread such nonsense."

"I didn't mean to anger you, Jess," Lee said.

"I'm not angry, Lee, but I am dismayed. There's simply no basis to that at all. Let's drop it. The program Saturday morning has really shaped up, thanks to you. See you then."

She walked me outside.

"I forgot to tell you," she said, "that Lennon-Diversified is donating money to refurbish the kids' reading room."

"That's wonderful. It can use some sprucing up."

"Money!" Lee said. "It always comes down to money. Fortunately, Joseph Lennon picked Cabot Cove to relocate his business. He's so generous."

I headed home, where I showered and settled in my den to do more work on the outline. But I couldn't concentrate. My mind kept shifting from the task at hand to Seth. His situation had all the marks of a "perfect storm." He loses a few patients and is understandably unhappy about it. At least one of those patients decides he's lost his touch as a physician and tells others, which prompts them to tell still others. Pretty soon, there are hundreds of people who've heard that Seth Hazlitt "is losing it," and is demonstrating signs of encroaching senility. That will cause more patients to seek other physicians, which will further depress Seth, and that, in turn, will fuel even more rumors. The classic vicious circle.

He didn't deserve it, and I made a silent pledge to myself to try and think of ways to counter it. I was immersed in that mental exercise when it was time to leave for dinner with Seth and Richard Allcott. Just what the doctor ordered—good food, good wine, and good conversation about more pleasant things. A relaxing evening.

At least that was my expectation.

Chapter Five

When I arrived at the restaurant shortly before six, Richard Allcott was already at the bar chatting with the resident bartenders, Randy and Kathy.

"The famous Jessica Fletcher," he said, sliding off the barstool and taking both my hands in his. "You look terrific."

"Thank you," I said. "I might say the same about you."

"Then by all means do," he said, smiling. "I'm always receptive to a compliment."

"I see you've already met Randy and Kathy."

"Bartenders are my favorite people," he

said. "They not only know how to make drinks, they have a finger on the pulse of wherever it is they ply their profession."

"And what did they tell you about Cabot Cove?"

"Just that if Jessica Fletcher wanted to run for mayor, she'd be a shoo-in."

We were greeted by the younger Joe DiScala, Joe Jr.

"Good evening, Mrs. Fletcher," he said. "Glad you'll be joining us tonight."

I introduced him to Allcott. As I did, the door opened and Seth entered.

"Dr. Hazlitt," Joe said, shaking Seth's hand. "Always good to have a doctor in the house in case a customer swallows a fork."

"Afraid I'm not a fork specialist, Joe. They'd be on their own."

We were seated at a corner table.

"I'm so pleased I decided to make a stop in Cabot Cove," Allcott said after we'd ordered wine, with Seth making the final selection at Allcott's insistence. "It's wonderful seeing Mrs. Fletcher again, and to have made your acquaintance, Doctor."

"It's Jessica and Seth," I counseled.

"Fair enough," Allcott said. "Please call me Rick."

"Jessica tells me that you spent years with the FBI," Seth said.

"That's right, Seth. Twenty years. Twenty very good years."

"You a lawyer or accountant?" Seth asked.

"No. The bureau dropped that requirement before I joined. I came out of the University of Wisconsin with a degree in English lit. I intended to go on for my master's and maybe even a Ph.D., but a friend had just joined up with the house-that-Hoover-built and suggested I might like it. No, it was more than a suggestion. He *challenged* me to apply, and I took the challenge. Glad I did. I liked what I did for those twenty years, catching the bad guys, making the country safer." He laughed and waved his hand over the table. "I know, that all sounds very Pollyanna, but it represents how I feel."

"Nothing wrong with following lofty ideals," said Seth.

"Do you have to retire after twenty years?" I asked Allcott.

"No. I could have stayed on. But my love of books and reading came back to haunt me. I decided to shift gears in my life and find the time to read all those books I never got around to. I don't regret that decision, although I will admit that I sometimes miss the action."

The conversation progressed smoothly as we enjoyed a lavish antipasto platter, followed by an entrée we all ordered on my recommendation, one of the restaurant's signature dishes, Chicken Peppino. Eventually, the subject of Joseph Lennon and his company became the topic of our conversation. After Seth and I had briefly recounted for Rick how Lennon-Diversified had relocated to Cabot Cove, and how its founder and CEO had become a highly visible citizen of the town—to say nothing of generous—Rick said, "Sounds like Cabot Cove struck it rich."

"Not always a good thing," Seth said.

"Oh?"

"Nothing's ever all good or all bad," my doctor friend continued. "You take the bitter with the sweet. Yes, sir, there's no doubt that Mr. Lennon has done some good things for the community. He—"

"Lee, at the library, told me this afternoon that he's putting up the money to refurbish the children's reading room," I threw in.

"That's nice," Seth said to me, then turned his attention back to Allcott. "You see, Rick, while Mr. Lennon is tossing his money around, he's also changing lots of things about Cabot Cove, changes that aren't necessarily for the better."

That led to a discussion about how growth, unless controlled, can do more harm to a community than good, and whether there's a danger in having a few people, especially those with deep pockets, exert undue influence over a town. It was a good debate, with Seth and Rick carrying the brunt of it. I was content to listen, and to offer an occasional comment.

I was happy that I'd thought to invite Seth to join us. His mood seemed bright throughout the meal—until Joe Jr. came to the table with a second bottle of wine, the same vintage and year as the one we'd ordered earlier.

"We didn't order another bottle," I said.

"Compliments of Dr. Boyle and his guests," Joe said.

We all looked in the direction of Joe's head nod. Seated at a large table at the opposite end of the room was Dr. Boyle, accompanied by Cynthia Welch, Lennon's son and daughter, and the young man named Dante who'd been at the presentation the previous day. Boyle raised his glass to Seth, whose response was a blank expression.

"Please thank Dr. Boyle," Seth said, "but we're getting close to leaving."

I watched Joe Jr. deliver the message to Boyle, who made a gesture that said it was irrelevant to him whether we accepted his gift or not.

"A colleague?" Rick asked.

"I suppose you might say that," said Seth.

Fortunately, Seth's mood picked up again. Over espresso and a fruit platter, the topic turned to baseball, something about which both of my male companions for the evening knew a great deal, and their views were passionate. It turned out that Rick was a Red Sox fan. Seth had been a Red Sox fan for as long as I'd known him, and their analysis of the current season was spirited and good-natured. They both vied for the check, ignoring my offer to add money to the pot. Seth prevailed, but only after it was agreed that we would enjoy another meal together at Rick's expense.

We'd been early arrivals and had our choice of tables. But as we got up and headed for the door, we saw that all the other tables were now occupied, and there was a short line of people waiting, undoubtedly pleased that we were leaving. Joe Sr. intercepted us and asked, "Was everything okay?"

"Ayuh," Seth replied. "Always is."

"Come back soon."

We stood outside the restaurant, reluctant to have the conversation end. "Is it just my imagination or has it cooled off a bit?" I asked.

"Humidity seems down a scrid," Seth said.

"You're not imagining it," Allcott said. "But I bet you have a fertile imagination to write books the way you do."

"That she does," Seth said.

Seated inside, I hadn't been as conscious of the contrast between the physical appearances of Seth and Rick as I was now. With them standing together I could see that Seth made two of the retired FBI special agent. Both Seth and I were taller than Allcott, who I noticed tended to rise up on his toes and lean forward and up, perhaps in an effort to make himself look taller.

"Drop you somewhere, Rick?" Seth asked.

"No, thank you," he replied. "I have a rental car in the lot over there."

"How did you get here tonight, Jessica?" Seth asked. "Ride your bicycle?"

"Your bicycle?" Allcott said.

"Jessica doesn't drive, but she does have a bicycle," Seth explained. "Not only that— the lady has a private pilot's license."

"You do?" Rick said. "You're constantly full of surprises. That's wonderful. You don't drive a car but you can pilot a plane."

"I'm a beginner pilot," I said. "Strictly a novice."

"Nevertheless, I'm impressed."

"Drive you home, Jessica?" Seth asked me as we walked to the lot adjacent to the restaurant.

"If you don't mind," I said.

"Seth, if it's okay with you, let me drive her," Rick said. "Give me a chance to see more of Cabot Cove."

Seth looked at me.

"That would be fine," I said. "Thank you."

I thanked Seth for dinner and said I'd be in touch with him tomorrow. He started to say something when a sound from behind a parked automobile caused the three of us to turn. Facing us was a young man dressed in black, including a dark woolen cap pulled down low over his brow. At first, I thought how odd it was to wear a hat on such a hot night. But then light glinted off the most striking feature about him—the very long, lethal knife in his hand.

"Money," he said. "Come on, give me what you have."

Seth pulled me behind him and took a step toward the would-be thief. "Listen to me, young man," he said, "put that foolish thing away and—"

The man lunged, swinging the knife in an arc in front of him, the blade of his weapon catching Seth on his wrist. Seth stumbled back and looked at his blood flowing freely onto the asphalt. Before I could do anything—go to Seth to help him, scream, run—Rick Allcott moved so quickly he became a blur. In what seemed an instant, the man with the knife was on his back on the ground. The knife had hit the pavement and slid a dozen feet away. Rick stood with his foot on the attacker's throat. "You make one move, jerk, and you won't breathe again."

"Gorry," Seth exclaimed as he pressed his good hand against the wound.

"We have to get you to a hospital," I said.

"What about him?" Seth asked, indicating the man beneath Allcott's foot.

A couple who'd just backed out of a parking space stopped. "What's going on?" the man behind the wheel asked.

"Please call 911," I said. "We need the police and an ambulance."

"Just the police," Seth said. "I don't need a hospital."

Allcott had turned our attacker onto his stomach and held his arms behind his back, causing the knife wielder to complain that he was in pain.

"You'll be in a lot more pain if you don't shut up," Rick warned.

By now, word of the assault had traveled inside the restaurant, and people flocked through the door to see what had happened.

"You okay, Mrs. Fletcher?" Joe DiScala asked.

A siren could be heard and grew louder.

I stood next to Seth, who was bleeding profusely despite his attempt to stem the flow by applying pressure to the wound. He sagged against me and I braced myself to provide support.

As a marked car from the sheriff's department screeched around the corner and came to a hard stop near us, Dr. Warren Boyle suddenly appeared at our side. He reached for Seth's hand to better see the source of the bleeding, but Seth said, "No, I'm fine."

"No, you're not," said Boyle. To me: "He's going to bleed to death if we can't stop the hemorrhage." He glanced around. "Get me a clean napkin," he yelled at Joe Sr., who ran into his restaurant and returned immediately with a white linen napkin.

Boyle pried Seth's bloody fingers from his wrist and wrapped the napkin tightly around the wound to form a tourniquet.

Two of Mort Metzger's uniformed deputies had leapt from their vehicle and raced to where Rick Allcott continued to subdue the man who'd tried to rob us. Allcott got off the mugger as the two officers yanked him to his feet. One slapped cuffs on him while the other looked to where Boyle and I stood with Seth.

"Where's the ambulance?" Boyle barked.

His question was answered by the wail of another siren. In moments, the ambulance pulled up next to the police car and two EMTs in white uniforms ran to us, just as Seth slumped to the ground.

"Seth!" I cried, leaning over him, holding his bandaged hand.

Boyle immediately dropped to his knees and checked Seth's vital signs as the EMTs hurried back to their vehicle, removed a gurney, and brought it to where Seth was now prone on his back. An EMT handed Boyle a roll of surgical gauze, and the doctor swiftly removed the white napkin with which he'd bound the gash in Seth's wrist, tossing aside the stained linen and rewrapping the wound. With considerable effort, the EMTs maneuvered Seth onto the gurney and carried him to the ambulance. I was about to climb in with Seth when one of the deputies stopped me.

"What happened here, Mrs. Fletcher?" he asked.

"I need to go with Dr. Hazlitt," I said.

"I'm afraid we can't let you go until we get a statement from you."

Rick Allcott joined us. He showed his ID to the deputy and said, "I think Mrs. Fletcher should be allowed to accompany Dr. Hazlitt. I can fill you in on what occurred here tonight."

"FBI?" the deputy said.

"Right." Allcott turned to me. "Go on, Mrs. Fletcher, before the ambulance takes off. He can get a statement from you later. I'll find my way to the hospital after I finish with the officer here."

I didn't hesitate. They were about to close the door to the ambulance when I scrambled inside. I looked back. Rick Allcott was walking with the deputy to the sheriff's department car. Dr. Boyle stood with his party from the restaurant, their attention on the ambulance as we left for the Cabot Cove Hospital Center.

The EMTs had hooked Seth up to an IV. A heavy pressure bandage had stanched the flow of blood, but he was unnaturally pale. His eyes were closed. I reached past the EMT and placed my hand on Seth's. "You'll be fine," I said.

His eyes opened and he said in a weak voice, "Ayuh, you bet I will."

Chapter Six

Seth was immediately whisked into the emergency room. I sat in the waiting room for what seemed an eternity, although the clock said it had been only twenty minutes before the young ER physician who'd processed Seth's arrival came through the doors and joined me on the couch.

"How's he doing?" I asked, trying to keep emotion from my voice.

"He's doing fine. The wound itself wasn't that severe, but the knife sliced into an artery. That's why there was so much bleeding. We've transfused him, and he's coming around just fine. I do want to keep him overnight, however. He should be ready to go home tomorrow."

"Whatever you think is best. I'm greatly relieved. And thank you for letting me know."

The doctor left, and Rick Allcott entered the waiting area, eyes scanning the room till they alighted on me. He walked swiftly to where I sat and squatted down in front of me, a concerned expression on his face.

"How's Seth?" he asked.

"Looks like he'll be okay," I said. "The doctor was just here. He says Seth lost a lot of blood, but they've given him a transfusion and he'll be fine."

"That's good news. And how are you feeling?"

"A little shaky, but I'll get over it. How did things end up back at the restaurant?"

Rick rose and took a seat next to me. "No problems. I told the local police what happened. Your sheriff arrived. Metzger?"

"Mort Metzger."

"Nice guy. He said that you and he are friends."

"We certainly are. He's close to Seth, too."

"Interesting guy—a cop in New York City before settling in Cabot Cove."

"That's true. We're lucky to have him. What about the man who attacked Seth?"

"According to Sheriff Metzger, neither he nor his men recognized him. They want a formal statement from you."

"Of course. I'll call Mort when I get home and—"

"No need," Rick said. "He's here." He nodded toward the glass door, through which we could see Mort striding into the waiting room.

"You okay, Mrs. F?" he asked.

"Fine, now that I know Seth will be all right." I filled him in on what the doctor had told me.

"How'd he get injured?"

"Warding off the man who tried to rob us."

"I hate to say it, but that was not too smart of the doc," was Mort's response.

"I thought it was very brave," I countered. Perhaps Seth had been foolish to try to deal with an armed thief, but everything happened so quickly—as it often does under such circumstances—that people reacted instinctively. Seth's instinct had been to protect me, and I couldn't criticize him for that.

"I know what the sheriff is saying," said Rick. "Better for a robber to take your money than your life."

"You didn't heed that philosophy," I said. "You didn't hesitate to attack him."

Allcott laughed. "My FBI physical training came in handy."

"Do you miss the bureau?" Mort asked.

"Sometimes," Rick answered, "but not often."

"I have to say it's a good thing you were there," Mort said. "The kid's an addict, strung out on drugs. He was looking for money from you to get his fix. When those guys are desperate, they'll do anything."

"How sad," I said.

While Cabot Cove hadn't been spared the presence of illegal drugs any more than other communities across the nation, we'd had virtually no violent crime connected with it. A few years ago, a young man who lived with his family outside town had been arrested for importing drugs from New York City and selling them. Obviously, there had been a market for him, supply reflecting demand as it almost always does. But I couldn't recall a single instance of someone armed with a weapon attempting to hold citizens up in a desperate attempt to feed a habit.

"Where's he from?" Allcott asked Mort.

"A town about fifty miles up the coast. We're running a background check on him now. He's not too bright. His little adventure will give him plenty of prison time to get straight. Aggravated assault, armed robbery, attempted murder."

"I don't think he intended to kill anyone," I said. "I think he was trying to scare us."

Mort looked quizzically at me.

"I'm not defending what he did," I said quickly.

"It doesn't matter to me what he intended; the results speak for themselves— the doc's in the hospital with what could have been a fatal wound, and that's what's going to get that stupid kid put away," said Mort. He looked at Rick. "Sorry your introduction to Cabot Cove was a negative experience. We like visitors to walk away with a better impression. Usually the town's a lot more peaceful than Washington, D.C."

"Or New York," Rick said. "Although if tonight is an indication, it's not as peaceful as I thought it would be. What's the murder rate here?"

"We get one or two a year."

"I don't have my fingers on the numbers," Rick said, "but Washington had more murders per capita than any other major city in the United States, almost three hundred the last year I lived and worked there."

The doctor tending to Seth reappeared and said we could see him for a few minutes. Allcott declined to join us, but Mort and I were led to the ICU, where Seth was tethered to an IV, along with other medical tendrils.

"Hello, Doc," Mort said as we stood beside the bed. "Some way to start the Fourth of July weekend, huh?"

Seth ignored the comment and asked about his assailant. Mort recounted what he'd told Rick and me.

"I figured he was high on something," Seth said. "Nobody in their right mind would pull such a dumb stunt, right there in the open with people around."

"The bad guys aren't always the brightest bulbs in the drawer," said Mort. "Mrs. F says you'll be fine."

"Of course I will. Gorry, no lully-brained youngster will ever get the better of me."

I sensed that Mort was about to give Seth a lecture about discretion being the better part of valor, and headed him off.

"Can I bring you anything tomorrow?" I asked.

"I'll be home tomorrow," Seth responded.

"Then I'll bring something to the house. You won't be up to cooking and—"

"I'll be cooking just fine, Jessica, and caring for my patients, too."

"Of course you will," I said, catching the small smile on Mort's face. We both knew Seth Hazlitt, M.D., only too well. "Right now," I said, "you should rest. I'll check back in the morning to see if you need anything, and get someone to give you a ride home—"

"Speakin' of rides, Jessica," Seth said, "my car is back there at Peppino's."

"I'll have my men pick it up and drop it off at your house, Doc."

It took a minute before we could find Seth's car keys in the pocket of his suit jacket, which had been hung in a small closet next to his bed, but we did, said good night, and returned to the waiting room, where Rick Allcott sat reading a magazine. Mort offered to drive me home, but Rick said, "I've already reserved that pleasure, Sheriff. I'm trying to soak in all of Cabot Cove that I can before leaving."

"Enjoy your stay, Allcott. Good night, Mrs. F. Glad things didn't turn out as bad as they could have."

We said good night to Mort just outside the hospital's main entrance and watched him drive off in his marked sheriff's car.

"Nice guy," Rick said.

"No argument from me. I don't know that I'm up to giving you a tour of Cabot Cove, but I'll take you the long way home."

"Sounds perfect."

We hadn't taken six steps toward where he'd parked his rental car when another vehicle sped into the parking lot and stopped with a screech of brakes. It was driven by John Shearer, the photographer from the *Cabot Cove Gazette*. Seated in the passenger seat was Evelyn Phillips, the paper's managing editor.

Evelyn had arrived in Cabot Cove two years ago and quickly transformed the newspaper from a lackadaisical publication to one with energy and verve. The former editors had assiduously avoided anything that even smacked of controversy, afraid of alienating advertisers. Evelyn changed all that, despite warnings from those already at the paper that advertising sales would be seriously affected. She applied solid journalistic standards while aggressively covering stories that had previously been off-limits, and let the chips fall where they might. At the same time, she maintained the small-town feel of the paper, focusing on upbeat local news that featured the town's citizens. Her approach worked. Fears that advertising sales would suffer proved unfounded, and the *Gazette* prospered.

Evelyn hopped out of the car, followed closely by Shearer, his camera in hand. Evelyn was a sturdy woman, about my age, with short-cropped gray hair. Perched on her nose was a pair of half-glasses attached to a gold cord.

"Hello, Evelyn," I said. "I know why you're here."

"I picked it up on my police radio," she said. "How is Seth Hazlitt?"

"Doing fine," I said. "They're keeping

him overnight as a precaution, but from the look of things, he'll be back home tomorrow and raring to go."

Evelyn looked at my companion.

"This is Richard Allcott," I said. "He's a friend visiting Cabot Cove for the Fourth celebration."

"Former FBI," Evelyn said flatly.

"That's right," Rick said. "Word sure gets around."

"Sheriff Metzger told me," Evelyn explained. "You were with Mrs. Fletcher and Dr. Hazlitt when it happened."

"Right," Rick confirmed.

"So," Evelyn said, pulling a slender reporter's notebook from her shoulder bag and poising a pen over it, "tell me about it."

"I'm sure you got everything from Mort Metzger," I interjected.

"I got the facts from him, but I need the human element. Dr. Boyle told me that you subdued the robber."

Rick didn't respond.

"It's a good thing you were there," Evelyn said, "and that Dr. Boyle was, too. He saved Seth Hazlitt's life. I just left him. He says it was a fortunate coincidence that he was at

Peppino's when it happened, and that if he hadn't been present, he doubted whether Dr. Hazlitt would have survived."

I thought back to the scene in the parking lot. It was true that Boyle had come to Seth's aid and had applied a pressure bandage prior to the EMTs' arrival. Perhaps his actions *had* saved Seth's life. If so, he was certainly owed a heartfelt thank-you. It also struck me, however, that Dr. Warren Boyle was not a modest man.

"Yes," I said, "Dr. Boyle was immensely helpful."

"What was your reaction when the man accosted you?" Evelyn asked me.

My laugh was forced. "Fear, of course," I answered. "But it all happened so fast that I really didn't have time to feel much of anything, Evelyn."

John Shearer started shooting candid shots of me and Rick Allcott as Evelyn turned to Rick. "You're now a local hero," she said.

"I'm anything but that," Rick said. "I'm here visiting Mrs. Fletcher and intend to just enjoy the weekend." He turned to Shearer. "And I would appreciate it if you'd stop doing that. Your strobe light is annoying." He said it in a way that left no room for debate. The young photographer lowered his camera and leaned against the car.

"Could you tell me something about your experience as an FBI special agent?" Evelyn asked Rick. "And about your relationship with Mrs. Fletcher?"

"I'm sorry," Rick said, "but I'm irrelevant in this whole matter. I was about to drive Mrs. Fletcher home, and I think we'd best do that—now!"

"Any final comment, Jessica?" Evelyn asked.

I shook my head. "Sorry, Evelyn, but you'll have all the information you need from Sheriff Metzger, and you obviously have spoken with Dr. Boyle. We have to leave."

"Who's the emergency room doctor who treated Seth Hazlitt?" she asked. "I'll want to get an update on his condition."

I gave her his name, and Rick and I went to his car. Safely inside, Rick shook his head and laughed. "So much for my visit to the bucolic Cabot Cove," he said.

"It may be hard to believe in light of tonight's events," I said, "but Cabot Cove is usually a quiet town. It's a wonderful place to live, where people not only know each other but look out for their neighbors—"

"A perfect example of small-town America, huh?" he said, starting the engine. "I'll take your word for it."

But Cabot Cove was changing. Did my description still hold true? Or was it just wishful thinking?

Chapter Seven

It was a fitful night's sleep. Try as I might, I couldn't shake the vision of the attack outside the restaurant, and of the injury to Seth. It kept playing over and over in my mind like a loop of videotape on a machine without a PAUSE button.

I finally gave up and got out of bed at five, my pajamas damp from the bedroom's uncomfortable temperature. I turned on the air conditioner in the kitchen, along with a small TV I have there, and put the kettle on. News of the attempted mugging had reached one of the Bangor TV stations. A female anchor reported that mystery novelist Jessica Fletcher and Seth Hazlitt, one of Cabot Cove's leading physicians, had been the victims of an assault outside a popular restaurant. I suppose they didn't have a photo of Seth in their archives because the only picture that flashed on the screen was one of me taken at a mystery writers' panel I'd chaired in Bangor earlier in the year. *Surely,* I thought, *there has to be more pressing news to report than a thwarted attack by a drug addict wielding a knife.* The anchor ended with, "According to eyewitnesses, the attacker was subdued by an unnamed man who'd been in the restaurant with Mrs. Fletcher and Dr. Hazlitt."

My thoughts shifted to Rick Allcott and the way he'd subdued our attacker. His action had been so quick that I was sure the knife wielder hadn't had a chance to use his weapon on him. The fury of Allcott's attack was especially surprising to me, considering his slight physique. He hardly looked like a man capable of making such a concerted physical response, nor did his demeanor give a clue to that capability. A good lesson learned, I thought, as I prepared my tea. As the saying goes, you can't tell a book by its cover—or a man by his appearance.

I heard the twin *thumps* of both newspapers landing on my steps, and fetched them. No surprise that last night's incident dominated the front page of the *Gazette*. Evelyn Phillips's story was straightforward, as her stories usually were, but I was dismayed by the accompanying pictures. One was a shot John Shearer had taken of me just outside the hospital. He'd caught me with a puzzled expression on my face, framed by lank hair, and— Let's just say it wouldn't be one I'd choose for the back cover of one of my books. More upsetting was a photo taken through a window of Seth Hazlitt in his hospital bed. You really couldn't make out that it was Seth, but the caption identified him. *What a terrible invasion of privacy,* I thought. Seth would be furious, especially because the photo was adjacent to a dramatic picture of Dr. Boyle in white coat, stethoscope draped around his neck, and evidently taken by a professional portrait photographer. I didn't relish hearing the explosion I knew would take place when Seth saw the newspaper.

Naturally, Mort Metzger was quoted at

length. So were Peppino's owner, Joe Di-Scala; the couple who'd been leaving the parking lot and witnessed the assault; Lennon-Diversified's Cynthia Welch; and, of course, Dr. Warren Boyle, who told Evelyn, "I can only say that it was fortunate that I had decided to have dinner at Peppino's that night, and was able to play a small part in saving Dr. Hazlitt's life. His death would have been a tragic loss to the Cabot Cove medical community."

As innocuous as the doctor's comments were, I had what I can only describe as a crawling sensation on my skin. I have nothing against anyone who takes advantage of situations to garner publicity, and by extension promotes his or her business. Maybe it was my love for Seth Hazlitt that generated within me an unreasonable dislike of Dr. Boyle. The man had never done anything to me to spawn such feelings, and I suffered a bout of guilt. Similarly, I had no tangible reason to dislike Joseph Lennon. He had demonstrated considerable generosity toward the town I love, and had gone out of his way to provide for its citizens. Certainly, Chester Carlisle's response to Lennon's largesse was extreme and uncalled-for. I may have witnessed Lennon in a particularly unflattering moment, but that didn't mean he was always cruel to his son. People often say things in anger that they regret upon reflection. I hoped that was the case with Lennon and his son, Paul. I was willing to give him the benefit of the doubt.

Still . . .

Maybe my feelings grew out of the changes that seemed to be swirling around me. I've always prided myself on being adaptable. When you travel as much as I do, you'd better be good at adapting to change. Had growing older diminished my flexibility, rendering me unable to go with the flow and to recognize change as inevitable, and often for the good? I hoped not.

I shook off my conflicted thinking (aided by the cool air from the air conditioner), showered, and settled in to resume work on the outline for my next novel. I waited until eight to call the hospital, and was connected to Seth's room.

"Good morning, Seth."

"Looks like another scorcher," he replied. "I can see the heat right through the window."

"I suppose so. How are you feeling?"

"Just fine, thank you. They say they'll be releasing me at ten. Did you read that flapdoodle in today's *Gazette*? I was near to popping my gourd when I saw it. What a nerve, taking a picture of me in the hospital."

I laughed. "You looked good."

"What was good was that no one could recognize me. And that handshaker Boyle, boostin' himself on my misfortune. Savin' my life, huh? Why, that man is lower than whale droppings, lower than—"

"How are you getting home?" I asked, trying to derail the gourd-popping I could see coming.

"Jim Shevlin is picking me up. Nothing like a hands-on mayor. He'll have my vote again, but I suppose he already knows that."

"I'm sure he does. What can I bring?"

"Yourself, Jessica. I have something I want to run by you."

"Oh?"

"And I won't be discussin' it on the phone. What time are you free this morning?"

"Anytime you say, Seth. I made a date to meet Rick Allcott for breakfast at nine. I want him to experience Mara's blueberry pancakes before he leaves Cabot Cove."

He chuckled. "He'll never leave once he tastes 'em. Interesting fellow. He took that young punk down without breaking a sweat."

"All that FBI training. We're lucky he was with us."

"You make sure to thank him for me."

"I'll do that."

He was silent a moment. "I suppose you want me to thank Boyle, too."

"He tried to be helpful, Seth."

I heard him cough and mumble something. "I didn't catch what you said."

Seth cleared his throat. "I'll call him later and express my appreciation."

"Yes, that would be a nice thing to do. Can you believe that tomorrow is the Fourth of July? The years just fly by."

"I wish the heat would break before the festivities," Seth said. "It will take a toll on our seniors, at least those foolish enough to stand outside. Are you planning to attend that rock-and-roll concert and the fireworks?"

"Are you suggesting that this *senior* shouldn't?"

"I'm suggesting nothing of the kind, Jessica. You'll come to my house after your breakfast with Mr. Allcott?"

"You should be home by eleven. I'll come by a little before noon."

"Have to get off now. The nurses are here to make sure I'm still alive. See you later."

I made some progress on my outline, which pleased me, and was about to phone for a taxi to take me to Mara's when Mort Metzger called.

"Sorry to bother you, Mrs. F, but I was wondering whether you'd be able to come by headquarters today."

"I'll make the time. What's it about?"

"Well, I never got a formal statement from you last night. I have to add that to the file."

"Of course."

"And the DA wants to put the fellow who attacked you in a lineup. He wants you and Mr. Allcott to see if you can pick him out. He wants Doc Hazlitt to participate, too, but I figured he probably wouldn't be up to it, at least not for a couple of days."

"I can't say for sure, but that's a good assumption, Mort. I'm seeing Seth around noon. I'll mention it to him. Does the district attorney really think a lineup is necessary? There were so many witnesses. Surely there isn't a question about who did it."

"That's the way I see it, Mrs. F, but it seems our young drug addict comes from a pretty well-to-do family upstate. His father's hired a hotshot attorney."

I sighed. "Of course I'll view the lineup. Have you spoken to Richard Allcott?"

"About the lineup? Not yet."

"I'm on my way to have breakfast with him. Maybe we can come by together after that. Will you be able to put together a lineup that quickly?"

"Shouldn't be a problem by, say, eleven. The kid's attorney is here in town, and I can press some of my men into service. Some of them are not much older than the kid."

"Eleven it is," I said, realizing as I did that I was making assumptions where Rick Allcott was concerned. Maybe being a former FBI agent would preclude his taking part in a lineup. I'd have to ask, and I wondered whether Mort had queried the defense attorney about it, too.

Rick Allcott was already at Mara's Luncheonette when I arrived. Judging from what I saw as I walked in—he was at the counter, chatting with townspeople, a half-consumed cup of coffee in front of him—he'd been there for a while and had made friends. He jumped off the stool and greeted me.

Mara, a pot of coffee in each hand, walked past us. "Good morning, Jessica," she said over her shoulder. "You don't look at all like you were the victim of an armed attack last night."

"Looks can deceive," I said. "It's very much on my mind." I turned to Allcott. "I see you've made yourself at home."

"Everyone wants to know more about what happened," he said, sweeping his hand toward his companions at the counter. "I've been filling in Barney Longshoot and Spencer Durkee here."

Evelyn Phillips won't need to put out her newspaper tomorrow, I thought. That pair were notorious gossips, not that they would admit to gossiping. They just liked to "discuss the news"—all over town.

We were interrupted by some people who wanted my version of events. I forced a laugh and waved them off. "I'd just as soon forget about it," I said.

"How's Seth Hazlitt?"

"Doing fine. He'll be home from the hospital this morning." I turned to Allcott. "Let's grab a booth before they're all taken.

"I'm sorry your initial visit to Cabot Cove turned out this way," I said after we'd been seated. "I'm sure you assumed that the baseball game at Fenway would be the most exciting part of your trip."

He grinned. "Not to worry," he said.

Mara served us coffee, and I ordered blueberry pancakes for both of us. "Mara, the owner, adds something special to the pancake batter," I told him, "that makes her pancakes extraordinary."

"What's her secret?" he asked.

"She refuses to reveal it."

"Nothing an ex-FBI man loves better than a mystery. I'll have to see if I can detect her secret ingredient. So, Jessica Fletcher, what's on tap for today?"

"How about a police lineup?"

His eyebrows went up. "About last night?"

I gave him a summary of what Mort had told me, and asked whether being a retired FBI special agent would keep him from participating.

He shook his head. "No problem as far as I'm concerned, although I assume the kid's lawyer will raise a stink."

"I suppose we'll just have to see," I said, and he agreed to accompany me to police headquarters after breakfast.

"You were right about the pancakes," he said, taking his final forkful. "Your friend Mara ought to start a franchise. They're the best. Haven't figured out the secret ingredient yet—I'll just have to order them again and again until I do."

"People have been trying to ferret out that information for years. Mara claims it's how she keeps us coming back. And I don't think she's wrong. Our chamber of commerce always mentions Mara's blueberry pancakes as one of Cabot Cove's many treasures."

Business was brisk at the luncheonette. Not only were the regulars there, but tourists streamed in and out, keeping Mara and her staff hopping. Our breakfast was interrupted a few times by people wanting to talk about the unfortunate incident and inquiring about Seth, but for the most part we were left alone.

"Seth wanted me to thank you for coming to his rescue last night, Rick," I said as we lingered over coffee. "I'm sure he'll thank you in person when you see him next."

He shrugged. "It was an automatic reaction, you know, like a reflex. Let's drop it. You and the doctor were telling me over dinner about this benefactor, Joseph Lennon."

"That's right."

"Who is he?"

"He moved his company to Cabot Cove and has been very active in the community. Not personally. But he's been extremely generous in funding various civic projects."

"I gathered from the conversation last night that his generosity isn't necessarily appreciated by everyone."

"That's true," I said. "There are his detractors who feel he's corrupting the town and using his money to reshape its character to his own liking."

"What does his company do?" Rick asked.

"No one seems quite sure," I replied. "The *Gazette* noted that the 'Diversified' in 'Lennon-Diversified' is like saying they have their fingers in a lot of pies. I remember hearing they had something to do with pharmaceuticals. At least that's what I've been led to believe. His philanthropic involvement with Cabot Cove is high profile, but that doesn't extend to his business."

"Interesting," Rick said.

As he said it, Chester Carlisle entered the luncheonette.

"There's one of Lennon-Diversified's leading detractors," I told Allcott as Chester came straight to where we sat. Now that he was closer, I could see what was written on the front of his yellow T-shirt: LENNON OR LENIN?

"Good morning, Jessica," he boomed. I saw that he had at least two dozen of the shirts draped over his arm.

"Good morning, Chester," I said.

"Care to buy a T-shirt? Got 'em in all sizes, only fifteen bucks."

"I don't think so, Chester," I said, wanting to add that he would probably end up fomenting trouble by parading around town in it.

"Who's your friend?" he asked.

I tried to ignore the question, but Chester slid into the booth next to me, hugging the pile of shirts to his chest. His breath smelled strongly of mouthwash. Had he been drinking? Were the rumors true?

"Chester," I said, "we were just about to leave and—"

"How about you?" Chester asked Rick. "Fifteen bucks."

"Sure," Rick said.

"Please," I said to Rick, "there's no need—"

"No, no, it's okay," Rick said. He pulled out his wallet.

"You look like a small to me," Chester said.

"Medium," Rick said.

"Suit yourself," Chester said, handing Rick a shirt. "They're roomy."

Rick handed Chester the money. "Now," he said in a low, firm voice, "it's time for you to leave."

Chester ignored him and said through a crooked grin, "What a' you think of the shirts, Jessica? I dropped a couple of them off at Lennon's building, gave 'em to the security guy there. Thought the guy would bust a gut. Got tossed out but got my point across. See if he can push us around next time—"

This time, Rick leaned close to Chester

and whispered something in his ear. The older man started to say something, but pulled back from Allcott. "Okay, okay," Chester said. "Take it easy. I don't mean no harm."

Chester got up and stood, as though not sure what to do or where to go next.

"Nice meeting you," Allcott said.

We watched Chester thread his way through a knot of people waiting to pay at the register, take an empty stool at the counter, and hold up one of his shirts for Barney and Spencer's inspection.

"I'm terribly sorry," I told Rick.

"Nothing to apologize for," Rick said. "Every town has someone like your friend."

"He's one of our council members, not really my friend," I said, sorry that I felt the need to make such a disclaimer. "He's not a bad man. It's just that—"

"Jessica, Jessica," Allcott said shaking his head. "It was nothing." He smiled and looked at the shirt he'd bought. "Nice souvenir to take back with me."

"I can think of better ones." I looked at my watch. "Time to head for police headquarters."

Mort Metzger was in the lobby to greet us when we arrived.

"Appreciate you doing this, Mrs. F," he said to me, "but I'm afraid we've got a problem with Mr. Allcott. The kid's attorney has turned thumbs-down on his taking part in the lineup."

"No surprise," Rick said. To me: "You go ahead, Jessica. I'll stroll around outside for a while."

"Shouldn't take more than a half hour," Mort told him.

"Good. I'll be back in thirty minutes."

I followed Mort to the rear of the building, where Cabot Cove's district attorney, Frank Curtis, waited along with the accused's lawyer, an intense young man named Jay Garland.

"All set?" Mort asked.

Everyone said yes, and we were taken into a darkened room with a large one-way pane of glass embedded in one wall. A dark maroon curtain covered it.

"You were one of the alleged victims?" Garland asked me.

"I was the victim of an attempted mugging last night, yes," I said, feeling a prick of annoyance at my experience being branded "alleged."

"The parking lot was dark, wasn't it?" Garland asked.

"There were lights," I answered.

"It happened pretty fast?" was Garland's next question.

"Yes, it happened fast," I said.

"Are you done examining the witness?" Curtis said scornfully.

"Go ahead," said Garland.

Mort instructed someone on the other side of the glass to open the curtain and to bring in the men who would be in the lineup. Now we looked into a brightly lighted room with thin horizontal black stripes set a foot apart on a white wall to indicate the height of the participants. A door to the side opened and four young men entered. One of them was our assailant. Not only did I recognize him, but the bruises on his face added weight to my identification. I also recognized two of the other men in the lineup, though. They were Mort's deputies, wearing dark civilian clothing similar to that worn by the young man who'd attacked us.

"Well, Mrs. Fletcher?" Frank Curtis asked. "Do you see your assailant among them?"

"Yes," I responded. "It's number three."

"Who are the others?" Garland asked Mort.

"A couple of my deputies and—"

"Your deputies?" Garland snarled. He turned to me. "How long have you lived in Cabot Cove, Mrs. Fletcher?"

"A long time," I said.

"Do you recognize the sheriff's deputies there?" He waved a manila folder in the direction of the lineup.

I glanced at Mort, who grimaced.

"Yes," I answered truthfully. "Numbers one and four."

"This is a joke," Garland said.

"I may recognize the sheriff's deputies," I said, "but that hasn't influenced my identification of the young man who attacked us. If you want someone who doesn't know the deputies, why not allow Richard Allcott to try? He'd never been to Cabot Cove before the attack and didn't know anyone in town."

"An ex–FBI agent?" Garland said, snorting. "Not on your life. I'm out of here." He stormed from the room.

"Maybe I shouldn't have used the guys," Mort said to Curtis, "but you wanted it done fast."

"Don't worry about it," Curtis said, slapping the sheriff on the back. "There were plenty of other witnesses besides Mrs. Fletcher. It's open-and-shut."

The others left the building, but I sat with Mort in his office until it was time for Allcott to return. The lineup had taken only fifteen minutes.

"Sorry it didn't go better," I said.

"Like Frank used to say, it doesn't matter. Ready for tomorrow?"

"The Fourth? I suppose so. You?"

"We're set to go. The state is supplying extra officers to handle the crowds. The town has really filled up for the weekend, lots of tourists here to catch the rock-and-roll show and the fireworks. I'll say this for Mr. Lennon—he knows how to throw a party. Looks like it may be bigger than the Lobsterfest, and that was a big deal."

Cabot Cove's annual lobster festival took place in the fall and attracted an enthusiastic crowd despite the fact that it was officially after the peak summer tourist season. The townspeople were very proud of the Lobsterfest, although it would need to go a far way to match the one in Rockland that took place more than a month earlier than ours and was world renowned. I hoped our folks would be equally as proud of this year's Fourth of July celebration.

I told Mort about Chester and his anti-Lennon T-shirts.

"Chester's going off the deep end," Mort said, shaking his head sadly. "T-shirts comparing Lennon with the dictator Lenin? That's really dumb. Had he been drinking?"

"I don't know."

Another shake of the head. "Best thing for him would be to sleep it off, to go to bed and stay there until the whole thing is over."

If only.

"What's on your schedule the rest of the day, Mrs. F?"

"I'm heading for Seth's house when I leave here. He's due back from the hospital. Jim Shevlin is driving him."

"Well, give Doc my best. I suppose there's no sense bringing him in for a lineup after what just happened."

I reminded Mort that he wanted a formal statement from me.

"How about you write one up and drop it off? I'll formally accept it when you do."

"Fair enough."

Mort laughed. "Should be a good one, considering that you write for a living."

"I'll do my best."

When I walked into the reception area, Allcott was coming through the door. "How'd it go?" he asked.

As we exited the sheriff's office I gave him a brief description, and he frowned when I mentioned the deputies in the lineup.

"Your sheriff should have anticipated the lawyer's objection."

"He was under pressure to set up a lineup quickly."

"Where are you off to next?"

"Seth's house."

"Mind if I tag along?"

"Of course not, only—"

He read my mind. "You'd rather be alone with your friend," he said. "I understand. I'll drop you off."

"Thanks for the ride—and for understanding."

As we drove, Allcott said he thought he'd spend the afternoon browsing around the town. "Free for dinner?" he asked as we pulled up in front of Seth's house.

"Afraid not," I replied. "I'm going to a friend's house. I can call and ask whether—"

"No, please. I think I'll make it a quiet night at the inn. Your friends, the owners, are serving up lobster tonight. I'll enjoy a drink in my rocking chair, a good dinner, and pick up where I left off in a book I'm reading—one of yours, as a matter of fact."

"I'm flattered."

"Maybe you'll sign it before I leave?"

"Happy to."

Following my directions, he pulled up in front of Seth's house and came around the front of the car to open the door for me. "My best to Dr. Hazlitt," he said. "See you tomorrow? Another round of blueberry pancakes?"

I laughed. "Not for me. Once a week is all my waistline can tolerate. But I'll meet you at Mara's at nine. We can go from there to the parade. It starts at ten."

"Great. A classic small-town Fourth of July parade. I love it."

I watched him drive away before knocking on Seth's door and opening it. "Seth?" I called.

"Back here," he responded.

I walked through the main part of the house to the small den, to which my friend often repaired when he wanted a quiet, peaceful place to read and think. He was leaning back in his favorite armchair, newspaper spread across his chest, glasses perched on the end of his nose. He started to rise.

"Don't get up," I said, sitting on a hassock. "Did I wake you?"

"Might have drifted off a bit. Hospital rooms are so damned noisy; can't get a wink in all night. Every time I start to doze off, here comes another nurse, poking me, taking my temperature or blood pressure. Amazing anyone gets well in a place like that."

"You look fine."

"I feel all right," he said. "Whoever's blood they gave me must have been an athlete, bright red and full of oxygen. Sure to give me plenty of pep."

"That's good to hear. Have they told you to take it easy for a few days?"

"Of course they did. They tell that to everyone. But I've got a full afternoon of patients."

"Maybe you should—"

"What, Jessica? Call Dr. Warren Boyle and ask him to cover for me?"

"Where's Dr. Jenny?"

"Downstate, visitin' her folks. She offered to come back up, but I told her no. And I'm not calling Dr. Boyle."

"I wasn't suggesting anything of the kind, and you know it."

"I'm not so sure you think it's a bad idea."

"I think it's a terrible idea. Now, you said you wanted to discuss something with me."

"Ayuh. You might recall that I told you I was speaking with someone from Bangor who specializes in selling medical practices."

"Yes, I do recall that."

"Well, I've made up my mind to go ahead and do it."

"And just what prompted this decision, if I may ask?" I said, knowing what he was about to say.

"Time marches on, Jessica, and it's passed this chicken-soup doctor by."

"Seth Hazlitt," I said, "that is absurd!"

"Oh, is it, now?"

"Yes, it is. You're at the top of your game, Seth. You have the benefit of experience to go with your insights and training. I remember when I attended that medical conference with you in Los Angeles. You received an award for your diagnostic excellence. You're the best diagnostician there is, and hundreds of people have benefited from it. Half of this town, at least those who go back more than a few years, have you to thank for their health and well-being. You're constantly attending conferences and seminars to keep up with the latest advances in medicine. You're not ready to retire, plain and simple. *You are not ready to retire!*"

A tiny smile crossed his lips. "The heat's got you all fired up this mornin', Jessica."

"No, *you* have me fired up, Seth. Should I stop writing because I'm on the wrong side of fifty?"

"Now, that's not a fair question, not an apt analogy."

"Of course it is. I'm at the top of *my* game, too. I have lots of fans out there who are waiting for my next book, just as you have lots of men, women, and children waiting for appointments with you. They *need* you, Seth."

He grunted and looked out the window at his garden, which he tended with care.

"Will you at least give it some more time before taking any action?" I asked, placing my hand on his good arm.

"Ayuh, Jessica. But not too much time. I suppose you know that Harriet is plannin' to retire."

"Yes, she told me."

"Not sure what I'll do without her."

"You'll find someone else just as capable and caring. That's what you'll do."

He folded the newspaper, put it aside, and slid forward on the chair.

"Need a hand?" I asked.

"I certainly do not, but thank you anyway."

He got to his feet and winced against a pain. "Back's been actin' up lately," he said. "Those god-awful hospital beds would cripple anyone."

"Want me to make some lunch, or pick something up?" I asked as we walked to the side of the house in which his medical offices were located.

"Not especially hungry, Jessica. You go on about your business. I've got to get ready for the first patient."

I said I'd be back in touch later that day. I stepped out into the heat of midday. I was satisfied that my little pep talk had had some impact on him, although I didn't suffer any delusions. A confluence of events had hit him at once, and his depression was very real. Like all of us (except for the young and foolish), he was well aware of his mortality. On top of that was the arrival in Cabot Cove of an aggressive young doctor who was energetically marketing his services, and by extension siphoning off patients from Seth, and probably from other physicians, too. My encouragement not to sell his practice and retire would have only a momentary impact.

That truth sat heavily with me all the way home.

Chapter Eight

Could it be?

When I awoke the following morning, the air coming through my window was actually cool. I got up, put on a robe, and stepped out onto my back porch. Sure enough, the oppressive heat wave that had gripped Cabot Cove and much of Maine for days had broken, just in time for our Independence Day celebration. The cooler air brought a smile to my face, and I sat on the porch and reveled in it.

It's remarkable how our lives are affected by weather. The heat and humidity had sapped everyone's energy, judging from the way people moved and spoke. I was no exception. This morning, my spirits had markedly picked up, and I looked forward to riding into town and taking part in the day's festivities, starting with the library panel.

I considered calling Seth to see if he felt up to joining Rick Allcott and me at Mara's, but thought better of it. Chances are he would have agreed, and it was undoubtedly better for him to stay at home and give his wound another day to heal.

Allcott was already at Mara's and engaged in conversation with a group of people, including our former sheriff, Amos Tupper, when I arrived. I joined them as Rick was finishing a story about one of the cases he'd worked on during his career as an FBI special agent.

"Good morning, Miz Fletcher," Amos said.

"Good morning, Amos. Been enjoying yourself?"

"Yes, I certainly have. The town has changed a lot since I was last here."

"Well, it's been quite a few years now," I said. "Change is inevitable, I suppose.

Would you like to join Mr. Allcott and me for breakfast?"

"Don't mind if I do, as long as the FBI won't be listening in on us." He laughed to reinforce that he was joking, and Rick laughed, too, although without much conviction. We took a booth that gave us a view of the dock and the flurry of boating activity that was taking place. It seemed that the break in the weather had injected a powerful dose of energy in everyone.

"Mr. Allcott told me earlier about what happened to you and Seth the other night," Amos said. " 'Course, I read about it in the *Gazette*, and that's all everybody seems to be talking about."

"That's past tense, Amos," I said, "and I'd like to keep it that way."

"How's Doc Hazlitt?"

"Doing just fine. He started seeing patients the day he came home from the hospital."

Thinking of Seth and the conversation we'd had the previous day threatened to dampen my mood, but I willed away any negativity.

"There's that old fool," Amos said, pointing out the window to where Chester Carlisle stood wearing his anti-Lennon T-shirt and hawking them to passersby.

"Oh, my." I sighed.

Chester's pile of shirts was considerably smaller than it had been the previous day, so he must have found some takers in town.

"I was chatting with Sheriff Metzger yesterday," Amos said. "He says Chester's become the town clown."

"I think that's overly harsh," I said, "although he has been acting oddly lately."

"Must be the booze," Amos said.

"That's just a rumor," I said. "One I hope isn't true."

Chester Carlisle had been a good and decent man for years, a valuable member of the community. Recently he'd become eccentric. Was it age? Had he begun to show signs of dementia of some sort? That was possible. Of course, if he had taken to drinking, that wouldn't help. I hated to see him become a laughingstock, and wondered if there wasn't some means of confronting him in the hope of bringing about a change. I made a mental note to ask Seth about that. Chester was, as far as I knew, still one of Seth's patients.

Allcott weighed in on the subject of Chester. "I'd be concerned about him if I were you," he said to me and to Amos.

"Oh, I am," I confirmed.

"Not just for him," Rick said, "but for the community. I've worked closely with some of the bureau's best criminal profilers, and people like your Mr. Carlisle, while viewed with amusement—you know, just a harmless old fool—can sometimes turn deadly."

"Deadly?" Amos and I said in unison.

Allcott nodded. "They keep deteriorating until one day they snap and hurt somebody."

"He's right, Miz Fletcher," Amos said, his expression suddenly serious. "He knows what he's talking about."

"I hate to think that," I said, and I meant it. At the same time, I couldn't dismiss what the retired FBI special agent was telling us. Maybe confronting Chester and getting to the bottom of his character change was more pressing than I'd previously thought.

The sound of a marching band tuning up drifted through the door as people arrived and left.

"The parade will be starting soon," I said. "Let's get a front-row seat."

The sidewalks up and down Main Street were filling up fast as we left Mara's and found a good location from which to view the marchers. The townsfolk always turned out for a parade, and we could see the whole range of Cabot Cove's population, from our most venerable senior citizens down to infants in carriages. Some people had brought lawn chairs and set them up along the parade route. Youngsters crowded together, sitting on the curbs, and waited for the parade to begin, waving little flags that had been distributed by the chamber of commerce. There were young fathers with children perched on their shoulders and mothers with babies on their hips. A group of teenagers hung out in front of the empty firehouse trying to look cool, and ended up chasing each other in and out of the empty bays. The fire trucks always led the parade.

Our civic organizations had worked for weeks building floats with a Fourth of July theme, and they could be seen at the end of the block getting ready to move. The route would take them down the length of Main Street, then bear left, snaking through some of the residential streets close to town, and reemerging at the dock, where a small stage, festooned in red, white, and blue, had been erected. A microphone and speakers had been set up. What would an Independence Day parade be without a few speeches at its conclusion?

We were joined by Kathy and Wilimena Copeland, and Ralph Mackin and his wife, Lorraine, at whose house I'd enjoyed dinner last night. Ralph was an attorney, as well as one of the town's judges.

"Do you think Joe Lennon arranged for the better weather?" Ralph asked jokingly.

"From what I hear, he's capable of it," was Amos's comment.

"They're starting," Kathy said.

The volunteer firemen on the hook and ladder pounded on their big brass bell and waved to the crowd as the fire engine slowly rolled down the street. They had placed a stuffed toy Dalmatian in the front passenger seat, its head sticking out the window. After the fire engine, walking behind a color guard, came Mayor Jim Shevlin and the town council, Chester Carlisle among them, looking cheerful for a change, and wearing a white cotton shirt that covered the message of his yellow T-shirt.

There's nothing like a parade to bring people together and to instill a sense of pride in where we live. The high school marching band in their colorful uniform, led by drum majors and majorettes and the school cheerleaders, strutted their stuff for an appreciative audience of all ages. The kids whooped and hollered, and the adults applauded, snapped pictures, and shouted greetings to their participating children as they passed.

"This is great," Rick Allcott said after the final float had moved past us, and the band's music began to fade. "Like something out of a Norman Rockwell painting."

"I'm so glad you're here to enjoy it," I said. "I suppose we'd better head down to the dock and be there when they arrive."

We joined the crowd and slowly made our way back to the dock. Chester Carlisle must have left the parade before its conclusion because he was there selling his T-shirts, or at least attempting to. The crowd around him seemed to be getting a kick out of what he was saying.

". . . and Mr. High-and-Mighty Joe Lennon will get his comeuppance, you mark my words. We don't need his kind here in Cabot Cove!"

A few people applauded, and someone said, "You tell 'em, Chester."

I started to move our little group away when Mort Metzger and a deputy suddenly stepped into the circle surrounding Chester.

"That's enough, Councilman," Mort said. "Time to move on."

"I got a right to be here like everyone else," Chester countered.

"Afraid not, sir," Mort said. "Got a call you're making a public nuisance of yourself. Besides, you don't have a permit to be selling things down here on the dock."

"Never heard of needing a permit." Chester's voice was harsher now, his posture more belligerent.

"Well, that's the law, and you probably voted for it. I'm going to tell you one more time, nicely. Please take those T-shirts and go home before you end up spending the Fourth of July in jail."

Chester pulled himself up to full height, which made him considerably taller than the sheriff. By now, of course, all attention was away from the stage and focused on the confrontation. I looked back at the stage and saw Cynthia Welch and the young man, Dante, who always seemed to accompany her. They were obviously to be part of the ceremonies when the parade arrived, and were both intently watching the scene playing out between Chester and Mort.

"Last chance, Chester," Mort said. "Either you leave peaceably, or I take you in."

"What the hell is going on here?" Chester barked. "Who are you working for, Joe Lennon or Cabot Cove? This is a free country, and I have a right to say what I want, and to wear any damn shirt I choose."

"That does it," Mort said, motioning to his deputy to grab Chester.

"Get your hands off me," Chester said, shrugging off the deputy. "I'm leaving, but I won't forget this, Sheriff. You and Mr. Joseph Lennon will pay for embarrassing me like this."

Chester, followed by some of his friends, stalked off and got in his silver Chevy Blazer. Cynthia Welch glanced at her assistant and the pair exchanged a private smile as Chester took off.

Mort turned to me. "Hated to do it, but this is no time for him to be causing a ruckus."

I was relieved to see Chester leave, although I hoped he wouldn't make trouble for Mort with the other members of the town council. The sheriff is appointed by the town council. Chester did have the right to be there and to make his statement about Lennon-Diversified, but perhaps not to sell T-shirts. I'm a fervent defender of the First Amendment and have taken a stand many times in its defense. Of course, there are always exceptions to free speech. It isn't okay to yell "Fire" in a crowded theater simply because you feel it's your right to do so. Then again, I also feel there's a time and a place for everything, and protesting Joseph Lennon at an event he was sponsoring would only tarnish our Independence Day celebration.

"Who called to complain about Chester?" I asked.

"Don't recall if he gave his name," Mort replied.

"You did the right thing, Sheriff," Allcott said.

"Appreciate that, coming from an ex–FBI agent," Mort said.

We all turned as our mayor, Jim Shevlin, took the stage and spoke into the microphone. "May I have your attention? The parade will arrive here shortly. In the meantime, I want to introduce Ms. Cynthia Welch of Lennon-Diversified, the company that's financed a lot of the events we'll be enjoying today. Speaking of that, don't forget that the rock-and-roll concert will begin at seven out at the industrial park, followed by a spectacular fireworks show put on by the world-famous Gruccis."

Cynthia took the microphone and launched into prolonged praise for her employer and its plans for Cabot Cove. Had Chester still been there, he might have heckled her speech. Of course, it was possible that he had simply moved to another location and could hear everything being said from the stage. Cynthia eventually introduced Josie Lennon and Robin Stockdale, who brought their youthful actors and actresses onstage for their pageant celebrating the meaning of Independence Day. The kids were charming, of course, and everyone seemed to thoroughly enjoy their performance despite the recorded rock-and-roll music. They left the stage to sustained applause and whistles as the parade finally arrived. The speeches continued until everyone had had a say, and the crowd finally dispersed.

"Where to?" Kathy Copeland asked me.

"Home," I said. "I have a ton of things to catch up on before heading out to the park this evening."

I'd taken my bike downtown, and, grateful for the break in temperature, I rode it back home, where after answering e-mails and other correspondence, I lay down on the couch in the study and promptly fell asleep, awakening at five to the ringing phone. It was Seth.

"How are you getting to the fireworks tonight?" he asked.

"Hadn't thought about it," I said sleepily.

"Wake you?"

"Yes, but that's all right. Time I got moving anyway."

"I'll pick you up at six thirty," he said.

"No, you won't. You have no business going out and—"

"I've never been known to miss a Fourth of July fireworks show, Jessica, and I'm not going to start now. Remember, the doctor knows best. Bring along a couple of those folding canvas chairs you have. Harriet packed a picnic basket for us. Nice of her. I'm packing those headphone contraptions so we won't have to actually listen to the music, if you can call it that."

I smiled but said nothing. He was obviously feeling a lot better than the last time I'd spoken with him.

"Jessica? You there?"

"Yes, Seth, I'm here. It sounds fine. See you at six thirty."

The conversation ended, and I took a shower, dressed in appropriate clothing for an outdoor concert and fireworks display (being sure to tuck some potent bug spray in my bag), pulled two chairs from where I kept them on the back porch, and went outside to enjoy some fresh air. It promised to be a spectacular sunset, judging from the vivid, striated colors already forming on the western horizon. I silently reminded myself, as I often do, how lucky I was to live in such a wonderful place and to be surrounded by good, caring friends. I hadn't been especially keen on attending the concert—the downtown parade was always my favorite part of the Fourth—but I do enjoy a good fireworks display.

I leaned over to pull some weeds from around my petunias, and tossed them in a bucket by the corner of the porch, dusting off the dirt from my hands. There was something gnawing at me that I couldn't put a finger on, a vague, unsettling feeling that took the edge off my excitement.

Silly, I thought, focusing on the fact that Seth was feeling better.

"On with the show!" I said aloud as I returned to the house to wash up and get ready for Seth's arrival. I looked forward to a relaxing evening beneath the stars.

But it was not to be.

Chapter Nine

Although I caught Seth wincing once or twice from a stab of pain where his arm had been cut, he was otherwise in what could only be described as a jovial mood when he picked me up—at least jovial for him. I wanted to ask whether he'd had a change of heart about selling his practice, but thought it better not to bring up the subject and possibly spoil his elevated spirits.

The large grassy area to the right of the Lennon-Diversified building, now a public park, was already filling with tourists and townspeople, who'd set up folding chairs of every variety and color or spread blankets on the ground. It was a glorious night, with a welcome crispness to the air. We chose a spot next to where a number of friends, including Kathy and Wilimena Copeland, had gathered for a communal picnic dinner. Spirits were high, and the sounds of laughter, which had been noticeably absent during the oppressive heat wave, were again heard. Naturally, many people stopped by to inquire about Seth, who assured them that he was feeling fine. I wondered whether he'd decided to come this night to make the point that he was still capable of handling his usual busy medical practice. If so, his attempt was successful. The outpouring of concern and affection for him was heartwarming, and I had to believe that it would confirm to him that he was very much needed.

As the time approached for the band to start, I looked around for Chester Carlisle, hoping that he'd taken Mort Metzger's sage advice and stayed home. I didn't see Chester, but there were some of his bright yellow T-shirts here and there in the crowd. I found it ironic that people were willing to enjoy the concert and fireworks, courtesy of Joe Lennon's generosity, but at the same time felt the need to thumb their noses at him.

Amos Tupper joined us, using a spare chair that Jack and Tobé Wilson had brought with them. Jack was one of Cabot Cove's leading vets, and Tobé worked alongside him in their practice. She could be seen now and then around town walking their pet pig, Kiwi, one of many animals they personally owned and upon which they lavished care.

Seth's nurse, Harriet, had prepared fried chicken, salad, rolls, and miniature crab cakes as appetizers. Seth had contributed a thermos of lemonade to go along with the iced tea I'd brought and the walnut cookies I'd baked for dessert. All in all, it was good being with close friends to celebrate this monumentally important day in our nation's history and the remarkable events that led up to it.

Cynthia Welch, Lennon-Diversified's VP, stepped onto the stage, followed by Joe Lennon and his son and daughter. Mayor Shevlin was up there, too, along with a few members of the town council—but not Chester—and various other community leaders.

"Where's your friend, Mr. Allcott?" Seth asked.

"I don't know," I said. "We hadn't made any plans for tonight. I was going to call the B and B where he's staying—Blueberry Hill—but I fell asleep. I'm sure he's around here someplace. He obviously doesn't have any trouble making friends."

Ms. Welch's voice boomed through the myriad immense speakers set up for the band. "Good evening, and happy Independence Day."

The crowd cheered.

She introduced Joseph Lennon, who stepped forward and doffed his baseball cap in recognition of a slightly less enthusiastic cheer. Welch went on to extol the virtues of her boss and his company, careful to wrap her comments into praise for the Cabot Cove community and its leaders. Mayor Shevlin waved at everyone, but was not given an opportunity to say anything. Like most speakers, Welch rambled on a little too long before introducing the Lennon children, Paul and Josie. Paul didn't have much to say. He welcomed everyone on behalf of the company and quickly turned the mike over to his sister. He could be heard saying, "Make it snappy; they're almost here."

Josie gushed about how thrilled she was to be able to introduce the band, "but first we have a surprise for you." She cupped her hand over her eyes and looked up into the sky. The roar of jet engines filled the air, and seconds later four F-16 fighter planes, their wingtips looking as though they were touching, came from over the water and thundered above us, eliciting a sustained gasp from everyone, young and old alike. As the rumble of the engines faded, the audience broke into a spontaneous ovation.

"That man must have a lot of influence," Amos said, to nodding heads all around.

Josie grinned. "And now, ladies and gentlemen, my favorite band in the whole wide world—the Snake Days!"

"The *what*?" Seth asked as the five members of the band bounced onto the stage and got ready to perform their first number. *"The Snake Days?"*

I confirmed that he'd heard right, as the drummer, who sat behind the largest set of drums imaginable, began a rhythm for the rest of the young musicians. They launched into a raucous, deafening song that didn't have a discernible melody, at least to my ears, but whose beat got everyone in the audience moving, toes tapping time and hands coming together in unison.

"Here," Seth said, handing me a set of headphones with foam earpieces, similar to those distributed on planes when the movie comes on. "Got 'em from one of my patients. Says she uses them when her kids are whining." I smiled and placed them over my ears, providing some defense against the music's electronic assault. As the concert progressed, I took note of others in our vicinity. The younger people obviously liked the performance better than our older citizens, numbers of whom removed themselves from in front of the bandstand to positions farther away from the speakers. They were replaced by the band's teenaged fans, who crowded together at the bottom of the stage, clapping and jumping in time to the beat. All in all, everyone seemed in a festive mood. I do admit that when the band completed its final tune of the evening, and the leader shouted good night, a wave of relief came over me. I handed the headphones back to Seth, who simply said, "Snake Days, indeed! Nothing but a lot of noise!"

I didn't debate it with him, both because I agreed—and because it wouldn't have mattered if I didn't.

It was now dusk, and in the sky, a band of pale blue hugged the western horizon. It was time for the fireworks. The first few rockets shot up from where the Grucci technicians plied their trade behind the stage, followed by an increasingly rapid barrage that filled the nighttime sky above the stage and over the water with a cacophonous report. I put my hand out and Seth dropped the headphones back in my palm and I replaced them on my ears. Even muffled, I could still hear the customary *oohs* and *aahs* that accompanied the dazzling displays, each launch louder and more colorful than the last.

I do love watching the luminous trails of light as they soar into the sky, and the vibrant sprays that cascade over our heads. At the same time, with each explosion and flash, I can't help but think of people in war-torn areas of the world for whom hearing such thunderous blasts is part of a frightening daily routine. For them, it's not a show. It's grim reality.

"That was terrific," Amos said as the acrid odor of spent explosives drifted over the area.

"Not for dogs and cats," Tobé Wilson said. "I hope everyone had their pets secured. We get in a lot of strays on July Fourth. There are always animals who break loose and run away, terrified by the noise."

As we started packing up, Rick Allcott approached. "Here you are," he said. "I looked for you earlier, but with this crowd—"

"I'm sorry," I said. "We should have arranged to meet someplace."

"No problem," he said. "I fell in with a nice group of people, all tourists like me."

I introduced him to the Wilsons and the Copeland sisters, who were folding their chairs.

"How's the arm, Doctor?" Allcott asked Seth.

"Just fine, sir. Just fine."

"Looks like you're getting ready to call it a night," Allcott said. "I hate to see it end. Anybody game for a nightcap?"

"Afraid not," Jack Wilson said. "I've got some early surgery to perform tomorrow."

"Don't forget the pancake breakfast at the firehouse," Willie said.

"We'll be there," Tobé said. "At least I will if Jack can't make it. Will we see you there, Jessica?"

"Wouldn't miss it for the world," I said, and bade them good night.

"Are the firemen's pancakes as good as Mara's?" Rick asked.

"Not even close," Seth said, "but the town supports the volunteers just the same."

"They're not bad," I said, tucking the dishes and paper napkins back in the basket. "Just no secret ingredient."

"So, Seth, will you join us for a drink?" Rick asked.

"Nope, but thanks. I'll need a good sleep to get over that infernal music. The Snake Days! Hah!" He looked at me. "You should go, Jessica. Allcott's been deprived of your company all evening. Ought to give the gentleman a little more of your time, since he's only here for a short stay."

I've known Seth Hazlitt long enough, and well enough, not to prolong a discussion once he's made up his mind about something. Besides, even if there had been no Snake Days music, he needed to catch up on his sleep.

"We'll just help you bring everything back to the car," I said, "and then we'll be on our way."

"Mind if I join you?" Amos Tupper asked.

"Sure! The more the merrier," Allcott said.

"You're always welcome, Amos," I said.

We carried the chairs and picnic basket to Seth's car and loaded them inside. "I'll drop your chairs off tomorrow," Seth said.

"No rush," I said. "I won't need them until next year's Fourth of July. Drive carefully." We watched him pull away.

"Where to?" Amos asked.

"I certainly don't want any more food," I said. "I feel like I've eaten an entire fried chicken. If you don't mind, what I really need is a good walk. That folding chair gave me a crick in the back." I arched against a stiffness in my back and neck.

"I'm up for that," Rick said.

"Me, too," said Amos.

We left the parking lot and strolled back to where we'd witnessed the concert and fireworks. There were still a few stragglers sitting in their chairs or on their blankets, evidently not wanting to end the evening either. The band's "roadies" were busy breaking down the equipment on the stage, and members of Cabot Cove's sanitation department had begun their cleanup work. I spotted Mort Metzger issuing orders to some of his uniformed officers, and we went to him.

"Quite a show, huh?" Mort said after dismissing his men.

"Spectacular," Amos agreed.

"What are you folks still doing here?" our sheriff asked.

"Walking off fried chicken," I said.

"I never had a chance to have dinner," Mort said, his eyes scanning the diminishing activity. "Fried chicken sounds pretty good just about now." He waved his arms in the air. "Hey, kids, get away from those wires on that stage." He hurried off to keep several youngsters out of harm's way. I hoped he'd be able to get home soon and grab some dinner.

Rick Allcott, Amos Tupper, and I walked down to the water's edge and strolled along, away from the Lennon-Diversified building. Light from a waning crescent moon danced off ripples in the water. Because we were outside town and its downtown lights, the sky was especially clear, millions of stars shining against an almost black scrim.

"Miss being sheriff here?" Rick asked Amos.

"Once in a while," said our former top law enforcement official, "but I get to travel some. Keeps me from being bored. Went on a safari tour to Africa coupla months ago with the senior center."

"Amos! How exciting," I said.

"It was."

"Always wanted to visit Africa," Rick said. "Sounds like an ideal retired life."

"Also do some bass fishing, and some woodworking."

"That's right," I said. "I'd forgotten that you'd started building furniture when you were here, Amos."

"I really enjoy it," he said with a gentle laugh. "I love the feel of the wood and the look of the grain. Then again, Miz Fletcher, I sure do miss the people in Cabot Cove. Finest bunch of people I've ever known. It was good to see Doc Hazlitt feelin' better."

"He's a trouper," I said.

"How about you, Allcott? You miss being an FBI agent?" Amos said. "You seem a little young for retirement."

"I put in my years," Rick said. "Sometimes I miss the action, but on lovely nights like tonight, I remember what I enjoy most about being retired—peace! There wasn't a lot of it when I was with the bureau. Nothing like in Cabot Cove. I can understand why you choose to live here, Jessica."

"It's my little slice of heaven."

"Even with the growth, and the changes that come along with it?" Rick asked.

"Even with that," I said.

I estimated that we'd gone almost half a mile before Amos suggested we turn back. Now we were walking toward the Lennon-Diversified building, whose marble facade caught the moonlight, giving it an ethereal aura, like some religious temple in another part of the world, or an imposing marble government building in Washington, D.C., home of many such edifices.

"Anyone care for a cup of coffee or tea back at my house?" I asked.

"Sounds good to me," Amos said.

"Count me in," said Rick.

As we started up the gentle hill toward

the lot where Amos and Rick had parked, we heard the sound of sirens.

"Some fool must'a had too much to drink and wrapped himself around a pole," Amos offered.

"Or around someone else's car," Rick said.

"Oh, dear," I said. "I hope not."

The sound came closer, two sirens now. We were within a hundred feet of Rick's car when flashing lights came into view. A few seconds later, their source became evident as two marked cars raced down into the lot from the road. One was Mort Metzger's sheriff's vehicle. They came to a halt a dozen feet away, and Mort and three deputies exited.

"What's going on?" I said.

"Got a report of a body down behind Lennon's building," Mort said.

"We were just down near there," I said.

"Did you see anyone?"

"No," we chorused.

Mort led his men down the hill. We didn't make a conscious decision to follow them. Amos, Rick, and I simply fell in line, our reflexes on autopilot. We saw the men disappear around the rear of the office building, where exterior lights had come to life, bathing the sweeping veranda, promenade, and dock in harsh white light. Two people stood together on the dock as Mort and his officers narrowed the distance between them. We stopped a respectful distance away, but close enough to hear what was said. I recognized one of the men awaiting the sheriff's arrival by his uniform, a Lennon-Diversified security guard. The other person was the young man, Dante, who seemed always to be at Cynthia Welch's side.

"Where?" Mort asked in a loud voice.

"Down there," the guard replied.

They all headed in the direction indicated by the guard, the far end of the dock. We moved with them.

"Right there!" the guard announced, and pointed toward the water.

Flashlights were trained on the object of their focus, and we strained to see what it was. We knew it was a body, of course, because Mort had said it was. The question was, Whose body was it?

After a few seconds, Mort retraced his steps in our direction.

"Who is it?" I asked.

"Is he dead, Sheriff?" Amos asked.

"Afraid so," Mort responded.

Rick, Amos, and I stared at Mort.

"Joe Lennon," he said flatly.

"Strange time a night to go swimmin'," Amos said.

"You folks didn't see anything at all?"

"No," I said. "Nothing."

"Well," Mort said, "I'd appreciate it if you'd stay around in case you remember something. I've got to call Doc Hazlitt."

"Why Seth?" I asked, thinking our friend was probably in bed already.

"The ME's out of town on vacation," Mort explained. "I need a doctor here."

It wasn't long ago that Cabot Cove didn't have a medical examiner. Instead, we had a coroner, the last one being the owner of the town's largest funeral home. This wasn't unusual, I knew. Most towns and smaller cities have laypeople who function as coroners—morticians, fire chiefs, taxidermists. But as Cabot Cove grew, the town council voted to fund the office of a medical examiner. Our first—our current one—moved here after a successful career as the medical examiner in Worcester, Massachusetts. He'd retired from that post and readily accepted our position because it promised not to be too heavy a load on him in his retirement. Prior to his arrival, Seth had functioned as ME on occasion, as had other physicians in town. Seth was board-certified as a forensic medical examiner, one of many certifications he held.

"I'm sorry to get Doc Hazlitt out so late," Mort said, "what with him being hurt and all."

"Isn't there another doctor who practices nearby?" Rick asked.

"Dr. Boyle," Mort replied. "Don't want him involved in the investigation, though," he said as he walked away and placed the call to Seth.

Of course, I reasoned. Dr. Boyle was intimately involved with Joseph Lennon. Mort was being prudent in not bringing Boyle into it, at least not at this juncture.

We sat on a low wall until Seth arrived, carrying the bag that he kept ready for when he was called out on ME duties.

"Mort says he's got a floater," he told us before going down to where the body had been discovered.

"I know," I said. "I'm sorry he had to call you so late."

"No bother at all. I was still up," Seth said. "I'd better get to work."

He returned a half hour later.

"No doubt about it?" I asked. "It is Mr. Lennon?"

"Ayuh."

"A homicide?" Rick Allcott asked.

"Not at liberty to say," Seth replied. He leaned in closer. "But I'd guess he didn't put the bullet in his head himself. I have to get down to the morgue and get the process started."

As Seth got in his car and drove away, an ambulance arrived, manned by two EMTs, who handled the removal of Lennon's body. It was placed in the rear of the ambulance and the driver sped away. Mort came over to us.

"Looks like you picked a fine time to come back to Cabot Cove, Amos," he told our former sheriff. "This is going to be a tough one."

"Any help I can provide, I'm happy to," Amos said.

"How was he killed?" I asked, knowing the answer but looking for confirmation.

"Looks like he was shot, but that's unofficial, Mrs. F."

As he said it, one of his deputies came from the crime scene carrying a clear plastic evidence bag. I pushed away from the wall and stopped him. "What's that?" I asked.

"What's what, Mrs. F?" Mort said, joining me.

I pointed to the portion of a yellow T-shirt visible through the plastic. Some of the lettering on it was also readable—. . . NON, NOT LENIN. "Oh, dear," I said. "That's one of the T-shirts Chester Carlisle was selling."

"I know," said Mort. "Looks like Chester and I had better have a little chat. We found that shirt floating in the water next to Mr. Lennon."

Chapter Ten

Murder has a way of changing one's plans.

Rather than having tea or coffee at my house, we followed Mort to headquarters, where we were offered a cup of station house brew, which we all politely declined. I knew from previous experience that the coffeepot at our sheriff's office had likely been on all day, and the result was a viscous liquid closer to shellac than anything Juan Valdez would have been proud to offer. Of course, Amos knew that, too, as did Rick, from having spent a portion of his professional life in station houses.

We settled in Mort's office, and he asked us to write out a statement of what we'd seen during our nocturnal walk. That reminded me that I'd promised to write a statement regarding the attack in the parking lot at Peppino's. *I'll deal with that later,* I decided. The statements we gave concerning what we'd seen on this night were uniformly short. We'd seen nothing.

"Did you ever get any dinner, Mort?" I asked.

"Got called away just as I was sitting down."

"You must be starving by now," I said.

He patted his stomach. "I guess I can afford to lose a pound or two. I'll get something later."

"You said that yellow T-shirt was found with the body?" Rick said.

"That's right. Two of my men are picking Chester up as we speak."

"It was a gunshot?"

"Right again. I suppose nobody heard it because of the fireworks."

"Or the concert," I said. "The music was very loud. I wonder—"

"You wonder what, Mrs. F?" Mort said.

"I wonder if it was planned that way, that

whoever shot Mr. Lennon intended for the report of the gun to coincide with the noise of the fireworks display so it wouldn't be noticed."

"If that's true," Rick said, "how would that same someone know that Lennon would be outside his building when the fireworks were going on?"

"Good point," Amos said.

"Since he was hosting the concert and the fireworks, it's not unreasonable to assume he would want to stay for those activities," I said. "It could have been relatively easy to draw him away with a message."

"That's true, Miz Fletcher," Amos said. "Hadn't thought of that."

"Okay, if we're speculating, he could have been shot inside his building," Mort said, "and the killer could have used a silencer so even if we hadn't had fireworks, the gun wouldn't have been heard."

"That's a possibility," Amos said. "What about that, Miz Fletcher?"

"I doubt whether an outsider would have been able to kill him inside the building," I said. "I know from experience that security there is extremely tight. And if the assailant used a silencer, that would indicate it was a professional job. The yellow T-shirt would tend to contradict that theory."

"Why's that, Miz Fletcher?"

Rick answered, "Mrs. Fletcher is probably thinking that if someone wanted to implicate Chester by leaving his T-shirt on the scene, that person would have to be someone who knows the people in town, not a stranger sent here for the sole purpose of killing Joe Lennon."

"Exactly," I said.

"Unless, of course, it *was* Chester," Mort said, "which, frankly, is what I believe. He was bad-mouthing Lennon left and right, carrying on like a commuter stuck in rush-hour traffic on the Long Island Expressway."

An officer poked his head through the door. "Got a reporter on line two, Sheriff. Won't speak to nobody but you."

"Here we go," Mort said wearily, slowly shaking his head and staring at the light on his desk phone. A second line lit up, followed immediately by the third and final one.

"I think we'd better leave," I said.

"Hang on. Let me just take this," Mort said. He looked at Amos. "How much longer were you planning to stay, Amos?"

"End of the week, or close to it," Amos replied. "I can stick around if you think you can use me."

"I've got a feeling I'm going to need all the help I can get on this one," Mort said as the officer reappeared and announced that there were media calls on all three lines.

"I'm happy to give a hand," Amos said.

"Good. I might deputize you."

Rick Allcott said, "I'm willing to help out, too, if that makes any sense."

"And you know you can count on me," I said. "Not that you need my help."

"I'd better start answering these calls," Mort said. "Appreciate it if you'd hang around a while."

We went from his office to the central waiting room. Seth Hazlitt had just arrived. "What are you doing here?" he asked.

We explained.

"Looks like I'm back in the saddle," Amos said proudly. "Mort's going to deputize me."

"Do tell," Seth said, peering over his glasses, his brows flying up. Seth had always liked Amos personally—everyone did—but he was never especially impressed with Amos's law enforcement abilities when he was sheriff of Cabot Cove. Of course, that was back when Cabot Cove was a much sleepier place than it is now. Amos's primary strength was his warm relationship with virtually everyone in town, and his ability to cajole potential lawbreakers into not making fools of themselves. Mort Metzger had some of that ability, too, but Amos had honed it to perfection.

"What's your initial finding?" Rick asked Seth.

"Keep it in this room?" Seth responded.

"Of course," we replied.

"The deceased was shot at close range, no more than nine or ten feet, I'd say. A single shot. The bullet's still in his brain. Once it's removed, the lab folks will analyze it."

The door opened and the *Gazette*'s Evelyn Phillips and her photographer, John Shearer, burst into the room.

"Is it true?" Evelyn asked. "Joe Lennon has been murdered?"

"You'll have to ask that question of the sheriff," Seth said.

Shearer started snapping pictures of us.

"Cut that out!" Seth growled. "I think it's time we got out of here."

"Good idea," I said. "The offer still stands for tea or coffee back at my house."

"I'm more in the mood for something stronger," Rick said.

"I have that, too," I said. I pulled Seth aside. "Shouldn't you be getting home, Seth? You're only out of the hospital one day."

"Stop your fussing over me, madam! I'm fine."

"Then you're well enough to come and have coffee with us."

Seth frowned at me. "Got any of that ice cream left that I like?"

I smiled. "There might be some in a corner of the freezer. You'll have to come and see."

"I have to fill out my preliminary report for the sheriff. I'll be by after that."

I went to Mort's office, where he was fielding media calls. He capped his hand over the mouthpiece and looked up at me. I quickly told him we were leaving, and where we'd be.

He nodded and returned to his caller.

"I'd best stay here," Amos said when I returned to the waiting room. "Mort will want to deputize me tonight, and I'd better be on hand."

"Suit yourself," I said, looking at my watch. "Come by later if you like. I don't think any of us will get to bed early tonight."

Rick drove us to my house. I put on the kettle for me and poured him a snifter of cognac.

"You've had quite a visit to Cabot Cove," I said absently as I rummaged in the cabinet for a box of herbal tea. I didn't want caffeine keeping me up when I finally did get to bed.

"Almost as exciting as a home run in the bottom of the ninth with two outs to win the World Series," he said, chuckling.

"I'm having trouble believing this," I said. "Our Independence Day celebrations have always been joyous events with happy endings. I suppose I could accept someone dying because of an auto accident, or a fall at home, but *murder*? Of one of Cabot Cove's leading citizens?"

"He may have been a leading citizen, but from what you've told me he wasn't the most popular guy around town."

"Controversial, yes. Heavy-handed in his support of some of our institutions? Again, yes. But who would hate him enough to kill him?"

"What about your town character, Chester? He of the yellow T-shirts?"

"He comes easily to mind, of course," I said, "because of the shirt found at the scene. But why would Chester shoot Lennon? He didn't even know him—he just resented some of the things he'd done. It doesn't make sense."

Rick said nothing. He sat back in the easy chair and sipped his cognac.

"I remember what you said at Mara's," I said, "about someone slipping off the deep end." I wrapped my arms about myself against a chill that had nothing to do with the temperature in the room.

We continued talking, the subject changing now and then, but always coming back to the events of that evening. I found myself waxing poetic about Cabot Cove and what it meant to me, and to everyone else I know fortunate enough to call it home. Rick was a good listener, and encouraged me with my tales. At one point, I outlined what I knew about Chester Carlisle, which was quite a bit. I stressed that he'd always been a productive and positive force in the community.

"Except for those yellow T-shirts trashing Lennon," Rick said.

I agreed that finding one of the shirts at the murder scene was, at best, problematic for Chester, but I also pointed out that he'd been *selling* the shirts. "Dozens of people might have bought those shirts, Rick. You did."

"So I did."

"I suppose it will be up to Mort and his men to learn who the others were."

"The only person who can testify to that is Chester," Rick said. "Whoever killed Lennon obviously won't admit to having purchased one."

Again, I agreed. My guest had a logical mind, no surprise considering his years with the Federal Bureau of Investigation. We were still discussing Chester when Seth arrived.

"Tea or coffee?" I asked him after the three of us settled in at my kitchen table. "A drink?"

Seth shook his head, scowling at me.

"Can I interest you in some ice cream?"

"Ayuh. You can."

I smiled. Seth was an inveterate ice cream lover. I always keep some handy in case he stops by. "Rick, would you like ice cream, too?"

"None for me, thanks."

I set a bowl of coffee-and-vanilla ice cream in front of Seth, along with a spoon and a napkin.

"Much obliged," he said.

"Rick and I were discussing the murder, and the possibility that Chester Carlisle might have been involved."

"Chester?" Seth said.

"You know about the T-shirts," I said.

"Damned fool," was Seth's reaction. "He's gotten in-creasingly ornery the last year or so, but he's no murderer."

"Mort is bringing him in for question-ing."

"I suppose he has to, but you'd have a far way to go to convince me that Chester Carlisle is a killer. He might annoy some-one to death, or give him a poke in the nose. But murder? Not possible."

"I hope you're right," I said. "Lennon was probably killed by someone passing through town, someone who doesn't live here, like that young man who attacked us." I silently hoped that was the case.

I expected Seth to fade fast, considering what'd he recently gone through, but he remained alert and fully engaged in the conversation. The emphasis eventually shifted from Cabot Cove and the night's tragedy to Rick's life as an FBI special agent. He was in the midst of a story about having led a task force that had indicted a major financial services firm for fraud when there was a knock at the door.

"Hello, Amos," I said. "Come in. We're still here."

"What's new at headquarters?" Seth asked our former sheriff.

"Have you been deputized?" I asked.

"I sure have been, Miz Fletcher." He turned to Seth. "They brought Chester Carlisle in."

"We knew they would. Mort told us that," I said.

Amos shook his head. "Boy, things have sure changed since I was runnin' the show here. Mort's got that fancy new audiovisual system down at headquarters. Everything Chester said was videotaped, and recorded, too."

"He's already been interrogated?" I asked.

"Yes, ma'am. Mort had me sit in on it, wanted my insight. I'll tell you, old Chester Carlisle has got himself in some bucket of worms."

We looked at him to continue.

"I suppose that now that I'm an official deputy, I shouldn't be talking about the case to outsiders. But I know and trust you folks." He stopped and looked at Rick All-cott.

Rick held up both hands. "Who's more trustworthy than me? I'm ex-FBI."

"Well, that's all right, then," Amos said. And in a tone intended to thwart any listening devices that might have been installed in my house, he whispered, "They found the gun used to kill Mr. Lennon."

"That was quick," Seth said. "Where was it?"

But I'd already guessed the answer.

Amos straightened up. "In Chester Carlisle's car."

Chapter Eleven

Amos's announcement that the murder weapon had been discovered in Chester Carlisle's car brought all conversation to a standstill. It was Seth who broke the silence. "How do they know it's the gun used to kill Lennon?" he asked. "The bullet's still in Lennon's brain. They've got to match it with the weapon, and that'll take time."

"That's right, Doc," Amos said, "but how much of a coincidence is it that Chester's got a handgun? He claims it's not his, says he's never owned one. Seems to me that he's incriminating himself left and right."

"You're jumping to conclusions, Amos," I said.

"Well, I'm not the only one," he responded sheepishly. "Sheriff said the same thing to me."

"Mr. Carlisle denies owning it?" Rick asked.

"Yes, sir. Flat-out denies it."

"Have they done a GSR—a gunshot residue test—on him?" Rick asked.

"First thing Mort did, used the adhesive strips that come in the testing kit. Has to send it out for some new specter testing or something like that."

"It's called a SEM test," Rick said. "Scanning electron microscopy."

"That's it. 'Course if old Chester washed his hands or used some other cleaner, the gunpowder might not show up. Mort's gonna hold him as a suspect. He's got a few days until he has to officially charge him."

"Has Mort begun questioning people at Lennon-Diversified?" I asked. "They obviously had easy access to Mr. Lennon, and would have known his schedule."

"Only one I know of was the guard, Miz Fletcher," Amos said. "He's the one who reported the body." He looked at the empty bowl next to Seth. "Was that ice cream?"

"Yes. Would you like some?"

"I would. My throat's a little sore."

We talked for another half hour until everyone, as though cued, announced it was time to leave. I watched them drive off in their respective cars before switching on the TV to listen to the news as I washed up the few dishes, glassware, and cups. As late as it was, I wasn't about to get ready for bed leaving dirty dishes in the sink. I was drying the snifter in which I'd served Rick's cognac when the news anchor came on to announce that a suspect had been detained in the murder of industrialist Joseph Lennon. "His name has not been released," she said, "but we have it from good sources that he is a longtime resident of Cabot Cove. The victim had recently moved his corporate headquarters to Cabot Cove. Stay tuned for more details as they become available."

The room was cool when I climbed into bed; maybe I wouldn't need that air conditioner I'd ordered after all. I lay awake for the next hour listening to neighbors setting off their own mini-fireworks displays and the gleeful sounds of children, up too late, laughing. I could see occasional bursts of a rocket in the sky outside my window and heard the accompanying explosions, and as Tobé had predicted, the frantic barking of dogs.

At what point in the Grucci fireworks display had another explosion gone unnoticed? The loud crack of a handgun being fired, its deadly missile finding its mark in the head of Joseph Lennon, his body tumbling into the water? I visualized that scene, over and over, until sleep finally trumped my imagination.

I slept soundly, but not long enough. I looked at the clock radio on the table next to the bed—six a.m. Since I'd gone to bed so late, I'd intended to sleep in that morning, at least until seven. I considered staying in bed. Maybe I'd be lucky and fall back to sleep. But it didn't take more than a few minutes before I gave it up, threw on my bathrobe and slippers, padded into the kitchen, and made some tea to go with a bowl of mandarin oranges I had in the fridge. *What day is it?* I silently asked myself. *Sunday,* I answered. The proverbial day of rest. There wouldn't be any rest for many

Cabot Cove citizens, including Chester Carlisle, Mort Metzger and his police department, and anyone and everyone else involved in the Lennon murder investigation.

I waited until eight to call Seth to see whether he'd be going to the firehouse pancake breakfast, a post– Independence Day tradition.

"I'll pick you up at nine fifteen," he said.

When we arrived, children were clambering all over the fire trucks, which were parked on the street in case they were needed for their true function. The front of the fire station was filled with people crowding around the long folding tables that had been set up in the driveway. Red, white, and blue plastic tablecloths fluttered in the breeze, kept from flying away by the plates and platters of pancakes, sausage, bacon, scrambled eggs, fried potatoes, and an assortment of home-baked goods. The doors of the station house had been thrown open, and more folding tables were set up inside to accommodate those who preferred to eat their pancakes and sausage sitting down— including Seth and me. Aside from the food, everyone gathered outside the firehouse seemed to have one thing on their mind: Joseph Lennon. There were, of course, myriad theories, and the town's rumor mill was already in high gear and picking up steam. To my dismay, too many in the crowd had already mentally tried and convicted Chester Carlisle of the killing. I pointed out to some that it was too early to come to such a conclusion. But while those with whom I spoke feigned agreement, I sensed that the door was closed. Word had already spread that a handgun found in Chester's car was the murder weapon; the fact that sophisticated tests would have to be conducted before any weapon could be linked to the shooting seemed irrelevant to them.

Seth and I found two spaces at a table and slid into the seats. To my consternation, Agnes Kalisch sat across from us next to Audrey Williams, Elsie Fricket, and Mary Carver, whom I knew from the Friends of the Library group. A patient of Seth's for forty years, Agnes had dealt him a serious blow when she switched to Dr. Boyle. Seth was gracious, however.

"Agnes," he said, nodding at her. "I hope you're feeling well. Those pills Dr. Boyle gave you help your fatigue?"

Mrs. Kalisch glanced at her companions, coughed delicately, and wiped her mouth with a napkin. "Actually, they haven't started to work yet," she said. "Dr. Boyle says they take some time, and I should have faith. He says they'll kick in any day now."

"For your sake, I hope they do," Seth said. "What's he giving you?"

"I don't know, supplements of some kind. Big capsules. They're a little difficult to swallow. They come in a silver and red bottle. Do you know them?"

"I doubt it," Seth said. "You have to be careful with supplements. They're not regulated by the government. Some manufacturers are not as meticulous as others in what they put in them."

"Dr. Boyle says he has them made up especially for him," Agnes said. "Mrs. Carson is taking them, too."

Seth's brows rose. "I didn't know she was suffering from fatigue."

"Oh, she isn't. She has a bad back. But Dr. Boyle says his capsules will help her, too."

Seth carefully cut his pancakes. "An all-purpose panacea, no doubt," he muttered under his breath.

"What was that?" Agnes asked.

"Nothing. Nothing. Give her my regards." He speared a bite of sausage.

Agnes took her empty plate and left the table. Mary Carver's eyes followed her. "She's not doing well, Dr. Hazlitt," she said. "Loses her energy every afternoon. I'm worried about her. Did you see the dark circles under her eyes?"

"Ayuh, I saw them."

"Can't you help her?"

Seth's lips were tightly pressed together as he shook his head. He looked up at Mary, and I could see the sadness in his eyes for just an instant. Then it was gone, his expression stern again. "Not if she doesn't want me to."

Mary followed Agnes Kalisch out, and Audrey and Elsie left soon after, all apparently ill at ease with the conversation. It looked as if Seth and I might be left alone, but two seats were soon claimed by Rick Allcott and Amos Tupper.

"You're lookin' a bit green about the gills this morning," Seth said to Rick. "You feel okay?"

"Not enough sleep," Rick replied. "You guys kept me up way past my bedtime. I'm usually an early-to-bedder. I'll make up for it tonight."

"How did you two hook up this morning?" I asked.

"We agreed to last night," Rick said. "I offered to help Amos and the sheriff any way I can, and thought I'd stay close in the event there was something I can do. It looks like there isn't, but I'm available."

"What's new in the case, Amos?" Seth asked.

Amos glanced around the firehouse before answering. He leaned in close and said in a low voice, "Lennon's family is really putting the pressure on Mort. His wife flew back from wherever she was—someplace up in Canada, I think—and showed up at Mort's office bright and early this morning. Mort's been up all night talking to those vultures from the media. I offered to take over handling those calls, but he says it's his job. I suppose it is, but the man's got to get some sleep."

I was aware that a lot of people were milling about inside and that many eyes—and ears—were trained on us. Word that Amos Tupper, our former sheriff, had been deputized by Mort had made the rounds, along with all the other scuttlebutt about the murder. Amos had now become a prime source of information to further fuel the rumors.

"That's not all," Amos continued. "Somebody who works at the Lennon company— some big-shot VP, I guess—is putting up a fifty-thousand-dollar reward for information that leads to nailing the murderer. Seems silly to me, considering we've already got Chester behind bars."

"Amos!" I said, unable to keep exasperation from my voice. "You know he's innocent until proven guilty."

"I know, Miz Fletcher, but sometimes solving a murder isn't as complicated as you make it in your books. I'll give Chester the benefit of the doubt, but I'll be—" His cell phone rang. Amos patted his pockets till he located the one that held his phone.

"Hello? Yup, Sheriff, I'm at the firehouse with Allcott, the doc, and Miz Fletcher. Sure. Want us to bring you some breakfast? Okay. Hold on."

He handed the phone to me.

"Good morning, Sheriff."

"Morning, Mrs. F. Hate to interrupt your meal, but I was wondering if I could ask a favor."

"Of course."

"Think you and the others could come by headquarters after you leave the firehouse?"

"I can't speak for everyone here, but I'll be happy to."

"I've got a videotape of the questioning I did of Chester Carlisle last night. Nope, correct that. We've got a DVD recorder now. No more tapes. Anyway, I thought you might pick up something from it that I didn't see. Wouldn't mind if Allcott was here, too. He mentioned that he attended the FBI's training on criminal profiling, serial killers, things like that. Just between us, Mrs. F, between the press, the victim's family, and that lady executive from Lennon-Diversified, there's a lot of pressure on my back. It's worse than trying to squeeze into a subway car at five o'clock. I could use some extra hands."

I held the phone aside and asked Rick and Amos if they'd come with me. They readily agreed.

"Come with us, Seth?" I asked after Amos concluded the call.

"No. Mort asked for you three, didn't ask for me. Besides, I've got a pile of paperwork to wade through today. That's all I seem to do these days, fill out forms, copy forms, send out forms. Give me a call later and tell me how things are going."

"We will," I said.

"And you," Seth said, pointing at Rick. "Try to get a nap in this afternoon. I don't like your color."

"He looks fine to me," Amos said.

"But you're not a doctor. Do I tell you how to do police business?"

"I'll get some rest, I promise," Rick said, ushering us outside.

Amos and I filled two paper plates for Mort. If he'd been up all night, it was likely he'd never had a chance to eat. As we left the pancake breakfast, Evelyn Phillips intercepted us. She and her photographer had been standing with a group of newspeople, including a remote truck from a Bangor TV station. She broke away from the group when she saw us and approached me.

"So, Jessica, come on, what's the scoop?"

"The scoop?"

"Have you learned anything more? We can't let those Bangor folks beat us at our own story."

"I'm not an investigator, Evelyn. Nothing I say would be official."

She stepped in front of Amos, blocking his path. "You're official. I know that Sheriff Metzger deputized you," she said. "What's the latest with Chester Carlisle?"

"Can't discuss an ongoing case."

Evelyn guffawed. "Don't tell me you haven't shared what you know this morning with Jessica Fletcher."

Amos scooted around her, keeping an eye on the other newspeople. They had been watching Evelyn, and now moved away from the remote truck and closed in on us.

"No comment," Amos said, sounding terribly official indeed.

Evelyn turned to Rick Allcott. "Is the FBI now involved?" she asked.

Rick flashed a wide, warm grin. "No comment," he said.

"Oh, come on," Evelyn said, rolling her eyes. "The citizens have a right to know."

"Then they'll have to get it from Sheriff Metzger," Amos said, leading us to the parking lot.

The other newspeople dropped away when they saw Evelyn turn back to the firehouse.

"Can you imagine the gall of that woman?" Amos said. "She tried to get Mort to let her interview Chester last night in jail."

"Evelyn's just doing her job," I said. "I enjoy reading her accounts of what goes on in Cabot Cove, although I must admit I'm not exactly happy when I find myself in the middle of one of her stories. However, she's a good journalist and has really turned the *Gazette* around since she's been here."

"If you say so," Amos muttered. Obviously I hadn't changed his view.

Mort was waiting for us in the reception area at headquarters.

"Glad you folks could come," he said, lifting off the paper plate I'd used to cover his breakfast. "For several reasons. This looks great." He bit down on a piece of bacon and closed his eyes in pleasure. "Mmm. Thanks!" he said, wiping his fingers on a napkin. "Got the preliminary autopsy report back. It's pretty straightforward. Nothing in the lungs. One shot. Gone! Lennon was dead before he hit the water. We had them send the bullet to ballistics."

"How's Chester?" I asked.

"Complaining, claiming he had nothing to do with Lennon's murder. I got him dead to rights, but I want to be certain I'm not missing anything. Ready to watch my questioning of him last night?"

"Ready as I'll ever be," I said.

Amos, Rick, Mort, and I sat in one of the interrogation rooms. Mort turned on a TV monitor and adjusted the lights so there wasn't a glare on the screen. In the film, Chester sat at a table opposite Mort. Amos was in a chair a few feet behind Mort. The camera shot the scene from slightly above them. The sound was not wonderful, but their words were audible, at least enough to be understood.

MORT: So, Chester Carlisle, you've been read your rights under the law. Do you understand them?

Chester nodded.

MORT: Okay, would you please spell your name for the record.

Chester spelled his name.

MORT: You've agreed to answer some questions without a lawyer present.

CHESTER: C'mon, c'mon, let's get this over with. I want to go home.

MORT: I know you're not happy to be here, but I've got a job to do. Joseph Lennon was shot to death tonight, and you're under suspicion of murder.

CHESTER: I already told you I didn't do it.

MORT: Yet you've made it pretty clear how much you hated the man.

CHESTER: I didn't like the man. Won't deny that. Damned rusticator comes to town flingin' his millions around and taking over everything.

MORT: He wasn't a tourist. He moved here.

CHESTER: For how long? He's probably got homes from here to the Pacific. Cabot Cove was just a place for him to flaunt his money, ruin the place for everyone else, and then leave us with that white elephant on the water. What are we going to do with that marble palace once he moves on to the next playground?

MORT: I don't want to argue the merits of Lennon-Diversified. I want to know if you killed the man.

CHESTER: I told you I didn't. Why in hell would I shoot him?

MORT: Because of what you just said about not liking what he's done to the town.

CHESTER: That doesn't prove anything.

MORT: What about your T-shirts, Chester? The one you're wearing, and the ones you sold comparing Mr. Lennon to that Soviet dictator Lenin?

Chester chortled, which brought on a wheeze and then a coughing spasm. He took a white handkerchief from his pants pocket and blew his nose lustily.

CHESTER: Pretty clever, weren't they? Got the point across real good. These shirts were just for fun, Sheriff. Can't you take a joke?

MORT: I'll be asking the questions, Chester. Now, where were you last night during the fireworks?

CHESTER: Home.

MORT: I've got two people who say they saw you down watching the fireworks.

CHESTER: Who said that?

MORT: Never mind who. If I have to, I'll bring them into a court of law and they'll swear they saw you there, Chester, and I bet I'll have half a dozen more swear to the same thing by tomorrow.

Chester screwed up his face, scratched his head, and tugged at the round collar of his shirt.

CHESTER: Well, maybe I did come down for a little while. I got a right to see the fireworks, don't I? Paid for them with my tax dollars—at least they used to. I didn't stay long. Burned me up to see that ugly building. Any fireworks sponsored by that bastard Lennon are—

MORT: Go on, Chester.

Chester must have realized that a display of temper wasn't going to do him any good. He crossed his arms and slumped down.

CHESTER: I've got nothing more to say.
MORT: You might be interested in knowing that we found the gun that was used to kill Joe Lennon.
Chester sat up straight.
CHESTER: Godfrey mighty! Why didn't you say so? That's good news. Whoever owns that gun is the guy you're after. Lets me off the hook.
AMOS: Not so fast, Chester. That gun—

Mort put up his hand to silence Amos.

MORT: I'll handle the questioning, Deputy Tupper. Now, Chester, that gun I just mentioned was found in your car.
CHESTER: That's a lie.

Chester sprang up from his chair and it looked like he might physically attack Mort.

Amos got to his feet, too, but Mort again waved him off.

MORT: Sit down, Chester, and if you do that again, I'll have you cuffed.

Chester flopped back down into his chair.

CHESTER: If someone took my rifle to kill Lennon, he had'a had stolen it when I wasn't looking.

MORT: I didn't say it was a rifle.

CHESTER: A shotgun, then.

MORT: Didn't say that, either.

CHESTER: I don't own a handgun, Sheriff, never have, never will. I got a rifle to go hunting now and again, and a shotgun I use to keep those pesky squirrels away from the bird feeder, but I've never owned a handgun in my life.

MORT: You know what I think? I think you're lying. I think you hated Joseph Lennon so much, you got a handgun. You took that handgun to the fire-works, and maybe waited till Mr. Lennon walked behind his building, and you followed him, and when you got him in front of you, you held him at gunpoint until a rocket went off and no one would hear. And then you shot him. In the head. That's what happened, isn't it?

CHESTER: That's not true!

MORT: You shot him and then you went home and pretended that you'd never gone to the fireworks. But you lied about that. And if you lied about that, why shouldn't I think you're lying right now about killing him?

CHESTER: Because I'm tellin' the truth, dammit. I want a lawyer. You're tryin' to get me to confess to something I didn't do.

MORT: You can get a lawyer. That's your legal right, Chester. But I'm betting your fingerprints are all over that gun, aren't they? And if you wiped them off, we'll find another way to prove that it's your weapon.

CHESTER: This isn't right, Sheriff. I didn't kill nobody, and you know it. Someone is trying to blame me for something I didn't do. Amos, you've known me for years. I wouldn't kill anyone.

AMOS: Just because you didn't before doesn't mean you wouldn't now. People change.

MORT: You got a lawyer in mind, Chester? You can call him if you want.

CHESTER: Only lawyer I know is the town attorney. Fred Nidel. Handles the county's business, too. But I don't think he'd want a piece of this.

MORT: Maybe he can suggest somebody. You can use that phone over there.

The screen went black. Mort shut off the DVD and turned up the lights.

"Well, what do you think?" he asked.

None of us spoke for a few seconds. Then I said, "I believe him, Sheriff. I don't think he killed Joseph Lennon."

"Based on what, Mrs. F?"

"I can't put a finger on it exactly. But it's too neat. It's too easy to point at Chester because he's been so vocal in opposing Lennon's activities in town. And if he killed the man, why would he leave the murder weapon in his car for anyone to find it, or allow himself to be seen at the scene of the crime, for that matter? Here's a man who spent a good portion of his life devoted to community service. Just because I don't always agree with his point of view doesn't mean I overlook his contributions to Cabot Cove, or in any way doubt his sincerity. He may have a misguided way of expressing his discontent, but that doesn't make him a murderer. I'm sorry, I just don't buy it. I know that's not really helpful, but that's my visceral reaction."

"Visceral?" Amos said.

"Gut instinct," Mort translated.

Amos turned to Rick Allcott and asked what his reactions were.

"I'm reluctant to disagree with Mrs. Fletcher," he said, "considering her track record for solving crimes. I—"

"She's been wrong sometimes," Mort said, casting a swift glance at me. I smiled and nodded.

"But," Rick continued, "your Mr. Carlisle comes off to me like a guilty man."

"That's the way I see it, too," Mort said.

"From my experience, I'd say he could be classified as BPD."

"What's BPD?" Amos asked.

"Borderline personality disorder," Rick

replied. "Carlisle exhibits many of the symptoms: impulsive acts, recurring threats,
unstable deportment, ego defense, rage,
tantrums, obsession, self-deception, mood
swings. All the signs are there and I'll tell
you this: A lot of crimes are committed by
BPD individuals. Better be careful, Mort, or
he'll get off on an insanity plea."

"I don't care what he pleads," Mort said,
"as long as I got the right guy."

"You've got the right guy," Rick said.
"Think about this. Here you have a man, a
pillar of the community for many years,
and now he's getting on in years. He's retired, so he doesn't have that same sense
of self-worth he had when he was younger
and earning money. He serves the town,
but his opinions aren't sought anymore.
People lose respect for him, maybe ridi-
cule him behind his back, or even to his
face. It rankles. He takes up a cause no
one else cares about, makes a fool of himself in public. He gets angry, obsessed
with the one he thinks is causing him to
lose face with his peers. You take all these
factors and put a gun in his hand. It's no
surprise to me that he uses it."

I hated to admit it, but Rick had come

far too close in his description of Chester's recent behavior. And as a former FBI agent, he'd been exposed to a lot more criminal profiles than I had. I shouldn't have doubted his assessment, but something still didn't ring true.

"I certainly don't have your experience with the criminal personality, gentlemen," I said, "and I'm far from infallible. But I just feel it's too soon to assume you've caught the killer. After all, there are others who might have had the motive, to say nothing of the opportunity, to shoot Mr. Lennon. Have you spoken with his wife and his children?"

"His wife was in Canada the night of the fireworks," Mort said.

"Presumably," I countered. "I'd talk with her anyway. And what about others who worked closely with him? Miss Welch and her assistant. And there's Dr. Boyle."

"Dr. Boyle?" Mort said, sounding as though I'd lost my mind.

"Who's Dr. Boyle?" Amos asked.

"He's a new doctor in town," Mort said. "The way I understand it, Mrs. F, is that he owes his practice to Lennon. Hardly a motive to kill his benefactor."

"All very true," I said. "And I don't mean to tell you gentlemen how to do your jobs, but if I were in your place, I think I'd do a lot more investigating before I decided to indict Chester Carlisle."

I sensed from the expression on Mort's face that I'd gone too far. He didn't need me to tell him how to proceed in a murder investigation, nor was it my place to do so. Still, I felt I'd been right in what I'd suggested. Based upon everything I knew so far, which admittedly wasn't much—and despite Rick's analysis of Chester Carlisle's personality and motives—I was immovable in my belief that my good friend the sheriff had settled on the most obvious of suspects without first ruling out others.

"I assume you've interviewed people close to the victim," Rick said.

If Mort was annoyed with yet another intrusion into his "business," he didn't show it. He pulled a narrow notebook from his pocket, flipped up a few pages, and replied, "I checked with the guys from Grucci. No one saw anything. I've already spoken to the wife, and the security guy for Lennon-Diversified. Whatshisname? Moss. Roger Moss, the one that found the body. We tested his gun. It was never fired. I've got others coming in this afternoon." Mort peered at me. "And I'll be questioning Dr. Boyle and his staff tomorrow. Okay, Mrs. F?"

I returned his smile.

Mort turned to Rick Allcott. "I'm especially interested in your take on things, Agent Allcott. You obviously have a lot of experience in judging character and criminal behavior."

"Happy to help in any way I can," Rick said, rubbing his hands up and down his arms. He looked apologetic. "It's a bit chilly in here."

"I got the air conditioner cranked way up because of the temperature this past week," Mort said. "Probably can turn it down a notch now that the heat wave's broken."

Amos stayed with Mort. I asked Rick to drop me at the Cabot Cove airport. "I'm in the mood for a flight," I explained. "I have my private pilot's license, but don't get nearly enough time to use it."

"I'm impressed," he said.

"So am I," I said, laughing. "There's

nothing like an hour up there by myself to put things into perspective."

"Care for a passenger?"

"I don't think so," I said. "But thanks for offering. I'll get a lift home from Jed Richardson. He's a former airline pilot who settled here in Cabot Cove and runs his own air charter service. He gave me my flight instruction."

"Well, in that case, I think I'll go grab that nap Seth suggested. I am feeling a little 'peek-id' as you Mainers say."

I studied his face. He did look washed-out. "Feel better," I said.

Jed had left a sign on the window of his office that he'd be back in fifteen minutes. I told Rick I was content to wait, and watched him drive off after we'd agreed to touch base by phone later that afternoon. It was a beautiful day, and I passed the time waiting for Jed by walking up and down the row of small private planes parked at the airport, which was growing all the time.

Our local airport had served as an air base during the Second World War. The town had allowed grass to grow over the longer runways that could accommodate larger aircraft, but smaller jets of the varieties used by corporations and companies that sell shares in the use of such planes were able to land there. And there was talk of rehabilitating the original tarmac, of reclaiming the longer runways, and of reopening the portions of the airport that had gone to seed. Not everyone was happy about that. Those opposed cited the increased noise. Others saw the runway extension as a way to induce more companies to relocate to the area. Most agreed that new business was good for Cabot Cove. Where agreement stopped was in just how fast the town should grow—and how far.

At the end of one row of planes was a twin-engine jet with LENNON-DIVERSIFIED painted on its sides and tail. I'd seen it parked at the airport before, and Jed had told me that it was the largest jet aircraft certified to land and take off on the existing runway. It was a sleek plane, state-of-the-art in every way. It was too high off the ground for me to peer into one of the oval windows, but I was walking around admiring the design when I saw Jed pull up in his red pickup.

"Hello, there, Jessica," he said as I approached. "What brings you out here today?"

"I thought I'd put in an hour of solo, keep current."

"Love to accommodate, but both my one-seventy-twos are in the shop. How about tomorrow morning?"

"Don't think I can, but we'll make it soon. I was just admiring the Lennon plane."

"A beauty, isn't it? A Gulfstream II. Boy, that was some shock to hear about Mr. Lennon. I understand that Chester Carlisle has been arrested."

"He's being questioned—along with others," I said. "I imagine that plane will be getting lots of use ferrying company people in and out. Losing your founder and leader can throw a company into turmoil."

"I haven't seen any action here today," he said. "The crew—they're top-notch pilots, former airline types like me—flew in late yesterday from Bangor."

"Was Mrs. Lennon with them?"

"I believe she *was* on the plane."

"I've never met her," I said. "It must have been a terrible shock for her to— Wait a minute! You say she flew in *yesterday*? *Before* the fireworks?"

"Yeah. A problem?"

"No. It's just that Mort Metzger was led to believe she arrived this morning. Do you have contact with the crew?"

"Sure. We talk when they come out here. Hangar talk." He laughed.

"I always enjoy being around hangar talk," I said.

"They gave me a nice tour of the equipment yesterday before they went into town. Asked me to get them a replacement bulb for a gauge in the cockpit. That's where I was." He held out his palm to show me a small glass bulb that looked like it belonged in a dollhouse. "Had a devil of a time finding this. Had to go halfway to Hades."

On the side of the nose of the jet, Jed used a hook to pull open a door that folded down to become a stairway. He trotted up the steps, ducked inside, and turned around. "Want to see this baby close up?"

"I'd love to," I said, following him into the cabin.

The jet was narrow but fitted more like a living room or RV than a commercial plane. There were two seats together, plush recliners in cocoa-colored leather, facing a pair of the same with a low table between them. Across the aisle were single seats facing each other with pull-down tables latched to the wall. Beyond them was another set of seats and after that a long upholstered bench that would have looked like a sectional sofa if not for the retractable seat belts every two and a half feet. Opposite the bench was a stand-up bar, complete with a brass rail six inches from the floor, and a brown leather padded rim around the top on which drinkers could rest their elbows.

"All the comforts of home, huh?" Jed said.

"I don't know about you, but I don't have a bar in my home."

"The bench pulls out to become a bed, and there's a full bathroom in the back, shower and everything. Have a look around; I'll be done in a minute."

He climbed into the pilot's seat and I

followed him into the cockpit and peered over his shoulder as he unscrewed a portion of the paneling and replaced the bulb.

"How fast can this go?" I asked.

"Well, it's a long-range plane. It can zip along at five hundred miles an hour at fifty-one thousand feet."

"Goodness!"

"You said it. They even have a flight attendant. Can you believe it?"

"Why would they need such a long-range plane?"

"Well, as I understand it, they're back and forth to Africa, so that would explain it."

"Is that where they came from?"

"No, I think they came in from Vancouver yesterday."

"Do you think you could confirm that Mrs. Lennon arrived in Cabot Cove last evening?" I asked.

He shrugged. "I suppose so. I think the crew is scheduled to fly out about an hour from now. I'll ask."

He maneuvered out of the seat, we climbed down the steps, and Jed folded the stairs up into the plane.

"Sorry you didn't get a chance to fly today."

"Maybe I'll be back tomorrow. Not sure how my schedule is running."

"Call before, Jess. I'm liable to get busy."

"I will."

"Need a lift back into town? Ronnie has to run an errand for me, pick up something at FedEx."

"Thanks, Jed. That would be great."

Ronnie, who'd just graduated from high school and who aspired to a flying career, had started working for Jed at the airport, washing and fueling planes, and running errands, all in exchange for free flying lessons. I asked him to drop me at Seth's house, where I found my friend toiling over a pile of papers.

"The computer doesn't help?" I asked, taking a chair across the desk from him.

"Helps plenty, but what do you do with a printed form? Can't put it in a computer like you could a typewriter. Didn't think of that when I got rid of my old typewriter, so I'm left with doing things by hand." He sat back, rubbed his eyes, and asked how things went at police headquarters.

"Rick Allcott and I watched Mort's recording of Chester under questioning."

"And?"

"Mort and Rick are convinced that Chester did it. But I can't get my head around to their way of thinking. Seth, I just don't believe Chester killed Joseph Lennon."

"Your instincts in such things have always been pretty good."

"Only pretty good?"

"Better than that. If Chester didn't do it, then who did?"

"That's what I'm determined to find out, Seth, and I need your help."

Chapter Twelve

The same security guard was at his post when I entered the Lennon-Diversified building Monday morning. The day was cool and overcast, and when the taxi dropped me off in front of the entrance, I was surprised to see that the stage for the rock concert had already been dismantled and carted away.

"Good morning. Roger, isn't it?"

"That's right, ma'am."

"I was sorry to hear about your employer."

"Thank you."

"Had you worked for Mr. Lennon for a long time?"

"Yes."

"You were working the night he was killed?"

"Yes."

"I understand you were the one who found his body."

"Do you have an appointment here, ma'am?"

"I do."

"Then go straight ahead to the reception desk, and Mrs. Koser will assist you."

Mrs. Koser? I thought. I know a Mrs. Koser.

"MaryJane! I didn't know you worked for Lennon-Diversified," I said when I reached the reception desk at the far end of the atrium. MaryJane was the wife of Richard Koser, a local photographer and dedicated man about the kitchen.

"Hello, Jessica. Been here a whole two months."

"I thought you were retired," I said.

"I *was* retired, but when these folks came to town, I applied and here I am." She lowered her voice. " 'Course, don't know if the job'll keep, what with Mr. Lennon dying and all."

"You don't think they'll close the business, do you?"

"Never can tell with these people. They don't talk much." She eyed the security guard, who was advancing toward the desk. "You have an appointment, Mrs. Fletcher," she said in a voice that would carry to the other side of the lobby. "Let me call in to announce you." She lifted the phone and Roger turned, heading back toward the front door.

MaryJane put a hand over the receiver and whispered to me, "Do you have an appointment, Jessica?"

"I don't," I whispered back, "but is Ms. Welch in?"

"Oh, yes. They're all in."

"I was hoping to talk with her. Do you know her?"

"Well, not to have coffee with. She's too *high check-rein* to talk to the likes of me, with her diamond earrings and fancy suits. No appointment, huh? I'll try, but they're very fussy about appointments here. Can't think of why they couldn't be a bit more flexible." She dialed a number and waited until someone picked up.

"Dante, I have Jessica Fletcher here and she would like to see Ms. Welch. That's right. Is she available? Okay, I'll have her wait." She looked at me. "He says he'll check and let me know."

I looked around, but there wasn't a bench or chair anywhere other than the one MaryJane occupied. *Either they rarely have any visitors,* I thought, *or they never keep them waiting. Or if they do, they don't care if a guest is uncomfortable. Maybe that's their way of discouraging visitors.*

"How's Richard?" I asked. "Is he still experimenting with new dishes?"

"Oh, you know Richard. He's the reason I'm here."

"He is?"

"He was getting ugly about me being underfoot. According to him, I was no help and all hindrance in the kitchen. I figured if I didn't want to get in hailing distance of a divorce, I'd better get out of the house. Never liked to cook, anyway."

"So you came to work here."

"I did. It's not much of a job, but it keeps me out of trouble. Plus, I get a lot of reading in." She held up a paperback novel. "Tried talking to that one"—she nodded toward Roger—"but he's tighter than a clam and not nearly as much personality. Mr. Lennon kept him on a short leash."

"What exactly do they do here?" I asked. "I heard the company had something to do with pharmaceuticals."

"From what I've seen, it's shipping, mostly."

"Shipping what?"

"Their drugs and medicines. They come in from their other offices and they ship them out from here."

"So it's similar to Federal Express shipping all their packages from Memphis, Tennessee. They're using Cabot Cove as the central shipping place to distribute their products."

"How did you know? That's how they described it to me when I first came."

"But why the strict security?" I said, thinking aloud. "And why be so secretive?"

"Beats me. They don't have a lot of people wandering through, anyway. Which reminds me—I thought I saw you here t'other day."

"Yes, I was here with Kathy Copeland. She was feeling a little faint from the heat, and we came in to cool off."

"That was quite a little dustup they had that day. Thought Ms. Welch would pop her embroidered buttons."

"She did appear upset."

"Upset is an understatement. She was slamming around here all afternoon. She and Mr. Lennon had a real knock-down drag-out. I could hear them shouting all the way out here. She was expecting to get a promotion and he's giving it to Paul instead. That's his son. President. He's making him president. Or was. I guess Paul'll still get to be president if Mrs. Lennon wants him to. She's here now. Never even stopped to say hello to me, even though I hailed her when she first arrived. Now, Paul, he's a nice kid, but not too much up here"—MaryJane tapped her temple—"if you know what I mean. At least not a real corporatey type like her—Ms. Welch, that is."

The double doors on the side of the lobby opened with a loud clunk, the sound reverberating through the empty marble space. Dante strode toward the reception desk. He was impeccably dressed in a three-piece suit and looked very "corporatey," as MaryJane had described Ms. Welch.

He addressed me. "Is there something I can help you with?"

"I'm Jessica Fletcher," I said. "We haven't been formally introduced, but I was at the Independence Day committee meeting at city hall last week when you and Ms. Welch made your presentation."

He stared at me, but there was no recognition in his eyes. In fact, his expression said he was clearly uninterested in anything I might have to say.

"Yes, well, I was hoping to get a chance to speak with Ms. Welch today. Is she in?"

"And what did you wish to talk with Ms. Welch about?"

"It's a private matter. If you would just tell her—"

He interrupted me with, "I'm Ms. Welch's personal assistant. She's a very busy woman, and sees people only by appointment. I handle her schedule, and you do not have an appointment, Mrs. Fletcher."

"Well, then, I'd like to make an appointment to see Ms. Welch."

"She's not making any appointments at this time."

"Sounds like a catch-22," I said.

"I beg your pardon?"

"*Catch-22*, the Joseph Heller novel. You know, the one about the army and its circular rules. I can't see Ms. Welch without an appointment, but Ms. Welch isn't taking appointments, and I can't see her unless I have an appointment."

He gave me a blank look.

"Never mind," I said. "It's better in the original."

MaryJane stifled a snort.

"Perhaps I can see Mrs. Lennon," I said. "I'd like to extend my sympathies. It must have been quite a shock to her—"

"Mrs. Lennon is in mourning and is not accepting visitors. I don't believe there is anyone here, Mrs. Fletcher, who has a vacancy in their appointments. Perhaps if you called ahead next time."

"I'll keep that in mind, Mr. . . . ? I'm afraid I didn't catch your name."

" 'Dante' will do."

"Thank you for your courtesies, Dante. I'll be sure to make an appointment the next time, that is, if Ms. Welch is making appointments."

I said good-bye to MaryJane and

walked to the front door, which Roger held open. I could feel Dante's eyes on my back, and was certain he didn't leave the lobby until he had seen me exit. The day felt warm and pleasant, especially after my cool reception in the marble halls of Lennon-Diversified. But I was not dispirited. Stopping there had been a last-minute decision since I was in the vicinity. Seth had referred me to Dr. Boyle, and it was he whom I'd come to see. Luckily, I had an appointment.

Boyle's medical offices were a short walk around the corner from the front entrance of Lennon's building, and a world away in interior design. Whereas the company had a virtually empty atrium clearly discouraging anyone who was not expected, the doctor's office had been designed to impress the citizenry of Cabot Cove. It was warm and welcoming, with modern plush chairs, flowering plants, and neat wooden racks filled with the latest sports and decorating magazines. I even spotted a copy of *Modern Lobstering* on one shelf. A coffee and tea service sat in one corner, and patients waiting to see the popular doctor were invited to help themselves to something to drink and to cookies I recognized as being from Sassi's Bakery.

I didn't know the nurse at the front desk, but she greeted me at once.

"I'm Mandy, Dr. Boyle's nurse. If you would kindly fill out these forms, we'll have you in the examination room in no time. I can tell by your face that you're not feeling tip-top. Oh, yes, I can see those things. Dr. Boyle will have you up to snuff in no time at all."

She handed me a plastic clipboard, a sheaf of papers, and a pen, and disappeared into a back room.

I waded through all the papers, wondering if I did indeed look ill, left the completed forms on her desk, and made myself a restorative cup of tea. Next to the little refreshment center was a bulletin board that held clippings of articles on Dr. Boyle that had appeared in the *Gazette*, as well as copies of the ads he had placed in the newspaper. A plastic bin hanging on the board was filled with leaflets showing Dr. Boyle standing beside some impressive piece of diagnostic equipment.

I sat down with my tea and opened one

of the brochures. Inside were more pictures of Dr. Boyle, a very photogenic man, and three short paragraphs describing the doctor's medical philosophy but giving no hint of his background or where he had practiced before establishing his office in Cabot Cove. I studied his face. Unlike the photo of Joseph Lennon that I'd seen in the paper, Boyle had a pleasant expression, with no hint of anything untoward in his eyes.

As if I'd conjured him, the door to the back room opened and the doctor himself emerged, ushering Agnes Kalisch out. She was holding a small shopping bag filled with bottles, and from what I could see, all of them had silver and red labels.

"Miracles take time, my dear," he said. "Just keep up with the treatment. I'm certain we'll start to see some improvement in your blood work by the next visit."

"I hope so," Agnes said, sounding less convinced and looking more wan than when I'd seen her at the pancake breakfast.

"I guarantee it," he said. "You can pay the nurse on your way out."

Mandy was back at her desk to take

Agnes's money. When she'd completed the transaction, Agnes turned to me.

"Hello, Jessica. I'm surprised to see you here."

"How are you feeling, Agnes?"

"Not too well, I'm afraid. But you heard the doctor. Miracles take time."

"What does he think is causing your problems?"

"He said it might be an electrolyte imbalance. That's what these are for." She held up the shopping bag.

"May I?" I said, pointing to one of the bottles.

"I guess."

I read the label. The pills contained an assortment of minerals and vitamins. What was most interesting to me was the fine print at the bottom, which indicated that the pills that Dr. Boyle expected to provide a "miracle" for Agnes were manufactured by Lennon-Diversified Industries. *How convenient,* I thought. *Help set up the doctor's medical practice, and he can sell your products to his patients.* I replaced the bottle in Agnes's shopping bag and wished her well.

"Mrs. Fletcher?" Mandy said from her

desk. "The doctor will see you now." She gathered up my forms and opened the door to the back of the office. "Just follow me."

She led me down a carpeted hall with bright white walls on which were hung framed photographs taken in Maine— picturesque scenes of fishermen mending nets, colorful coastal villages, and sunsets on the water, all looking as if they had been cut from a coffee table book. Signs off to the right pointed to DERMATOLOGY SUITE and underneath in smaller letters, MASSAGE THERAPY and TANNING SALON.

"I see you're another one from Dr. Hazlitt's office," she said, leading me into a small examination room. "We've been getting a number of his former patients recently."

I bit my tongue to keep from saying anything that might tip her off that I was not a "former" patient at all.

"Fatigue, huh? And forgetfulness? You poor thing. Dr. Boyle has pills that will fix you right up. I don't know why more doctors don't provide dietary supplements. But then, they don't have the contacts Dr. Boyle does. His are formulated to his specifications."

"Ah. How interesting."

She took my blood pressure, pulse, and temperature—"All normal. That's a good sign"—marked them on a form in a folder, tucked the folder into a basket hanging just outside the door, and closed the door. I had spotted two documents that appeared to be degrees or certificates and hopped off the examining table to take a closer look. I had just put my glasses on when Dr. Boyle arrived. "Checking my credentials?" he said, chuckling. "Hello, hello. Nice to see you again." He shook my hand and guided me back to the table, then went to the sink and used a foot pedal to start the water. "How's Dr. Hazlitt feeling?" he asked as he washed his hands.

"He's—"

"He called me the other day to thank me. He didn't need to, but it was nice to hear from him."

"Yes, I'm—"

"Not every day I get a chance to save a life so dramatically. Of course that's what medicine's all about—saving lives. That's why we all go into the field, to help people, and I've been moderately successful, if I do say so. Got the latest equipment, and I've made sure to get trained on it, so it's second nature. Not everyone bothers, you know. So, are you here scouting my practice so you can report back?"

"Oh, I don't—"

"Don't blame you. I would, too, if my practice was starting to bleed patients the way his is. But you need to keep up with the times. Can't rely on chicken soup and hunches."

Hunches! Until these last comments, I had been starting to think perhaps Seth had misjudged the man, that he wasn't such a bad fellow after all, perhaps a little taken with himself, but there was room for all kinds of doctors in a town. However, when he began to gloat about the patients he had drawn away from Seth, and belittle my good friend's considerable knowledge, Dr. Boyle lost me altogether.

A buzzer sounded and he pushed a button on a wall panel. Mandy's voice came over the intercom. "You have a call on line one, Doctor." He excused himself to me and picked up the phone, saying briskly, "Dr. Boyle here."

I knew from the way his voice dropped that the person on the other end of the line was not a patient or a fellow physician. It was a personal call. "I can't," he said softly. "I'm with a patient right now. . . . All right." Then, aware I was listening in, he raised his voice. "Give me fifteen minutes and I'll see what I can do."

"Sorry about that," he said, rinsing his hands again and drying them on paper towels, which he tossed into a steel trash can. "Now, let's see what we can do for your fatigue and forgetfulness."

Fifteen minutes later, I was carrying my own little paper bag that Dr. Boyle had filled from a sizable closet stocked with bottles bearing silver and red labels as well as the usual medicine samples that most doctors have on hand. He walked me to the front desk. "Call me anytime if you have a problem, and I'll see you next week. If you follow a strict regimen with these pills, you'll be feeling tip-top in no time."

"Thank you, Doctor."

"Not at all. Mandy will set up your next appointment."

I put the bag of pills down and took out my wallet. Mandy was typing furiously into the computer. "Your insurance will pay for the office visit," she said. "But it's one hundred ten dollars for the pills."

"One hundred ten dollars?"

"Yes. I know they're a little pricey, but they're certainly worth it if they work."

A big if, I thought. I began to regret my charade.

She punched some more keys. "Just give me a minute, Mrs. Fletcher. If I don't keep the medical records up to date, he gets annoyed."

"Take your time," I said.

The phone rang. Mandy gave me an apologetic look, picked it up, and listened for a moment. "Yes, Mrs. Thomas. I'm sorry, but Dr. Boyle doesn't make house calls. Yes, I understand." She put her hand over the receiver and whispered to me. "I'll be with you in a sec."

"That's okay," I whispered back. "I forgot to ask Dr. Boyle a question. Won't be a minute. I'll just go find him." I left my bag on her desk and opened the door to the hallway.

"Wait! Mrs. Fletcher." Mandy rose and called after me, but I knew the phone would keep her. She sank back into her seat. "Yes, of course, Mrs. Thomas. I understand, but—"

The door closed behind me and I walked

down the hall, the carpet muffling my foot-
steps. I could hear voices. A man and a
woman. I presumed the man was Dr. Boyle.
But who was the woman, and how did she
get there? She certainly hadn't come in
through the front door and the reception
area.

I walked to the room in which I'd seen
the doctor. The door was open. It was
empty. I peered into an office just beyond it. No one was there. At the end of
the hall was a large section that held
some of the doctor's modern diagnostic
equipment that I'd observed on a tour
when he'd first opened his practice and
invited the public to see what he offered.
The voices were louder. I looked around
the corner. Dr. Boyle was talking to a
woman whose back was to me. Dressed
in a linen suit, she wore her dark hair
pulled into a chignon, but I couldn't see
her face.

"No more after tomorrow," she said.

"You don't have to stop. You're going to
be in charge now."

"That remains to be seen," she said.

"Don't play me. You can't back out after
all I've done for you," he hissed. Spying

me, his face changed from a frown to a surprised smile. "Mrs. Fletcher," he said, his voice rising.

The woman stiffened and quickly moved past him through a door on the other side of the room.

He rushed forward. "Is there a problem?"

"Oh, Dr. Boyle," I said, feigning innocence, "I'm so sorry to interrupt you, but I had a question."

"Yes, of course," he said, firmly taking my elbow and swiftly propelling me back into the hallway and toward the exit. "What was it?"

He opened the door to the reception area and all but threw me into it, glaring at Mandy. "Mrs. Fletcher had to come find me. Where were you?"

Mandy colored. "I'm so sorry, Doctor. I had a phone call and she went into the back before I could catch her."

"Next time, make sure our patients' questions are all answered before you take phone calls," Boyle said, barely containing his anger.

"Of course." She looked at me, stricken. "Mrs. Fletcher, I'm so sorry I neglected to ask if all your questions were answered."

"That's all right, dear," I said, picking up my bag from her desk.

"What was it you wanted to know?" she asked.

"Oh, dear me," I said, looking from one to the other. "I'm afraid I've already forgotten."

Chapter Thirteen

I'd been remiss in not writing up my report for Mort on the attempted mugging, and when I got home, I went straight to my writing room, meaning to give him a detailed account of the incident, at least as much as I could remember. I powered up the computer and clicked on my Internet browser. It opened on Google. I'd meant to bring up my word-processing program. Instead, I stared at the search engine, my fingers hovering over the keys. At last I typed in Warren Boyle's name and waited for the results. There were lots of Warrens and many Boyles, but no record of a Dr. Warren

Boyle in Massachusetts, site of the previous headquarters for Lennon-Diversified, or anywhere else that I could find.

Next, I typed in "Lennon-Diversified" and scrolled through the listings that came up. One article from our own *Cabot Cove Gazette* was an interview with Joseph Lennon. I'd read it when the paper first came out, but now I gave it more attention in light of what I knew, and didn't know, about our new corporate neighbor. *Give Evelyn credit,* I thought. She'd asked lots of questions about the company, but it was clear from her piece that Lennon was intent on discussing his community contributions and gave short shrift to his corporate activities. I wondered why. The possible answer came several pages into Google, when a reference to Lennon-Diversified showed up in a legal document filed by the Food and Drug Administration. The privately held company had been investigated for fraud, but nothing had been proven, and Lennon-Diversified was never charged. Obviously, its owner preferred to talk about his good works rather than any flags raised about his company's past.

There were several more references

to Joseph Lennon's civic philanthropy—
indeed, the man gave away a lot of money—
in other communities where his company
had offices, but aside from offers to buy
him out that had been rejected, I found little of interest.

Chastising myself for procrastinating, I
closed Google and focused on finishing
the write-up I'd promised Mort. It took less
time than I had anticipated, and when I
completed it, I printed out the one-page
report, tucked it in my shoulder bag, turned
off the computer, and went into the kitchen
to put on the kettle for tea. It was only then
that I noticed the light on my telephone
answering machine. I pushed the button
and heard a message from Jill Thomas,
who with her husband, Craig, ran the Blueberry Hill Inn.

"Jessica, I'm so sorry to put this on you,
but one of our maids entered Mr. Allcott's
room this morning to clean it and found
him shivering under the covers. We think
he has the flu. When he checked in, he
told me he was a friend of yours. I'm not
sure what to do. I called, but couldn't get
a doctor to come see him this morning—
I guess house calls are a thing of the

past—and Craig is out of town, so I can't leave the inn to drive Mr. Allcott myself. Would you please call me back when you get this message?"

I dialed the number Jill had left, and she picked up immediately. "Oh, thank goodness it's you, Jessica."

"How is he?" I asked, realizing it must have been Jill who'd called Boyle's office while I was there.

"I think he's gotten worse since I left you the message."

"What makes you say that?"

"I ran in to check on him. He's burning up with fever, and he's mumbling. I can't understand what he's saying."

"We have to get him to a doctor."

"Even if I could get someone to cover for me, I'm not sure I could manage to get him dressed and in the car. And if he's contagious . . ." She trailed off.

"I understand," I said. "You did the right thing by calling me."

"We always take care of our guests, but I've never had someone so ill staying with us."

"It sounds as if he's too sick for you or me to handle," I said. "Let's get the EMTs to take him to the hospital. I'll call Seth Hazlitt and ask him to meet me there."

"Seth. Of course. I should have thought of him. I called that doctor that advertises in the paper. Thank you, Jessica. I'll call 911 right away."

We said good-bye, and I called Seth, explained the situation, and agreed to wait to hear from him before calling a cab to take me to the hospital. "No use in Nick haulin' you over there if Allcott's contagious and you can't see him," he said.

"You'll call me as soon as you know something?"

"Ayuh. You'll be the first to hear."

I poured my tea and set it on the kitchen table, but I was too agitated to sit. I was sorry Rick was under the weather, of course, but there were some things that had been nagging at me ever since he arrived in Cabot Cove. I'd been meaning to corral him for a talk, but we'd almost never been alone. The one instance when we had an opportunity to talk was right after Joe Lennon's body had been found, and it was not the appropriate time to express what was bothering me.

When in doubt, clean, I told myself, and

while my tea grew cold, I picked up a sponge and scrubbed the kitchen sink, even though I'd gone over it pretty thoroughly earlier in the morning. I'd finished all the countertops and was starting on the refrigerator when Seth called back.

"You're too late," I said. "I've just ruined a perfectly good manicure cleaning everything in sight. How's the patient? Is it the flu?"

Going straight to the point, Seth said, "What do you know about your friend here, Jessica?"

"Not much more than you," I replied. "We met a few years ago in Washington at a conference on forensics that the FBI held for writers. I hadn't heard from him after that until he called from Blueberry Hill to tell me he was in town. Why do you ask?"

"He doesn't have the flu."

"Then what does he have?"

"Malaria."

"Malaria?"

"Ayuh. Told me he picked it up in Alaska. 'Mosquitoes as big as birds up there.' I can believe it. But he didn't get malaria from those mosquitoes no matter what size they are. It's too cold up there for *Plasmodium falciparum.*"

"That's the malaria parasite, I take it?"

"You are correct. That's the one responsible for the most severe form of malaria, which is what I suspect our patient has. Even with the right mosquito, if the temperatures aren't high enough, the parasite cannot complete its growth cycle. And Alaska is not known for its balmy weather."

"If he didn't contract malaria in Alaska, where did he get it? And why would he lie about it?"

"That's the mystery," Seth said. "That's your department, not mine. Fortunately, we had an antimalarial drug in the hospital pharmacy. I'll fix him up. When he's lucid, you can ask him."

"When do you think I can see him?"

"Not sure. Right now he's still in the emergency room. We don't have a bed for him yet."

"Is the hospital that full?" I asked.

"No, we have room, but the EMTs forgot to bring Allcott's wallet, and Admitting wants his insurance information before they make him at home in the medical unit."

"Oh, for heaven's sake."

"That's the health-care bureaucracy for you."

"Why don't I go over to Blueberry Hill? I'll get his insurance card and bring it to the hospital."

"Was hoping you'd volunteer."

"You know you could have asked."

"Didn't want to impose."

"You never impose. I'll call a cab and have the driver wait while I find Rick's wallet. I'll see you in the emergency room."

"I'll be here," he said. "Must be a full moon. I had two other patients pop in while I was tending Allcott."

Jill Thomas was printing out the bill for a couple from Danbury, Connecticut, who were checking out of the inn. "I hope you had a pleasant stay," she said, handing them the itemized sheet.

"It was wonderful, Jill. Cabot Cove is so charming. Maria said it would be. That parade was just like the ones I remember as a child. And the fireworks. Wow!"

"I'm so glad you came for the holiday," Jill said. "You must say hello to the Moreys for me when you see them. Jack and Maria

are old friends. Please thank them for rec-
ommending us." Catching sight of me, Jill
smiled and said to her guests, "Would you
please excuse me for a moment?" She
pulled a key from the board behind her
and reached out to hand it to me. "It's
number four, Jessica," she said. "You don't
mind if I don't go up with you, do you?"

"Not at all," I said. "Take care of your
guests. I won't be long."

I climbed the stairs to the second floor
and looked for the room numbers. Blueberry Hill was more properly a bed-and-
breakfast than a true inn, although Craig
had added extra bathrooms to the six-
bedroom Victorian house to make it more
appealing to visitors. The floors were oak,
stained a dark color, and creaked pleasantly when walked on. Jill had installed
etched-glass wall sconces and laid a beige-
and-blue Oriental runner over the boards
to lighten up what otherwise would have
been a gloomy hallway. The walls were
cream-colored, and the paneled doors and
trim matched the stain of the floors.

I found number four, inserted the key,
and let myself into a large bedroom with
a four-poster bed. The linens had been

stripped off, and a new set lay on the mattress until Jill or the maid could get to it. I imagined Jill wanted to air the bedding before she remade the bed, perhaps even spray some germ killer, although I don't know how effective it would be on fabrics. Opposite the bed and under a window that looked out over the rear garden was a small desk with a lamp and a chair. To the right was a tall armoire. The room had no closet. I peeked into the bathroom, but there was only one personal item in sight. Rick had placed his black leather Dopp kit on top of the commode. It was open and contained the usual toiletries—toothbrush, toothpaste, floss, comb, deodorant, nail clippers. I zipped it up and took it with me, figuring he would appreciate being able to brush his teeth when he was feeling better.

I didn't find his wallet in the desk drawers, so I opened the armoire in hope of better luck. It was a large piece of furniture, mahogany, with an arched top and double doors kept closed with a lock and key. Inside, a rod to hang clothing spanned the top half, and six drawers, three on each side, filled the bottom. A pair of sneakers and two pairs of shoes sat on top of the drawers. Rick had several jackets, slacks, jeans, and a Windbreaker hanging up, and the drawers contained folded shirts, shorts, socks. It was a full wardrobe, and surprisingly more than I would have expected he'd need for an extended weekend. I patted down his jackets and slacks in case he had left his wallet in a pocket. Finding nothing, I went drawer by drawer until I'd checked them all. By chance I moved one of his sneakers and found it heavier than I expected. I pulled back the tongue and there inside the toe were Rick's wallet and passport. I flipped open the passport to his picture. It had been taken several years ago, and a younger face than I'd seen the other day looked back at me. Inside, pages were stamped by the countries he'd visited: France, Germany, Sierra Leone, the Czech Republic, and on the last page, Zimbabwe. *What an interesting life an FBI agent has,* I thought.

I picked up the other sneaker. Something metal had been stuffed in the toe. I shook it out. It was an ammunition clip. I don't know why I was shocked. Rick was a former FBI agent, after all. But the evidence that he still carried a gun was disturbing.

He was on vacation, wasn't he? Why would he need a gun to watch a baseball game or attend an Independence Day parade? And where was the gun this ammunition fit into?

I checked to make sure Rick's insurance card was in his wallet, placed it and his passport in the Dopp kit, then locked the room and returned the key to Jill at the front desk.

"I hope you found what you needed," she said.

"I did."

"Mary and I were nervous even going into his room. After the EMTs took Mr. Allcott, we stripped the bed right away. If one of us gets sick, we're really in trouble. It's so busy this time of year."

"Are you all booked up?"

"We've been booked since April. I've had to turn people away, even local businesses that needed rooms. I told that fellow from Lennon-Diversified that we couldn't guarantee a room for his company visitors with all the advance reservations."

"Someone from Lennon-Diversified was asking for a room?"

"Yes, what was his name? Something foreign sounding."

"Dante?"

"That's it. Such a nice young man. He wanted to see the rooms anyway, in case we got a cancellation. Mr. Allcott has the biggest room, but he'd just gone out, so I couldn't ask him to show it. I gave Dante the keys to two and three instead. He must have liked them; he said if we got a vacancy to let him know."

Nick held the door of the taxi for me, and I slid into the backseat. "We're off to the hospital now, right?" he said.

"Yes," I said.

"Got everything you need, Mrs. Fletcher?"

"Yes," I said again. *And more*, I thought.

Chapter Fourteen

Since the sheriff's office was on the way to the hospital, I asked Nick to wait while I ran inside to deliver my eyewitness account of the attempted mugging that resulted in Seth's injury. Mort was sitting at his desk reading a report.

"Nice to see you, Mrs. F," he said. "Put it right there." He nodded at a pile of papers, to which I added mine. "I was just reading a lab report and thinking about you. Have a seat."

"I wish I could," I said. "I have a taxi waiting outside—"

"Don't you want to hear the results of Chester Carlisle's GSR test?"

"GSR?" I said. "Oh, right. The gunshot residue test. Well, yes, of course." I perched on the edge of the chair, hoping he would be brief.

Mort turned the report around and offered it to me. "See this?" he said, pointing to the concluding paragraph. "Says 'positive' for gunshot residue. That's enough for me to keep Mr. Carlisle in jail on suspicion of murder."

I sighed. "I don't suppose these kinds of tests can tell the difference between a gun fired in a crime and a gun fired to scare squirrels away from the bird feeder, can they?"

"You're a tough one to convince," Mort said. "But I feel a lot better knowing I've got the right man. We now know that Chester fired the gun we found in his car, and as soon as we have the ballistics report back, we can prove that's the gun that was used to kill Lennon."

An argument was on the tip of my tongue, but I thought better of it.

"By the way, Mrs. F, Maureen said if I saw you to invite you to dinner tonight."

Maureen was Mort's second wife and an enthusiastic, if not exactly accomplished, cook. She was famous, or perhaps "infamous" was the right word, for her culinary experiments, which was why a box of Charlene Sassi's doughnuts could always be found in Mort's office. I cast around for an excuse. "That's very nice of her, but—"

"She invited Amos Tupper to come, and she likes to have even numbers at the table. Frankly, Mrs. F, you'd be doing me a real favor."

I'd received more gracious invitations to dinner before. But it would be an opportunity to discuss the case further, and Mort and Maureen were good friends. "Of course," I said. "How nice of Maureen to think of me. What time would you like me there?"

We arranged for me to be at the Metzgers' house by six. I thanked Mort for letting me see the test results, and left to apologize to Nick for keeping him waiting.

Only two chairs were occupied when I entered the seating area outside the hospital's emergency room. In one, a little girl with a tearstained face sat in her father's lap, clutching a well-loved doll. What looked like a kitchen towel was wrapped around her hand and I assumed that whatever injury she had sustained was underneath the covering. Several seats down, a teenager sprawled in his chair, flipping through a sports magazine. Two skateboards were on the floor next to his feet. From his demeanor I gathered he was waiting for someone who was already inside receiving help.

A triage nurse sat behind a glass window, which she slid to one side when I approached.

"I'm looking for Dr. Seth Hazlitt," I said. "Is he available?"

"Are you Mrs. Fletcher?"

"Yes."

"He's with a patient right now, but he told me you'd be by. You have Mr. Allcott's insurance card?"

I handed her Rick's card.

"If you don't mind waiting, Mrs. Fletcher, Dr. Hazlitt said he'll see you when he's free. He shouldn't be too long."

"I don't mind waiting," I said.

"I'll let him know you're here."

I sat across from the little girl and smiled at her. She looked at me with sad eyes and held up her bandaged hand. "I have a boo-boo."

"I see that," I said. "I'm so sorry."

Her father smoothed her flyaway hair and looked at me. "Caught her hand in a door, racing after her brother," he said. "She knows she's not supposed to run in the house. Don't think it's anything more'n a bruise, but didn't want to take the chance."

"I don't blame you," I said.

"Wanna see it?" the little girl asked.

"Now, Chloe," her father said in a soft voice.

"That's all right," I said. I looked at the little patient. "If you would like to show it to me, I'll be happy to see it."

She unwound the cloth to reveal a small hand clutching a plastic bag of frozen corn. "Mama put cut corn on it," she said.

"Cut corn?" I asked.

Her father looked sheepish. "We use the frozen corn for all the kids' bruises and sprains. We don't eat it. That bag's just for sprains and bumps and anything that needs icing. It's more flexible than ice cubes."

"What a clever idea," I said.

Chloe held up her hand. It was a little red from holding on to the frozen bag, but didn't look to me as if there were any serious injury.

At the sound of the glass window sliding open, we all turned our heads. "Mr. Fry, the doctor will see Chloe now," the nurse announced. Father and daughter walked to the double doors that led to the ER examining rooms. Chloe turned and waved to me, and I waved back. "Good luck," I called.

A few minutes later, a young man with a sling came through the same doors and used his good arm to signal his friend. "It's nothing," he said, going over to him. "Just a bone bruise."

"Yeah, but what about that?" his friend said, eyeing the sling. "Can we still practice?"

"We'll work around it."

His friend shrugged. "Your funeral," he said, picking up the skateboards.

I hope not, I thought, as they walked out of the waiting area, leaving me alone with my thoughts. Young people can be so cavalier about their health. The exuberance of youth combined with the unfounded but absolute conviction that nothing bad will happen to them spurs them to take the kinds of chances those of us with more experience would never attempt. That could explain why so many extreme sports had worked their way into the public consciousness, even appreciation, in recent years. Seth and I had cringed while watching snowboarding competitions in the last Olympics. And I knew from the Cabot Cove Gazette that the town council was contemplating a skateboard section in the local park. "Better to give the skaters a recreational environment in which to practice at their own peril," Mayor Shevlin had been quoted as saying, "than deal with the property damage, not to mention personal injury risks of them riding down the banisters in front of the high school." Even though the mayor's logic was sound, I didn't believe the proposal stood much of a chance of passing. And I wasn't sure how I would have voted were I sitting on the council in their place. I could hazard a guess at how Chester Carlisle might vote, if he ever returned to his seat on the council.

Seth interrupted my musings.

"Ah, good to sit down," he said, sinking

into the chair next to mine and running a hand over his close-cropped white hair.

"Busy day for you?" I said.

"Not bad."

"How's the injury?" I asked, nodding at his still-bandaged wrist.

"Just a flesh wound, as they say in the movies." A small smile played around his lips.

"What is it, Seth? You look like the cat that ate the canary."

"Damnedest thing, Jessica," he said. "A man spends most of his life in a small town taking care of its citizens, builds a practice, has what you could consider moderate success—"

"I'd say it's more like a great deal of success."

"Mebbe. But then it all falls apart. Patients begin to think he's an old fogey, accuse him of not keepin' up with the times. All the experience and knowledge he's built up over the years count for little, and patients start dropping away."

"Is that what you think has been happening?"

"Ayuh. I do."

I knew he had more to say, so I waited.

Seth cleared his throat, and straightened in his chair. "Then you get in a case like Allcott. Everyone here thought he had the flu." He waved a hand around, indicating the emergency room staff. "They didn't stop to think it's not quite the right time of year for flu. Usually pops up in the fall and later. They wanted to send him back to Blueberry Hill and let him sweat it out. Not much you can do for the flu once someone gets it. Give 'em a pill for the aches, tell 'em to gargle with salt water—it's an old remedy, but it works. And lots of rest." He paused. "Seeing as it's contagious, however, don't imagine Mrs. Thomas would've been too happy to have Allcott staying at her place with the flu."

"She wasn't."

"Don't blame her. Same symptoms, you know—chills, fever, headache, muscle aches."

"But you suspected it might be something else?"

"I did. Sounds funny, but after the EMTs brought him in and I had a chance to examine him, I kind of had a hunch it wasn't flu."

I smiled, thinking of Dr. Boyle. "But your

hunches are based on a depth of knowledge of medicine, on years of taking care
of people."

Seth nodded, his eyebrows raised.

"So how did you determine it was malaria?"

"Simple, really. I asked him if he'd ever
had malaria before."

I laughed. "No one else had thought of
that?"

"Oh, they might have got around to it at
some point. Also did a blood smear and
told the lab to look for it." He glanced at his
watch. "We'll need another one in six hours,
just to confirm it. But in the meantime, we
have him on quinine and tetracycline. And
I've got a new drug on order. Should be
here by tomorrow."

"So if you've had malaria once, you can
get it again?"

"You can treat some kinds of malaria
and it goes away and never returns. With
other types, you may get long periods between relapses, sometimes years and
years," Seth said. "His is the kind that
doesn't usually relapse, but it does recru-
desce."

"That's a new word to me," I said.

"It simply means the symptoms can re-appear several weeks after the initial treatment."

"And if it wasn't for your hunch, what would have happened?"

"If we'd sent him back to Blueberry Hill, he mighta gone downhill real fast. Could've died. Malaria is deadly, especially for the weak—it kills three thousand children a day in Africa."

"A *day*?"

"Outrageous, isn't it? With all the modern medicines we have. Don't get me started on that."

"I won't. Is Rick in danger of dying?"

"I doubt it. Allcott seemed relatively healthy before, so he should do well, but you never can tell. Treating malaria is tricky. Can't even trust the drugs used for it. Whether they work or not depends on where in the world he contracted the disease. In some places the bacteria has developed resistance to chloroquine, the usual treatment. If he picked up the disease in the Caribbean, say, then it might work. But if he first got sick after visiting a country in sub-Saharan Africa, it would be another story."

"He was in Zimbabwe three weeks ago," I said.

"He tell you that?"

"No. I found his passport when I looked for his wallet."

"Three weeks sounds about right. He could have gotten sick there, been treated, and thought he was cured. But once we get him properly medicated and on the road to recovery, he should be fine. Thanks to you bringing in his insurance card, he's now resting comfortably upstairs."

"Thanks to your diagnosis, you mean."

He smiled. Evidently, the identification of a disease rarely seen in Cabot Cove had given his ego a much-needed boost. He was feeling more assured, more confident in his medical skills, and more like the old Seth I was happy to call my friend. I didn't say it—at least not yet—but I was hoping this experience would help him see he wasn't ready to sell his practice and retire.

"When do you think Rick will be up for a visitor?" I asked.

"I'd wait a day. The nurses gave him something to help him sleep. Like with the flu, rest is what he needs most now."

"I brought his toiletry kit," I said. "Perhaps you could have someone take it up to him."

"Do it myself," he said, taking the black leather bag from me. "I'd like to check on him before I get back to the office. If you can wait a bit more, I can drop you off at home."

"I can wait." It was what I'd been doing a lot of today.

He rose from the chair, straightened his shoulders, and headed for the ER's double doors.

I jumped up. "Oh! Wait. I almost forgot." I opened my bag, pulled out a bottle of the supplements Dr. Boyle's nurse had charged me over a hundred dollars for, and handed it to him. "This is my treatment for 'fatigue and forgetfulness.'"

Seth held up his glasses so he could read the ingredients on the label. "Don't see much of anything here. Won't hurt, but don't know if it'll help you, either. You'll have to let me know."

"Oh, for goodness' sake, Seth. How would I know? I don't have fatigue to begin with."

He chuckled. "What about forgetfulness?"

"If you're going to give me a hard time, I'm going to forget I was planning to invite you to dinner next Friday."

Chapter Fifteen

"It's stuffed steak pinwheels in curry sauce with rosemary mashed potatoes. I kind of combined two recipes I saw a lady make on TV." Maureen proudly placed a big platter on the table next to the salad bowl. She slid a steak pinwheel onto my plate, together with a scoop of the potatoes, and passed me a pitcher of curry sauce.

"Wow," said Amos when she handed him his plate. "This looks terrific. I didn't know you were a gourmet cook."

Maureen beamed. "Not exactly gourmet, but I do play around with the recipes like the fine chefs do. You have to know how to substitute if you want to be a really good cook."

Mort took his plate and set it down in front of him. He glanced at me with a pained expression and ran a finger inside the collar of his shirt. "Well, here goes," he said, taking up his fork and starting on the potatoes.

"How are they?" Maureen asked.

"I never had mashed potatoes that crunched before," he said. "What's in them?"

"It's rosemary," his wife replied. "I didn't have a sprig of fresh rosemary, so I had to use the dry instead. You're supposed to take it out, but I figured it would be okay if I left it in."

"It's a very interesting flavor," I said, pushing aside the little spikes of rosemary to get to the potato.

"Kind of like getting splinters in your mouth," Mort said.

Maureen frowned.

"I'm sure the meat will be better, hon."

Amos was wolfing down his dinner. "I haven't had a good home-cooked meal like this in a long time. What's in the curry sauce?"

"It's a secret ingredient," Maureen said.

"No secrets in this house, please," Mort said.

"Oh, all right. It's a combination of curry sauce mix, chicken broth, and apple sauce. It also calls for coconut milk, but I didn't have that, so I improvised and substituted piña colada mix."

"Are you sure it goes with the steak and garlic stuffing?" Mort asked.

"It's the combination of sweet and savory that gives it its piquant essence," Maureen said.

I pushed the sauce to the side with my fork, and concentrated on the salad. I'd brought cookies from Sassi's Bakery and hoped Maureen hadn't planned an elaborate dessert like the Kwanzaa cake recipe she'd tried from a television show last January.

"Got the ballistics report back today after you left, Mrs. F," Mort said when we'd finished eating and had cups of coffee in front of us.

"Oh?"

Amos nodded at me. "The ten-millimeter pistol we took from Chester's car was the gun used in the murder, Miz Fletcher. The bullet they took out of Joseph Lennon was fired from that gun."

"That may be," I said, "but it doesn't mean Chester fired that gun."

"It was found in his car, Miz Fletcher. The tooth fairy didn't leave it there."

"Probably not, but someone else might have. His fingerprints weren't on it, were they?"

"No, but he could have wiped them off, Mrs. F."

"He could have, Mort, but if he went to all the trouble to wipe off his fingerprints, why would he leave the weapon in his car for the police to find?"

"Mebbe he wasn't thinkin' that far ahead," Amos said.

"The circumstantial evidence does point in his direction. I'll grant you that," I said. "But don't you find it a little convenient that the murder weapon was right there for all to see? And that Chester's T-shirt was found with the body? It seems to me someone went to a great deal of trouble to frame Chester Carlisle."

"Do you have an alternate theory, Mrs. F?" Mort asked.

"No, not yet," I had to admit. "Still, there

are too many little pieces that don't add up."

"What else, Miz Fletcher?"

I wasn't prepared to point a finger at anyone else, but there were some people whose actions would bear investigation. If I mentioned the secretiveness of the Lennon-Diversified staff, they would think I was grasping at straws. Was I? I wanted to speak with Joseph Lennon's wife and children, and perhaps the flight crew. And where did Dr. Warren Boyle spring from? And was Rick Allcott missing his gun? Amos had said the gun was a 10 mm pistol; I hadn't seen it, of course, but a pistol of that size is the type of gun issued by the FBI to its agents. "There are just too many unanswered questions," I said.

"Well, let us know when you suspect someone else," Mort said.

"I'll do that," I said.

Maureen sang out from the kitchen, "I hope you saved some room for my wonton surprise with cherry pie filling and wasabi peas."

The European-style house was on the outskirts of town. Custom-built for its wealthy original owners, it was an imposing building, very different from the narrow Victorians, like mine, that lined the streets leading to Cabot Cove's harbor. This house was built in three sections; the middle part was a rectangular block with three windows on the second floor overlooking the arched loggia that formed the entrance. Two pairs of French doors topped with fanlights flanked the recessed portico. A multicar garage with a steep roofline jutted out to form one end of the building, matched by a smaller, steep-roofed structure on the other end. I climbed the front steps and rang the bell. Inside the loggia, a glass transom and sidelights framed the paneled door, but it was impossible to see into the house, thanks to the wavy hand-blown cut glass used in the long windows.

Josie Lennon answered the door, looking more like a model in *Vogue* than a daughter in mourning. She was clothed dramatically, head to toe in black, with a butterfly-sleeved sheath, fishnet stockings, and patent leather high heels. She wore a jet necklace with matching bracelet and earrings. Her makeup was pale with the exception of her eyes, which were lined in black with dark brown shadow on her lids. It must have taken hours in front of a mirror to achieve this precise vision of gothic misery.

"Hello, Josie," I said. "I don't know if you remember, but we met at the middle school last week during rehearsals for the Independence Day events. I'm so sorry about your father."

She didn't say a word, but held the door open wider so I could enter. The house was kept very cold, even though outside the weather was pleasant, if not cool. I understood why Josie had selected a long-sleeved dress to wear, and regretted not bringing along a lightweight sweater for myself.

"I'd like to see your mother, if I may, to extend my condolences."

Josie drew in a long breath and let it out. "The last time I saw her, she was in the library," she said, and pointed to my left. "It's through the living room."

"Thank you."

Josie faded into the back of the house, and I followed the direction she had indicated, making my way past modern Asian-inspired furniture upholstered in beige brocade and arranged around a glass-and-steel cocktail table in front of a white marble fireplace. Floor-to-ceiling drapes in a bronze watered silk set off the French doors. When closed in the evening, as I was sure they would be, the drapes must have created a wall of shimmering fabric. Since they were open, however, morning sunlight poured in, making bright oblongs on the Persian carpet, like stepping-stones. It was an elegantly appointed room, with obviously expensive furniture and artwork, that must have been designed to create a serene atmosphere. Nevertheless, it appeared to my eyes to be a bit cold and unwelcoming. I wondered if Mrs. Lennon would be the same.

I didn't notice her at first when I walked through the archway from the living room. I was too fascinated by the surroundings. The library must have been Joseph Lennon's retreat from the soulless beige behind me. In this room, everything was decisively masculine, almost ironically so. Dark polished wood paneling, bookcases filled with leather-bound volumes, tufted chesterfield sofas, a stone hearth flanked with matching deep wing chairs, over which hung trophy heads of wild animals looking out on the room as if eavesdropping on the conversation, the faint aroma of tobacco—a pipe perhaps, not a cigar. All conspired to make a macho statement, and an excessive one at that.

Mrs. Lennon must not have had a hand in decorating this room, I thought. *Or if she did, she may have intended to give her husband an extreme version of what he wanted.*

"When you're finished gawking, you might introduce yourself."

"Good heavens!" I said. "Where are you?"

"I'm right here."

A face peered around the side of a chair, the wings of which had blocked her from my view. However, the brass fish-eye mirror on the opposite wall must have allowed her to see me enter. Mrs. Lennon was dark-haired and dark-eyed, and even though, unlike her daughter, she was without makeup, I could see where Josie got her exotic looks. She was dressed in a knit pantsuit in a color that would have blended well with her living room, and she had drawn a fringed scarf around her shoulders, probably to counter the frigid effects of the air-conditioning. Her hair was pulled back in an elaborate twist at the base of her neck.

"Have a seat," she said, and waved me to the wing chair opposite her. Between the chairs was a low leather table and a tray holding a china tea service, a carafe of water, a glass, a bottle of pills, and a little silver bell.

I did as instructed, saying, "Good afternoon, Mrs. Lennon. I'm Jessica Fletcher. I came to offer my condolences."

"The name is familiar. Maybe Joseph spoke of you." She had a slight foreign accent, although I couldn't place it.

"We had met on several occasions," I said. "I was sorry to learn of his death."

"Thank you, Mrs. Fletcher."

"Please call me Jessica."

"And I'm Denise." She squinted at me. "Jessica Fletcher, you said?"

"Yes."

"Would you be J. B. Fletcher, the author?"

I smiled. "I would."

Her face brightened. "I think I've read every one of your books, J. B. Fletcher.

My favorite is *The Corpse Was a Comrade*."

"That's very kind of you to say."

"No, no. It's kind of you to come, Jessica. I'm very touched." Her face fell. "Joseph's death was a great shock to me. I would never have expected it. It is supposed to be so safe in America. In my country, they wouldn't let a man go around threatening someone, but here . . ." She shrugged.

"I hope you won't think me rude if I ask where your country is," I said.

"Not at all. I'm from what used to be Rhodesia and what is now Zimbabwe. My ancestors were Portuguese and British and Ndebele. Like many native Africans, I am a mixture of many peoples."

"How interesting. Do you get to go back often?"

"Not often, but every now and then. We were there only a few weeks ago. Joseph loved Africa."

"Is that where you met your husband?"

"Yes." She looked up at the animal heads that were mounted on the wall. "My family led safari tours, and Joseph was one of our clients." She chuckled softly. "He didn't kill all these, if that's what you're thinking. I bought them from a company in New York. When we moved into this house, I wanted a room to remind him of me when I wasn't here. It's a bit over the top, no? But he likes to entertain in here." She stopped, realizing she'd spoken in the present tense. "It's going to take me some time to remember he's gone."

"I'm sorry I hadn't had an opportunity to meet you before," I said, "but I understand you were out of town. When did you get in?"

"Joseph wanted me to come for the fireworks—he was very proud that he was able to get that famous family to do the show—so I flew in on the Fourth from Vancouver. We have a home there."

"Were you at the fireworks? I saw your husband. Cynthia Welch introduced him. I would have thought she would introduce you, too."

She made a face at the mention of Ms. Welch's name. "No, I missed them," she said. "I had a migraine when we landed—traveling gives me terrible headaches—so I called Joseph and told him I'd meet him at home, and had the flight crew drop me off here. I went to bed early. Now I'm thinking that if only I'd gone to the fireworks, I might have kept Joseph by my side, or made him take me home early. None of this would have happened."

She was right, of course. Most incidents in our lives hinge on a matter of seconds. We move in one direction rather than another, and everything shifts. I thought of the attempted mugging from the other night and the attack on Seth, and how if we'd gotten in the car right away rather than standing outside the restaurant chatting, Seth might never have been injured. Then again, we might have been accosted anyway, and it could have been worse. He might have been killed. Each decision we make, each road we take, leaves another road not taken, as in the final line of the famous poem by Robert Frost that I used to teach in my English class.

"I hope you don't blame yourself," I said. "There was no way for you to know what would happen."

"No, I don't blame myself. I just think about what might have been." She was silent for a moment. Then she sighed. "Do you know you're one of only a few people from Cabot Cove who've come to see us, aside from the people who work for us?"

"I'm surprised to hear that," I said, wondering whether the mayor and members of the town council had stopped by to express their sympathies, or anyone from the other institutions in Cabot Cove that had benefited from Joseph Lennon's contributions. And if not, why not?

"I'm not surprised. Joseph was an aggressive businessman. He thought if he invested a lot of money in the towns where he set up his companies that would be enough to buy people's loyalty, to get them to forget whatever inconveniences a new business brings. Everywhere we had an office, he'd woo the politicians and the citizens, dazzle them with his money, support the local causes, get interviewed by reporters. Frankly, I think he liked the fuss, enjoyed being the center of attention. I warned him that everyone might not take to his style. But of course he didn't listen. And now, unfortunately, I've been proved right."

"Did your husband have any enemies that you know of?" I asked.

"That's funny," she said, giving me a small smile. "There was a sheriff here who asked the same question. And I'll give you the same answer I gave him. Not that I know of. The pharmaceuticals industry is enormous, and we occupy only a very small part of it, packaging and distributing drugs. So, no, I don't believe Joseph had any enemies. Except, of course, the horrible person who killed him. And did you see how fast they caught him? That's what offering a reward will do. We put up fifty thousand dollars. I told that sheriff about the money; I knew it would make him work harder."

I doubted if Mort would ever claim her reward money, even assuming he arrested the right person, which I didn't believe was the case at this moment. Mort took pride in his profession and would work hard to solve Lennon's murder regardless of whether or not a reward was offered. But there was no point in debating with Mrs. Lennon. In my experience, people who don't trust the police cannot be argued out of it.

"From what I've been told, he sounds like a deranged old man," she said. "Someone should have put him away before he went crazy."

"You mean Chester Carlisle?"

"Is that his name? All I remember hearing is that he was one of the ones who resented Joseph's trying to ingratiate himself into the community. Had nasty T-shirts made up ridiculing our name. Tried to get others to reject Joseph's generosity. And then when he couldn't sway them to join in his campaign against my husband, he shot him. What a sick, sick man. I feel sad for him."

She was not at all what I'd expected. Having met her husband and her children, I'd imagined a pampered society lady, someone as dramatic and demanding as her daughter, or perhaps as meek and insecure as her son. And she might still turn out to be one or the other, but somehow I suspected that wouldn't be the case.

"I'm sorry, Mother. I didn't realize you had company." Paul Lennon stood in the entryway, hesitant to intrude. He was wearing jeans and a polo shirt and seemed slighter than I remembered—or perhaps it was just the first time I was seeing him without a suit and tie.

"Paul, come in, dear. This is Mrs. Fletcher. Have you met?"

"Not officially," Paul said. "How do you do?"

"Very well, thank you," I replied.

He pulled up a hassock and sat at his mother's feet.

"Paul is going to take over the business for me," Denise said.

"Mother, I really think we should discuss this. I'm not sure I know enough to run the company by myself."

"You won't be by yourself," his mother said. "I will be by your side."

"But what about Cynthia? She'll expect—"

"I don't care what Cynthia expects. She is an employee. That's all. You are the heir, and Lennon-Diversified is your father's legacy."

"But the board—"

"The board will do as I say, or I will replace them." She looked at me. "I'm sorry, Jessica. We shouldn't discuss our boring business while you're visiting."

"Please, don't mind me," I said. "I know you have many important decisions to make."

"That is very understanding of you."

"Cynthia said she was coming by today to talk with you," Paul said, picking up a corner of his mother's shawl and playing with the fringe.

"I will talk with her, but I'm not going to change my mind. Your father and I discussed it last week, and we were in agreement. After that business several years ago, I never knew why he kept her on—or perhaps I do. She is young and pretty, after all." She leaned over and looked in her cup, which was empty. "Jessica, I must apologize to you. I never offered you any coffee or tea." She picked up the silver bell to ring it but changed her mind. "Paul, will you please ask the maid to bring in a fresh pot of rooibos tea and an extra cup and saucer?"

"Please don't fuss on my account," I said. "I'm fine as I am."

"I want tea for myself, Jessica, and you may have it or not as you like. Paul?" She leaned over and plucked the medicine bottle and glass of water from the tray before her son picked it up and left the room. "Joseph was always a little hard on Paul," she confided when he'd gone.

The scene I'd witnessed in the lobby of Lennon-Diversified sprang immediately to mind. Lennon had been more than hard on Paul. To my thinking he'd been cruel. "Why do you suppose that was?" I asked.

"Paul is not as assertive as his father was. But I think that with a bit more seasoning to build his confidence, he'll be fine. I'll train him." She opened the pill bottle and shook one out into her hand. "Warren gave me these to calm my nerves. Do you know Dr. Boyle?"

"We've met, yes."

"Joseph liked taking people under his wing and bringing them along, but he had high expectations. Unfortunately, he had a lot less patience with his own children. Josie has no interest in the business, so that was never a question, and Paul—well, he'll have to learn it now, won't he?" She swallowed the pill with a sip of water. "I don't imagine these things work if you don't believe in them. But I'd rather take an herb than a tranquilizer. In Zimbabwe, we have a great deal of respect for medicinal herbs. We even have pictures of them on our postage stamps."

She seemed to be drifting from one topic to another, and I tried to bring her back to a topic I was interested in. "Was

Dr. Boyle one of those Mr. Lennon took under his wing?" I asked.

"I beg your pardon. Dr. Boyle? Yes, he was one of Joseph's protégés. He didn't have the money to set up a successful practice, so Joseph agreed to help him out, provided Warren helped Joseph market his supplements. It was my idea. When you offer mineral supplements in the same office that houses state-of-the-art diagnostic equipment, patients tend to have more confidence in the pills. And I think it has worked well for him."

"Have you made this arrangement with other doctors as well?"

"No. Warren is the first. He's our test case, so to speak. Cynthia was the one who brought him to our attention. He had a little office in Massachusetts, and when we moved here, we set him up. The sales aren't much—he's only one doctor, after all. But the program has the potential to grow. Joseph and I talked about expanding the program to other medical offices, perhaps even others here in Cabot Cove."

I knew that Seth would never entertain the idea of promoting pills in exchange for receiving expensive medical equipment, no matter how advanced, and I hoped our other local doctors would feel the same. But you can never be sure of such things. Greed has a way of finding excuses.

I heard the doorbell ring just as Paul re-entered the room and placed the tray back on the table in front of his mother. She picked up a porcelain cup and saucer, poured tea from the china pot, and handed the cup to me. "Help yourself to sugar and cream," she said, as she poured for Paul and herself.

"Thank you," I said, sitting back with the cup and wondering if it was Ms. Welch at the door. My curiosity was satisfied a moment later when Cynthia strode into the room, Dante at her heels.

"Hello, Denise. I've brought the contracts I told you about." She crossed the room and Dante pulled over a chair for her. He stood behind it. "Joe and I agreed this was to go forward," she said, laying a sheaf of papers on the tray so they covered Mrs. Lennon's cup. Ms. Welch looked pointedly at me. Even though we'd met several times before, she said, "I'm sorry to interrupt your morning tea time, Mrs.—?"

"Fletcher," Dante supplied.

"Mrs. Fletcher. But Mrs. Lennon and I have some business to discuss. You don't mind, do you? You can come back another time."

"Mrs. Fletcher is my guest, and she isn't leaving, Cynthia. Anything you have to say to me you can say in front of her."

"Really, Denise. This is company business. I'm sure Mrs. Fletcher has no interest in our business."

Denise pulled her cup from underneath the contracts. "Do you mind staying while we finish with these?" she asked me. "It won't take long."

"Not at all," I said. "I'm at your disposal."

Cynthia looked down at her lap, nostrils flaring, and I could see she was trying to get her temper under control. Dante glared at me. Paul, on the hassock next to his mother, smiled into his teacup.

Cynthia straightened her shoulders and twisted her body in the chair, so she faced Mrs. Lennon, her back to me. Like Denise, she wore her dark hair in a chignon. I studied the hairdo. One of these women had been talking with Dr. Boyle in his office. I thought I knew which one, but couldn't be certain yet.

"This is the contract renewal for the new medication," Cynthia said. "We have four countries signed up so far. And I've spoken with representatives of that charity group to unload the last of the old formula."

"I know about the contracts," Denise said. "I have been in touch with the health department in Harare. There were some problems with a previous shipment, I was told."

Cynthia cleared her throat. "There weren't any problems. We investigated the complaints, and they were unfounded. The medicine works only on certain bacterial infections. Everyone knows that. We can't be responsible if someone has contracted a form of the disease resistant to the medication. I'm arranging to send the last shipment to the refugee camps. And the new orders will go out in a month. We just need your signature to proceed."

"Paul, have you read through these contracts?" his mother asked.

Paul shook his head.

"Why don't you leave these with us," Denise said to Cynthia. "That will give Paul a chance to familiarize himself with the responsibilities he is about to undertake."

"I think we both know who Joe wanted

to succeed him," Cynthia said between clenched teeth. The back of her neck was flushed a bright red, and I was certain that her face was the same. She seemed to have forgotten I was there, or else she thought to embarrass Denise in my presence to get even for allowing me to stay through this highly charged discussion.

"I am well aware that Joseph was very *fond* of you," Denise said, placing the emphasis on "fond" and leaving questions hanging in the air.

"It was more than fondness. He trusted my judgment. I have fifteen years of experience with this company. In the time I've been with Lennon-Diversified, company profits have doubled. I take great pride in that."

"So I have heard."

"Paul, you'll pardon my saying this, but you have only six months' experience, and only in the least important areas." She switched her gaze to his mother. "Frankly, Paul isn't capable of running a company this size. It will fail without me."

"Then I'm sure he will be able to count on you to help guide him in his new post. Isn't that so?"

Cynthia's hands were fisted in her lap, the knuckles white. "I'd hoped I wouldn't have to go over your head, Denise. I don't believe your decision is final. Several members of the board have indicated that they would welcome my taking over, that they would back me in a vote," Cynthia said, allowing a note of satisfaction to creep into her voice.

Paul looked up sharply. Denise put her hand on her son's shoulder to keep him from speaking, and the thought crossed my mind that Cynthia had underestimated Joseph Lennon's wife. Denise kept her voice soft, but her eyes were hard on the younger woman. "Just who on the board has made such promises?"

"Obviously, I'd rather not say at this time. But I assure you I will do my best to make sure Lennon-Diversified is positioned to do well in the future. And, of course, Paul will always have a place in the company as long as I'm in charge."

"How kind of you. But I am afraid you have counted your chickens a bit early. Perhaps if Joseph had lived, you might have been able to convince him to side with you, and together with a few board members, you may have outvoted me and gotten your wish. But now that he's dead, you see, Joseph's share in the company has been left to me. Together with my original votes, I currently have the controlling interest in the company. The board cannot overrule me." Mrs. Lennon let the news sink in before adding, "I will consider keeping you on, provided you sign an agreement promising to ensure that Paul learns everything he needs to know to take over. If this is too difficult for you, I will understand, of course." She stopped there.

Cynthia rose abruptly from her chair, her chest heaving. "I will . . . I will think about it and let you know."

Dante returned the chair to its original position.

"By tomorrow," Mrs. Lennon said. "And, Cynthia?" Her voice stopped Ms. Welch as she was about to walk out. "I've instructed Roger to let all the employees have the rest of the day off today and told him to lock up. Lennon-Diversified will be closed tomorrow in tribute to Joseph Lennon."

"But I've got deadlines to meet, shipments to get out."

"They can wait a day, while we honor our founder, and while you decide if you'll remain with the company."

Chapter Sixteen

Rick Allcott was sitting up in his hospital bed when I stopped in to see him. Tethered to several IV bags hanging from a pole, he looked drawn, but gave me a big smile. "Jessica, what a nice surprise. I hear I owe my recovering health to you and Dr. Hazlitt."

"You certainly may credit Seth," I said. "All I did was to bring in your insurance card."

"I'll bet it wasn't easy to find, either," he said. "And I'm especially grateful you thought to bring my toiletry kit. Can't tell you how wonderful it was to wash up this morning and use my own toothbrush. Thank you."

"You're welcome," I said. "How are you feeling?"

"A little weak, but I'll pull through."

"Malaria is a disease that takes quite a toll on the body, I understand."

"So you know about my diagnosis."

"An exotic disease in Cabot Cove is always news. It was all over the hospital in no time, and it was even mentioned in this morning's *Gazette*—without your name, of course."

"Too bad they didn't use my name," he said. "I haven't had my fifteen minutes of fame yet."

"It wasn't a front-page headline," I said. "It was a small item, reassuring the community that malaria is not contagious. I imagine Mrs. Thomas at Blueberry Hill was particularly relieved."

"She's a nice lady. I'm sorry if I scared her. Please, Jessica, pull up a chair. I feel rude being in bed while you're standing. I know you have some questions for me. I can see it in your face."

I wondered what it was about my face these days that caused people to assume they knew what I was thinking and feeling—first Dr. Boyle's nurse, Mandy, and now Rick Allcott. But there was no use fretting over whether my facial expressions were revealing my inner thoughts. I did have questions for Rick, and he was inviting me to ask them.

"I do have a few things I'd like to talk about with you," I said, taking the hospital-issue vinyl chair that was next to his bed.

"Fire away."

"I have a feeling you came to Cabot Cove under false pretenses. Care to comment?"

"It's your fault I'm here," he said with a smile. "Your portrayal of Cabot Cove was so appealing, I knew I'd have to see the town for myself. And it is indeed the perfect vision of small-town Americana, especially the parade that you so colorfully described to me at the conference."

"It took two years before the appeal of my hometown's description sank in and you decided to check it out in person?"

"I told you, I just retired and now I have the time to travel. Why would you doubt me?"

"You've been telling me one lie after

306 Jessica Fletcher & Donald Bain

another since you arrived," I said. "Either you enjoy spinning yarns, in which case I will start to doubt the impression I formed of you two years ago, or you're up to something and don't want me to know about it."

Rick laughed. "What have I lied about?"

"The Red Sox, for one."

"You don't believe I'm a Red Sox fan? I've been following them ever since I got a Ted Williams glove for my seventh birthday."

"You may indeed be a fan of the Sox, but you didn't stop in Boston to watch a game before arriving in Cabot Cove in time for Independence Day. They were on a ten-day road trip when you claim to have seen them in Fenway Park."

The smile on Rick's face became an ironic one. "I was hoping you hadn't checked their schedule."

"I didn't. News of their road trip was all over the radio and television. Maine doesn't have its own major-league baseball team. Everyone here follows the Red Sox."

"Is that all? All right, I didn't go to the stadium. I was eager to come up here. What's the big deal? I'm branded a liar for that?"

"When we were walking on the shore after the fireworks and Amos told us about his trip to Africa, you acted as if you'd never been there. In fact, you told us you'd love to see it one day."

"So?" His smile had now disappeared.

"Your passport was in the same sneaker as your wallet."

"And you looked at it?"

"I did. You visited Sierra Leone last year. That's in Africa. And three weeks ago you were in Zimbabwe, where you must have contracted an apparently difficult case of malaria."

"You're a hard lady to fool."

"Why would you want to?"

He leaned back against the pillow and sighed.

"You're not retired from the bureau, are you?" I asked.

His head came up. "Now why do you say that?"

"I think you're still working for Uncle Sam. You showed the police your FBI ID and you've obviously kept up with your martial arts skills; otherwise I doubt you'd have been able to attack and disarm that mugger so efficiently the night you saved Seth from further harm. I think you're working on a case in Cabot Cove, and unless I miss my guess, I'd say it has to do with Lennon-Diversified."

"Sheesh, Jessica. Would you consider coming to work for the bureau? We could use more investigators with your powers of logic."

"Compliments won't get you out of this, Rick."

"You're only partially right. I am officially retired from the bureau. Put in my twenty years, qualified for the gold watch, if the national budget would ever supply them. But the bureau does hire back its retirees as independent contractors, especially if they've been working on a case for an extended time. No sense in putting another agent through a steep learning curve if it isn't necessary."

"And you've been investigating Lennon-Diversified for a long time?"

"If I reveal a government secret to you, you have to promise you won't share it with anyone—not with Seth, not with Amos, not even with Mort."

"I won't make that promise if it's going

to hinder a murder investigation. Mort needs to be informed if a different governmental organization is asserting jurisdiction, especially if it's impeding work on his case. There's a man being kept in jail as we speak, who very well may be innocent. *Is* innocent, in my view."

"I can't speak for Carlisle's guilt or innocence."

"Can't you? I didn't see the T-shirt you bought from Chester when I was looking for your wallet. It wasn't among your clothes."

"It's in my car. Boy, you really went through my things, didn't you?"

"You might still be in the emergency room hallway if I hadn't."

"You're right. I apologize. I know you're upset, but I really can't discuss this with you. It's an official matter."

"Out of curiosity, where is the gun that goes with the ammunition clip I found in your other sneaker?"

I watched as color flooded Rick's face. "It was stolen from my room."

"Does Jill Thomas know?"

"God, no. I would never tell her I left a gun in the room. She would freak out."

"Did you report it to the police?"

He shook his head. "Look, Jessica, I can't think of anything more humiliating than an FBI agent's being relieved of his weapon. It should have been on my person, but with the hot weather, there was nowhere to conceal it. Besides, I figured no one would break into my room in Cabot Cove, of all places in the world."

"Are we going to discover that the gun used to kill Joseph Lennon and found in Chester Carlisle's car is FBI issue?"

Rick crossed his arms. "Before you accuse me, did you check to see if the gun they found in Carlisle's car is registered to him?"

"Are you trying to buy some time?"

"It's a legitimate question."

"No, it's not. Maine doesn't require gun registration, and as an FBI agent working in the state, I assume you know that. So I'll ask again. Was your gun used to kill Lennon?"

Rick threw his head back on the pillow. "I hope not, but it's possible."

"If it's the same gun, will the police be able to trace it to you?"

"No way. It's not registered, and there are no identifying marks on it."

"When was your gun stolen?"

"You mean when did I realize my gun had been stolen? The night of the murder, when I returned to Blueberry Hill from your house and checked to see if it was where I'd hidden it. That's when I discovered it missing."

"Yet you never reported the theft to Mort?"

"I had a feeling it might have been used in the murder, and I didn't want to claim it just yet."

"Could that be because you killed Lennon yourself and tossed the murder weapon into the back of Chester's car?"

"I know it may look that way to you right now, Jessica, but I swear that's not the case. And as soon as I get out of here, I'll go talk to Mort and tell him about the gun."

"How long are you going to be in the hospital?"

"Seth didn't say, but let *me* talk to your sheriff. It should come from me."

"Am I supposed to hold on to information about crucial evidence in this case until you feel you're well enough to walk out of here? How do I know you won't skip town and leave Chester languishing in jail?"

"Look. I'll call up the sheriff and see if I can get him to release the old man, or at least get him to let Carlisle out on bail. I offered before to work with Mort's office on this case, and I swear I'll help him find the real killer."

"I'll give you time to talk with the sheriff," I said. "But if you don't tell Mort your gun is missing, I will."

"What's this all about?" Seth stood in the doorway looking from Rick's face to mine. "Are you upsetting my patient, Jessica?"

"I think the upset is mutual," I said, standing.

"Well, visiting time is over for today. This man needs his rest if he's to get better."

"Then I'll leave him in your competent care," I said.

Rick looked at me imploringly. "I didn't do it, Jessica. Do you believe me?"

"I hope that's the truth, Rick," I said. "But I don't know that I'm ready to believe anything you say."

Chapter Seventeen

"Jessica? It's Jed Richardson. The Cessnas are back in service, and since I have some time, I thought I'd give you a call and see if you want to go up for an hour or two today."

I took the phone to the window and looked out at a beautiful blue sky. "You know, Jed, I think that's a wonderful idea. I need to keep my skills sharp. I'll see you in about an hour." Smiling, I hung up the phone.

Yesterday had been a long and difficult day. While my visit to Mrs. Lennon had been informative, my confrontation with

Rick Allcott had been just the opposite. I'd left the hospital feeling guilty that I'd harassed a sick man and frustrated that I hadn't been able to get answers from him. One thing was clear: The FBI was here in Cabot Cove on official business. Rick wouldn't admit it, but I was convinced it had to do with Lennon-Diversified. At one time the company had been the target of a fraud investigation by the Food and Drug Administration. Those charges had never stuck. Had the FBI sent Allcott to Cabot Cove to follow up? He had visited Zimbabwe around the same time the Lennons had been there. It couldn't be a coincidence. If Rick's gun had been used to kill Joseph Lennon—something I couldn't prove yet— who had fired the fatal shot? Rick? He'd been at the fireworks, but I had no idea with whom he'd met up or whether he'd left at any time and wandered off behind the building to confront Lennon.

Unless someone had seen him.

But the hundreds of people there all had their eyes trained on the brilliant displays. The loud pop of a 10 mm gun would never have been heard above the explosions in the sky. And if Rick's gun truly had been stolen, who could have taken it? Who had access to his room other than Jill Thomas and her maid? Dante had visited the inn to arrange for rooms for the company's visitors—or so he told Jill. According to my friend MaryJane, who worked at Lennon-Diversified, the company rarely had visitors. If Dante went to the inn to break into Rick's room, did that mean he knew who Rick was and why he was here?

Had Mrs. Lennon really gone straight from the airport to her lavish home, skipping the fireworks show altogether? She was now in charge of Lennon-Diversified. Had that been her goal all along? Had she believed her husband was cheating on her, perhaps with Cynthia Welch? She'd hinted that he had an eye for a pretty woman, and she was determined that her son would head up the company. While Cynthia Welch may have underestimated Denise Lennon, I certainly did not.

Or had Cynthia Welch tried an end run around both Lennons to ensure her place running Lennon-Diversified? Without his mother's support, Paul was no match for Ms. Welch's forceful personality. But then again, Paul had been badly treated by his father. Was Joseph Lennon's death merely the revenge of an abused child? Could Paul's sister, Josie, also have a motive? It didn't seem logical that she would kill the parent who supported her stage career, but murder is rarely logical.

And where did that purveyor of a closetful of pills, Dr. Warren Boyle, stand now that his benefactor was gone? Would he gain or lose by Joseph Lennon's death?

I'd gone home that night with my head ringing with questions but without any answers. I'd left a message at the sheriff's office for Mort, but I hadn't mentioned Rick's gun. Instead, I asked him to call Rick at the hospital and told him that Allcott had something he needed to discuss with him. I would give Rick a chance to come clean with Mort, and I hoped he'd do it.

A hot bath, a cup of tea, and a light dinner had done little to calm my mood, and I'd slept fitfully. But by morning I was feeling better. The prospect of going up in the air sounded delightful. Being at the controls of a plane heightens your senses, making you aware not only of the beauty of the landscape below but also of the infinite sky above and your small place in this universe. Perhaps alone, with only the buzz of the engine to intrude on my thoughts, I could unravel this twisted knot. And if I couldn't, at least I would have nurtured my spiritual side and achieved the practical goal of keeping up on my flying skills.

Jed was behind the counter when I entered his office. Two men in aviator uniforms lounged on his battered couch, flipping through the old issues of the *Cabot Cove Gazette* that were piled on a wooden coffee table that had been naturally distressed by years of boot heels propped on it.

"Remember this guy?" one of them said to his colleague, pointing to the paper. "Didn't he hitch a ride to Zimbabwe with Welch once?"

"Yeah. He looks familiar."

"Jessica, there you are," said Jed. "Hey, guys, remember I was telling you about J. B. Fletcher, our homegrown novelist and fledgling pilot? Well, not so fledgling anymore."

The two men dropped their reading material and jumped to their feet. "That's

Captain Andy Baron," Jed said as the taller of the two men shook my hand. "And his copilot, Jerry Fitzpatrick."

"Nice to meet you both," I said. "Please, sit down."

"Andy and Jerry are the crew for the Lennon-Diversified Gulfstream," Jed said.

"It's a beautiful plane," I said, taking a folding chair that was next to the couch. "Are you flying out, or did you just get in?"

"Out," Captain Baron said. "You heard about our boss, Joe Lennon?"

"Everyone in Cabot Cove knows what happened," Jed said.

"We were supposed to pick up Mr. Lennon's body and take it to Vancouver for burial, but the cops haven't released it yet. I think Mrs. Lennon wants to bring the kids back to British Columbia. That's where their principal residence is."

"Or else she'll have us fly to Zimbabwe. She's got family there," Jerry said. "We were told to fuel up, but not where we're going."

"Did Mrs. Lennon call you herself?" I asked.

"Never does," Andy put in. "It was someone from the office. We don't know the itinerary or even who we're carrying. We're stuck here waiting for our passengers. That's the life of a corporate pilot. You're on call all the time. It's always hurry up and wait."

"And wait and wait." Jerry winked at the captain. "But, as we always tell each other, the money is good and the plane is great."

"Were you the crew that brought Mrs. Lennon here?"

"Yeah, we always fly her. But if we have too many hours, a second crew takes over," Andy said.

"The company insists they follow the same FAA regulations as commercial pilots," Jed added. "They can't fly more than a certain number of hours per week, and not at all if they've had a drink within twenty-four hours of takeoff."

"It's nice," Jerry added. "A lot of corporate pilots never get a break. We know that once we hit our mark, we get some time off."

"When did you get in?" I asked.

"On the Fourth," he replied. "Just in time to see the fireworks."

"Great show," Andy said. "You see it, Jed?"

"Of course. Everyone in town was there."

"Was Mrs. Lennon there, too?" I asked.

Andy and Jerry looked at each other and shrugged. "I guess," Andy said. "Dante picked us up here and dropped her at the house before he left us at the hotel. She wanted to freshen up. I thought he was going to circle back to take her to the show. Mr. Lennon was expecting her. At least that's what Dante said."

Ronnie came into the office holding a box. "All fueled and ready to go," he told the pilots. "I did the windshield, too. And some guy delivered this package for you."

"Thanks, kid," Andy said, taking the box. "Appreciate the hard work." He handed Ronnie a folded bill.

"Thank you, sir."

Andy looked at the box. "It's addressed to Mrs. Lennon."

"Who's it from?" Jerry asked.

"Doesn't say. I'd better go stow this aboard."

"How about a couple of games of gin?"

Jerry asked. "I want to win back the money I lost to you last week."

"Never happen. You're a lousy card-player, but if you want me to take you to the cleaners again, I'm happy to do it. We should have a couple of hours before they get here."

The pilots stood and put on their caps. "See you later, Jed. Nice meeting you, Mrs. Fletcher."

"Nice to meet you, too," I said.

Jed came around the counter and handed Ronnie the keys to his truck. "I need you to go into town to pick up that fuel pump. The receipt's in the glove box." He turned to me. "You ready to go up, Jess?"

"You know, I've changed my mind, Jed. I'm going to hitch a ride into town with Ronnie. Maybe I'll come back a little later."

"You're sure?"

"Yes. I'm sorry if I put you out."

"No trouble at all. Women's prerogative. Just sing out if you change your mind."

"I will. Oh, do you mind if I take these?" I picked up the *Gazette*s the pilots had been reading.

"Help yourself. They're pretty old, though."

"That's all right. I like old news." I left Jed scratching his head, surely thinking I was daft, and walked out with Ronnie.

Chapter Eighteen

Amos was sitting at Mort's desk reading an adventure novel when I entered the sheriff's office. He put his finger in the book to hold his place when he saw me. "How do, Miz Fletcher?"

"Fine, thanks, Amos. How are you?"

"Not too bad. Nice and cool in here. Mornin' paper says we're in for another heat wave comin' through."

"I hope it's not as bad as the last one."

"Supposed to go up way past ninety tomorrow."

"Oh, my. I'd better stop by Charles Department Store to see if they got in the

air conditioners Jim said they had on order."

"Can't be worse than down south. Called
my cousin back home. He says it's hotter
'n blazes, but I've got an AC in my work-
shop, so I don't mind the heat."

"Does that mean you'll be leaving us
soon, Amos?"

"Mebbe. I'd like to wrap up this murder
case before I go, but it isn't lookin' promising right now."

"Why not?"

"Well, you should know. You left the
message for the sheriff. Mort spoke to Rick
Allcott this morning. Right after that, he
went on over to the hospital to get an official statement. Said he might have to let
Chester out on bail this afternoon. Chester
was mighty happy, I can tell you."

"I'm sure he is," I said.

"We're not too busted up about lettin'
him out, either. He was the most complai-
ningest prisoner I ever met. He griped day
and night. Nothin' was right. The bed was
too soft. The temperature was too cold.
The food was horrible, even though Mort's
wife has been making home-cooked
meals just for Chester. Glad I never had

occasion to put him behind bars when I was sheriff."

"Well, when you get to be a certain age, it's harder to adjust to changes in your life," I said. "Besides, I'm inclined to think no one is really comfortable in jail. I hope he gets to sleep in his own bed tonight."

"If he doesn't have air-conditioning at home, he may be sorry he left here." Amos folded down a corner of the page of his book and set it aside. "Is there anything I can do for you, Miz Fletcher? I don't imagine the sheriff will be back for some time."

"I wanted to talk to him about taking a look around inside Lennon-Diversified, but they're closed today in memory of Joseph Lennon."

"What do you expect to find?"

"I'm not sure, but the company was investigated for fraud in the past, and I have a feeling that whatever they were up to then may still be going on."

"What kind of fraud?"

"That's the problem. I don't know."

"Judge won't grant a search warrant without probable cause. Doesn't sound like you got any."

"I don't suppose the murder itself is

enough reason to justify examining the premises."

"Lennon was killed in back of the building. We could always justify examining the scene of the crime. Don't need a search warrant for that."

"Amos, you're brilliant."

"I am?"

"Is the crime scene tape still up?"

"I believe so."

"Any chance you could take me over there?"

"Now, Miz Fletcher, I'm not going to get in trouble with the sheriff, am I?"

"We'd only be going to take a look at the scene of the crime. What could he object to?"

"I guess he wouldn't mind. I could tell him you had some ideas about the murder. You're pretty good at comin' up with new ideas."

"Thank you, Amos."

He pushed himself up from the desk, tucked his book in a pocket, wrote out a note for Mort, and instructed the other deputy to be sure to give it to the sheriff when he returned from the hospital. Outside, Amos escorted me to an unmarked car and held open the front passenger door. "I hope I'm not going to regret this," he said.

Amos pulled into a space in the parking lot that served both Lennon-Diversified and the town park that the company's owner had given to Cabot Cove. There were several cars in the lot, and I noticed some people flinging a Frisbee on the greensward that had held the hundreds who'd come to watch the fireworks, courtesy of Joseph Lennon. It was a pleasantly warm afternoon, but I could feel humidity creeping in, a harbinger of the heat wave to come. We walked down the hill toward the cement footpath that wound around the building. I trotted to the front entrance and tried to open the door. It was locked. I cupped my hands over my eyes and leaned against the glass to see into the atrium. Sunlight filtered down from above. The hall was empty. The security guard was not on duty.

"We're not goin' inside," Amos said when I rejoined him on the path that led around the side of the building with the loading dock and to the back.

"Doesn't look like we could if we wanted to," I said. "Let's take a look at the crime scene and see if anything strikes us."

The yellow tape the officers had put up the night of the murder still circled the veranda and part of the promenade and dock where Joseph Lennon had been shot. Fluttering in the warm breeze, the tape was intact except at one corner of the building, where either it had broken away or someone had pulled it down; the free end lay curled on the stone blocks like a yellow snake. We walked through the gap, across the veranda, and down the steps toward the water. Dark stains on the dock showed where Lennon might have been positioned when the bullet hit him in the head, knocking him backward into the bay, and where his body had been dragged from the water back onto the dock before being carried away by the medical team.

If Rick's gun was the murder weapon, it strongly suggested premeditation. Lennon had died instantly. The autopsy hadn't shown any water in his lungs, which would have been there if he was still alive when he sank into the cold water. How clever the killer was to wait for a fireworks display to cover the murder. No one had heard anything, and no one had seen anything. Had there been an argument? Or had the assailant sneaked up behind Lennon as he watched the fireworks from the water-front, calling out his name at the last minute to cause the victim to turn in the killer's direction?

I pivoted at the end of the dock to take in the view of the Lennon building. It was a sleek marble block with a steel door that would likely allow employees to step out onto the veranda without having to exit from the front entrance. An addition jutted out on the right side of the building. A door on that side led to the office of Dr. Boyle. On the day of my appointment with him, I had left Lennon-Diversified and had walked around the outside of the building to get there.

"Seen enough, Miz Fletcher?" Amos said.

"I suppose."

We walked up the dock toward the building. I went straight to the steel door and tugged on the handle. It didn't budge.

"Locked," I said to Amos.

"Good! Ready to leave, Miz Fletcher?"

"Let's go this way," I said, "so we can see the other side of the building."

"Don't see how that's going to make any difference, but if you insist."

"Lennon-Diversified is closed today," I said. "I wonder if that means Dr. Boyle's office is also closed."

"Could be. It's Wednesday," Amos said, catching up with me as I strode along the rear of the building toward the doctor's office. "Lots of doctors close their offices on Wednesday. In Kentucky, it's hard to get time on the golf courses on Wednesdays."

We rounded the corner and walked up to the door leading to Boyle's practice. A sign on the glass said the office was closed for the day. Nevertheless, I pulled on the handle. To my amazement and Amos's consternation, the door was unlocked. I held it open for Amos.

"Now, Miz Fletcher, you said you were satisfied just seeing the crime scene. The sign says they're closed. No need to be goin' in and disturbing the place."

"You can wait in the car if you prefer, Amos. I won't be long. I'm just going to see if Dr. Boyle is in. I have one or two questions for him."

"I think I'll do just that," he said, patting the pocket that held his book. "But if you're not out in ten minutes, I'm comin' in after you."

"I won't keep you that long," I said.

The lights were out in the reception area, but the interior door to the examining rooms was unlocked. I walked down the carpeted hallway and called out Dr. Boyle's name. No answer. Dr. Boyle's office was dark and unoccupied. I flipped the wall switch on. His desk was clear, no stacks of files, or X-rays on the light box, or other materials to indicate he was working on what should have been his day off. I turned off the light and continued down the hall to the large area housing his diagnostic equipment. There were no windows in this space, and only the barest light filtered in to reflect off the large machines. Tiny spots of green and red on operating panels gave minimal illumination in the glass-enclosed computer room that overlooked the space. I squinted, waiting for my eyes to adjust to the gloom. It was here that I'd seen Dr. Boyle speaking with the woman who might have been Mrs. Lennon or Ms. Welch. She had hurried through a door on the opposite side of the room. Since his visitor hadn't come in through the front door and reception area, either she was already on the premises— perhaps working in a back room—or there was a connection from his office to the main building. I skirted the equipment, putting my hand up to keep from banging my head on a large metal arm that jutted out from its side. It swung out of the way.

The door I'd seen her go through was steel, like the one that led to the veranda in the back of Lennon-Diversified. Wouldn't it be ironic if I'd walked all the way through Dr. Boyle's office only to end up outside at the back of the building? *Amos would be happy about that,* I thought. I turned around and tried to re-create in my mind the directions I'd taken since entering Dr. Boyle's practice. I'd come in on the side of the building and walked straight through the door from reception. The new dermatology suite was to the right; the hallway to the examining rooms and Dr. Boyle's office angled to the left. No, it wasn't possible that this door led to the outside. If my calculations were correct, it would open directly into the back-room operations of Lennon-Diversified.

I put my bag on the floor, turned to face the door, leaned in, and placed my ear against the steel. There was a hum made by some machine, but I didn't hear any voices. I tried the doorknob. It rotated easily in my hand. I took a deep breath and knocked loudly but didn't wait for someone to open the door. I opened it myself.

Bright light left me blinking.

I let the door close behind me and took a step into the room, which was absent of any staff but filled with shipping materials and machinery whose functions were not clear to me. Everything I saw was oversized. There were huge tables piled with cardboard containers and enormous rolls of bubble wrap. Suspended on rods hanging from the ceiling were gigantic spools of clear plastic, the ends dangling. And there were wooden pallets all around me with boxes stacked higher than I was tall, all of them swathed in plastic wrap.

The hum I'd heard through the door came from a small machine, part of a labeling mechanism, or so it appeared. Brown bottles were lined up on a conveyor belt, and a roll of self-stick labels was arranged so that as the next bottle moved forward, the new label would be applied. The machine had stopped, but the motor was still running. Next to the machine was a vat of clear liquid—it looked like water—in which sealed bottles of pills were submerged. The liquid had dissolved the glue that held the labels on—apparently its purpose. A large trash bin lined in plastic held a soggy mass of labels. I plucked one from the bin and put on my glasses so I could read the silver and red label. It said LD CHLOROQUINE. I assumed the "LD" stood for "Lennon-Diversified." Seth had said chloroquine was an antimalarial drug. I couldn't reach the roll of new labels on the machine to see what they said, but a search around the mechanism yielded the same sealed bottles in an open box. A different label had been affixed to these. It read simply LD ANTIMALARIAL. *They're relabeling the bottles—but why?*

The sound of a conversation drifted in to me from somewhere, the voices becoming louder as the people approached the room. There wasn't time to retreat through the door I'd used. Instead, I ducked behind a pallet and hoped I wouldn't be seen.

"When's the truck coming?" a man's voice asked.

"Should be here any minute," a woman's voice responded, "but this is absolutely the last shipment. I can't take a chance on getting caught. It's just not worth it."

"Don't be such a worrier, sweetheart. You have a great future ahead of you. We'll take care of the mother and the kid, and you'll be back on top again."

"That's what you said the last time. I'm sorry I got involved with you. You must be mad."

"Don't pull a Miss Innocent act with me. I know all your secrets. I'm not alone in this. You've been with me every step of the way."

"I had no idea what you planned."

"You knew. You just didn't want to acknowledge it. You prefer to do your dirty work from a distance, don't you? But if you want to keep things the way you like it, you have to take action. You weren't unhappy when you thought it was going to benefit you."

"You're the one who was afraid things were going to change. I could have managed him and made it work. I've handled her before, and I could do it again."

"Well, it's too late now, and I'm not going

to lose everything I've worked for. I have a lot invested in this. With them out of the picture, we'll have a lot more leverage. Did you empty out the safe?"

"Yes. They should be on their way to the airport soon. They're flying out at five."

"Good. We just need to load up the pallets and get to Peppino's. I want to be drinking a martini when the news comes in."

A thunderous crash startled me, but my gasp was covered by the deafening noise made by the motorized crank lifting the giant garage doors. There was a loud *clunk* as the doors reached the ceiling, followed by a beeping sound. I peeked around the side of the pallet to see a large truck backing up. Cynthia Welch and her supposed assistant, Dante, watched as the truck nestled closer to the loading dock.

The truck driver and his helper vaulted themselves up onto the dock and began wrestling the first pallet onto the truck. If they intended to take all the pallets, my hiding place would be exposed.

"There are seven altogether," I heard Cynthia say. "These five, and those two over by the green door."

I glanced at the door I'd come through.

It was green. My stomach dropped. I didn't dare look out again. What if they saw me? How could I explain my presence? Warm air from the outside poured in, mixing with the cooled air inside. The air conditioner cycled on, and a cold draft flowed down over me from the register above my hiding place. I shivered. What would happen next? Were they armed? What if Amos blundered in? He'd said he would come after me if I wasn't back in ten minutes. How long had I been here? I looked at my watch. It was far longer than ten minutes. I was in trouble now.

"Okay, only two more pallets left."

Chapter Nineteen

"Hey, lady, we don't have enough room for those last two pallets."

"Are you sure?" Cynthia asked.

"Nonsense! I'm sure you can fit them in," said Dante.

"Look, man, I'm only the truck driver. Come see for yourselves."

Never had more welcome words been spoken. I was crouched behind the pallet farthest from the door. Praying that they were gathered around the back of the truck, I scooted over to the other pallet. My heart pounded. I stuck my head out to see where they were. Dante had climbed into the back of the truck and was directing the driver and his assistant on how to rearrange their load. Cynthia Welch, her arms crossed and foot tapping, watched the proceedings.

Keeping my eyes on their backs, I inched over to the green door, felt for the knob and pulled, opening a space just wide enough for me to slip through. Once inside, I held on to the door and closed it gently to keep it from slamming shut and alerting Dante and Welch to my presence. Then I grabbed my bag that I'd left on the floor and hastened through the doctor's office, out his front door, and up the hill to the parking lot. I flung myself into the passenger seat of Amos's car. "We've got to get to the airport," I said, breathing heavily.

Amos didn't look up from his book. "I'm almost to the end of the chapter," he said.

"Amos," I said, trying to catch my breath, "please put down the book. We have to go. Right now. The airport."

"All right," he said, a disgusted look on his face. "But I don't see what can't wait two paragraphs. The shark was just about to strike."

"We have to get to the airport right away.

I think a bomb has been planted on the Lennon-Diversified plane, and we've got to stop it from taking off."

"Well, why didn't you say so?" He threw the book into the backseat, started the engine, and pulled out of the lot in front of the truck that was lumbering up the hill from the loading dock.

"Wait! Slow down. I want to get the number of that truck." I released my seat belt, twisted around, and held on to the headrest, trying to see the numbers on the license plate.

"Make up your mind, Miz Fletcher. First you tell me to get to the airport as fast as I can, and now you're telling me to slow down. Which is it?"

"Both," I said, plunging my hand into my bag and groping for a pen. "Got it!" I slumped back in my seat. "Now, let's get to the airport." I scribbled down the truck's identification and snapped my seat belt into place.

Amos radioed Mort as we got on the highway to the airport.

"I'm in the patrol car," Mort said. "I was just about to drive out to Lennon-Diversified. Did Mrs. F come up with anything new?"

"Yup, she thinks there might be a bomb on the company plane. We're on our way to the airport."

"I'll meet you there," Mort said. We heard his siren over the radio, and soon heard it in person.

"Darn rental car wasn't made for speed," Amos said as Mort's cruiser passed us on the road. "I've got my foot to the floor."

I rummaged in my bag for my cell phone and dialed Jed Richardson. "Jed, it's Jessica. Has the Lennon-Diversified plane taken off yet?"

"Not yet. Mrs. Lennon and her son and daughter were a little late getting here. But I think they're aboard now."

"Jed, you have to keep that plane from taking off."

"You're breaking up, Jess. Could you repeat that?"

"Don't let that plane take off," I shouted into the phone. "Can you hear me?"

"Did you say not to let the plane take off?"

"Yes! Stop the plane. It can't take off."

"How am I supposed to do that, Jessica? They're already taxiing to the end of the runway."

"Jed! There's a bomb on board."

"You're breaking up again, Jess. Oh, looks like the police are here." The line went dead.

"Take that next right," I instructed Amos.

"But, Miz Fletcher, the airport exit is another half mile."

"This road goes to the end of the runway," I said, pointing. "Please. Hurry!"

Amos followed my directions, and we bumped over the unpaved road, reaching the far end of the runway. I could see the headlights of the Lennon company Gulfstream as it rounded the turn to take its place at the head of the runway. The whine of the engines reached our ears as the pilots revved them up in preparation for takeoff.

"Keep going!"

"There's no more road, Miz Fletcher, just grass."

"If you cross this section, you'll be right on the runway."

"But what if the plane takes off? They'll crush us."

"They should be able to see us. The only way we can keep them on the ground is to block their way. If you put your hazard lights on, that will help."

Amos pushed the button, and the front and back lights flashed on and off. We bounced over the grassy lane and skidded onto the tarmac. Then, racing along the side of the blacktop, we put our arms out the windows and waved them at the plane. Amos pressed his hand down on the horn, an ineffectual signal. It would never be heard over the aircraft's engines.

We saw Mort's cruiser off to the right, the red light spinning on the roof, siren screaming. He was trying to catch up to the plane. Not far behind him was Jed's red truck, horn blaring.

The jet started forward, picking up speed.

"Amos, pull in front of the plane. They'll have to stop."

"Miz Fletcher, if I live through this, I'll never complain about my quiet life again."

Amos jammed on the brakes and pulled the wheel sharply to the left. The car spun around and landed squarely in the path of the oncoming plane. We jumped out, waving our arms in the air, and ran to the side of the runway. If the plane hit the car, it would be totaled, along with the plane and the people in it. I saw the pilots gesticulating inside the cockpit as they managed to swerve to avoid hitting the car. The wind coming off the wings nearly knocked us down. I heard them reverse the engines. The tires shrieked as pressure was applied and rubber was left on the runway. But the plane came to a stop just before the blacktop ended and the grass began.

Mort's patrol car sped by us, Jed in close pursuit, and they pulled up next to the plane.

Amos and I got back in the car and drove to where the Gulfstream sat. The stairway had already been lowered and the captain came out of the plane yelling, his fist in the air. "What in blazes are you crazy people doing? You almost killed all of us."

"Get everyone off the plane," Mort yelled. "Right now."

"What is going on?" Mrs. Lennon stood in the doorway, her son and daughter looking over her shoulder.

"Now!" Mort yelled. "Hurry up. Get down here. Get in the car."

"You'd better have a good explanation

for this, Sheriff," Mrs. Lennon said, taking her time on the stairs. "Paul, call our lawyer. I want him here now."

"Move!" Mort shouted.

"I'm going as fast as I can," she said. "It's not easy to walk down these stairs in high heels."

Mort opened the rear door of the cruiser and waved Denise and her children in.

"Are we under arrest?" Paul asked.

"No time for questions," Mort said. To Jed, "Get that other pilot into your truck and drive the two of them back to the office. I'll meet you there."

Amos and I stood behind the open doors of his car. Mort jogged past us, and did an about-face at the last minute. "You'd better be right, Mrs. F, or we'll be in for a major lawsuit. My job won't be worth a dime if I stopped a private plane from taking off for no good reason."

I climbed in Amos's rental car and breathed a sigh of relief. He turned the car around and drove slowly away from the Gulfsteam. The sleek jet sat at the end of the runway, its engines off but lights on, the stairway hanging out of its side like a gaping wound.

"Miz Fletcher? Are you okay?"

"I'm fine. Thank you, Amos. You did a splendid job."

"Just so you're okay."

We followed Mort's patrol car and Jed's red truck up the runway. Because we were the last car in the procession, we were the first vehicle to feel the tremor when the Lennon-Diversified Gulfstream exploded, shooting flames a thousand feet into the air, the blast breaking windows in the airport office and, as I later learned, the reverberation heard in houses as much as a mile away. The smell of burning jet fuel filled the approaching night, the conflagration eerily illuminating, then scorching, the surrounding landscape. Our three vehicles rushed to shelter behind the airport hangars to escape the pieces of burning debris that floated down.

I can't say exactly how long it took, but the response of the Cabot Cove Volunteer Fire Department was swift and professional. Mort called in two more deputies and left Jed at the airport to supervise the cleanup in his office. The rest of us drove into town to sort out the events.

Only four days ago, Joseph Lennon had

been murdered while the fireworks he so generously financed marked the celebration of our nation's birth and thrilled the spectators in his adopted hometown with brilliant flashes of color lighting the night sky. A different spectacular explosion almost took the lives of his wife and children, as well as the pilot and copilot. Thankfully, they all escaped harm. Now it was time to bring those responsible for the murder and the attempted murder to justice.

Chapter Twenty

The sheriff's office was jammed with people, all talking at the same time, most of them on cell phones, some voices louder than others, trying to be heard over the insistent ringing of the telephones. Mort hunted around for extra chairs while Amos called Charlene Sassi at her bakery and asked her to send over coffee and dough- nuts. Mrs. Lennon, insisting she was fine, had collapsed in Mort's desk chair and was being tended to by the Cabot Cove EMS unit. Her son was on his cell phone, calling family members to report what had happened. The pilots were giving their version of the incident to the deputies. And Evelyn Phillips, who'd sent her photographer to the airport, paused in her interview with Josie Lennon to take a picture of the girl's mother with a cell phone.

Mort surveyed the scene, debating where to start, and I tapped him on the shoulder. "Mort, we need to talk," I said.

"Boy, Mrs. F. You sure called it this time. Incredible! How'd you do it?"

"I happened to be at the airport when the package was delivered to the pilots. It was directed to Mrs. Lennon, but had no return name or address. You may want to speak with Ronnie, who brought it in, but I think I already know who sent it. We should get over to Peppino's before they leave."

"Peppino's?" Mort said. "The bomber is at Peppino's?"

For a moment, all talk stopped. It was as if someone had turned down the volume on the TV. Then the room erupted noisily.

"You're not arresting anyone without me there," Mrs. Lennon said, pushing away the medical technician who was trying to take her blood pressure. "I have a right to know what's been going on. Is this the person who killed my husband?"

Evelyn Phillips used her cell to order her photographer back from the airport. "Meet me at Peppino's," she told him.

"C'mon, Mrs. F," Mort said. "You can tell me more on the way over." He ordered everyone to stay put. "Deputy Tupper, you're in charge."

Amos stepped in front of the door after Mort escorted me through. "Now, folks. I want you all to calm down," I heard him say. "We have Sassi's doughnuts coming, should be here any minute now." But he may as well have been speaking to a room full of moose, for all they listened to him. They bullied past Amos, squeezing through the door and dispersing to various cars. He threw up his hands and jumped in the back of Mort's car. "Thought you might need my help, Sheriff."

Joe DiScala was startled to see such a big group crowding into his restaurant. "Do you all have reservations?" he asked.

"We're not staying," Mort said. "I just want to speak with two of your patrons." He pulled me into the dining room, and I pointed out Cynthia Welch and Dante at a corner table. They were sipping drinks and seemed in good spirits. When Ms. Welch looked up at the commotion in the entry, her smile died away and her face paled. Dante's expression became somber, the light fading from his eyes.

Mort wound his way through the tables, with me close behind, and positioned himself in front of theirs. Amos had succeeded in keeping the others from following Mort into the dining room, but every customer was aware of our presence. They stopped eating and talking to stare at the drama unfolding in the corner.

"Unless you want to create an even bigger scene," Mort said, "I suggest you come outside with me."

"What is the meaning of this, Officer?" Dante said.

"I'm placing you both under arrest."

"What for?"

"A bomb went off tonight," Mort said, "and if not for quick action on Mrs. Fletcher's part, five people would have been killed."

"What has that got to do with us?" Dante asked.

"We think you planted the bomb."

"That's ridiculous," Cynthia said. "We're

businesspeople, not terrorists. I think you're going to find yourself very embarrassed, Sheriff. How would we know anything about bombs, anyway?"

"If we take a look at Dante's military experience," I said, "I expect we'll find the answer there. The fireworks people were complimentary about the Lennon company's 'very knowledgeable' staff. Soldiers working in the ordnance division become very familiar with explosive devices, don't they, Dante?"

"I don't have anything to say to you."

"Are you ready to go?" Mort asked.

"Wait a minute. Just what are the charges?" Cynthia said, her back rigid.

"We can start with conspiracy to commit murder," Mort told her. "Then we can add reckless endangerment and malicious destruction of property. How about using a destructive device in a crime of violence? I'm sure I can think up at least thirty or forty more counts, ending with premeditated homicide."

"You have no proof," Dante said.

"Who did we kill?" she said. "Look, everyone there is alive." She pointed to Mrs. Lennon and her children, who were watching from behind Amos's back together with the pilots, the EMTs, and the *Gazette* editor and photographer.

"Shut up, Cynthia," Dante said.

"The sheriff didn't say whom you *meant* to kill," I said. "But you just pointed out your intended victims. How would you know who they were if you weren't in on the plot?"

"What plot? There was no plot."

"Mrs. Fletcher will testify that she overheard you scheming to place a bomb on the plane that was supposed to take Mrs. Lennon and her children to Vancouver."

I wouldn't be able to do that, of course. The discussion I'd eavesdropped on hadn't been specific enough for any charges to stick, but they didn't know what I knew. Mort was taking a chance, but it turned out to be a good one.

"That should be enough to send you away for a long time," Mort said.

"I had nothing to do with the bomb," Cynthia said, rising. "It was him. He planned it. He sent it to the plane. I never knew it was taking place until it was all over."

"Shut up, Cynthia," her companion said,

grabbing her arm and pressing her back down into her seat.

"But you made no effort to stop him, did you? Even after you knew he'd killed Joseph Lennon to ensure your place in the company."

"Don't answer him, Cynthia," Dante ordered. "I want a lawyer," he said to Mort. "And we're not saying another word till we get one."

"Ms. Welch, you have an opportunity to save yourself from additional charges if you cooperate," I said. "The authorities already know that Dante stole the gun used in the murder of Joseph Lennon and put it in Chester Carlisle's car to throw suspicion on him." I was bluffing, but I hoped that Mort would let it go. He knew about the missing gun, but until now not who had taken it.

Cynthia looked at Dante. "I'm not going to jail for the rest of my life because of you."

"You bi—" Dante launched himself across the table at Cynthia and wrapped his hands around her neck. Mort gripped his arms but was unable to break the hold. Pandemonium broke out in the restaurant as other patrons left their seats, attempting to assist Mort. Amos tried to reach him but had to clear others out of the way. The man at the next table grabbed Dante by the waist and pulled, tumbling backward and sending a platter of spaghetti and meat sauce flying over the combatants before they were able to muscle Dante to the floor. Cynthia fell back into her seat, coughing and gasping, holding her neck. Red wheals were starting to rise where Dante had dug his fingers into her flesh.

"Am I bleeding?" she asked, staring down at the red stains on her suit jacket. "Did he stab me?"

"That's just spaghetti sauce," Mort said as he cuffed Dante with Amos's help. "Your boyfriend over here has matching decorations." Mort hustled Dante through the restaurant, to a standing ovation from the diners.

Amos took Cynthia Welch's arm and walked her out. Mrs. Lennon stepped in front of her. "After all we did for you," she said bitterly, "this is how you repay us."

"You did nothing for me," Cynthia said. "I made your company the success that it is. Me! Not you. Not Joe. You did nothing except collect the money and then order the board to drop me when you wanted your little boy to take the position that should have been mine. I earned it. I deserved it. And it would have been mine if you hadn't interfered."

"How naive can you be? That's business," Mrs. Lennon said. "It's not your company just because you worked there. You didn't own it. We did. We paid you for your services, paid you well, and you betrayed our trust. I told Joseph you were wrong for the position. I was right. And I was right to choose Paul to take over. At least I can trust him."

Not exactly a ringing endorsement of your son, I thought, but I didn't say anything.

Amos asked Denise to step aside so he could escort Cynthia to the squad car.

"Wait! Wait!" The restaurant owner hurried after us, waving his bill in the air. "Who's going to pay for their dinner? They had drinks and wine and the most expensive dishes."

"I'm certainly not paying for their food," Mrs. Lennon said. "They won't get another dime from the Lennon family." She put her arms around her children and walked out.

"Put it on my tab, Joe," said a man wiping spaghetti and sauce off his shirtfront. He'd been seated at the table next to the conspirators and had helped to subdue Dante. He grinned at me. "I'll pay for their dinner," he said. "I told the wife this was the most excitement I've had since coming to Cabot Cove."

Chapter Twenty-one

"Dr. Boyle testified before the FDA on behalf of Lennon-Diversified some years back, and after that the investigation was dropped. Then Boyle turns up in Cabot Cove with a ready-made practice financed by Lennon-Diversified. I knew they were paying him off. I just couldn't let that go."

Rick Allcott was looking much better than the last time we'd seen him, both Mort and I agreed. But Seth was not yet ready to let him leave the hospital.

"Do you have anything on Boyle now?" Seth asked. He was looking at his watch while he took Rick's pulse.

"We're still working on it," Rick answered. "We think he's involved with their latest scam."

"What scam is that?" Seth asked.

"The one Jessica uncovered."

Seth raised his eyebrows and peered over his glasses in my direction.

"While I was visiting Mrs. Lennon, Cynthia arrived," I said. "She said they had contracts for their new drug, and also that she had a way to get rid of the old one. She'd made a deal with a charity group to 'unload' it—I think that's the word she used—at their refugee camps. The camps would never take it if they knew what drug it was. So Cynthia's solution was to disguise the truth. She and Dante were relabeling the old drug and passing it off as a new antimalarial."

"Was the old medicine no good?" Mort asked from where he stood leaning against the wall.

"It's not that it's no good," Seth said. "It's that in many parts of Africa, it's no longer effective against the most common strains of malaria."

"Which means those folks could die if they didn't get the right drug," Mort said.

"Pretty low to victimize sick people like that."

"You know why she chose refugee camps, don't you?" Rick said.

"Ayuh," Seth said. "Apparently the Lennon people didn't think anyone would point to the drugs as a problem, since refugee camps are notorious for epidemics of myriad diseases. So many die anyway. No one would suspect it was because of an ineffective drug."

"Yet Mrs. Lennon knew something was up," I said. "She challenged Cynthia, saying someone in Harare had complained about drugs they'd sent before. Cynthia said it couldn't be helped if some people had a strain of the disease that developed a resistance to the drug. What she didn't say was that that resistance is already widespread."

"She and Dante probably figured the company would be hailed as a good Samaritan and could take a hefty tax deduction for the donation, making her look like a marketing genius, right?" Mort said.

"You hit it on the nose, Sheriff," Rick said. "She's been boosting profits in questionable ways for a long time."

"Mrs. F gave us the license number of the truck," Mort said. "We sent it on to the FBI so they can track down its cargo and make sure it never reaches that destination."

"We at the bureau think it was Boyle who came up with the idea in the first place, but I don't have any proof yet."

"It could be," I said. "He accompanied Cynthia to Africa on one trip."

"How do you know that?"

"Boyle's picture was in the *Cabot Cove Gazette*. The pilots recognized him, said that he'd hitched a ride with her to Zimbabwe."

"That's helpful to know," Rick said, smiling at me.

"What's going to happen to Lennon-Diversified?" Mort asked. "Is the town going to get left with an abandoned building down at the water?"

"I don't think Denise Lennon gives up that easily," I said. "She wants her son, Paul, to take over the company. They have a lot of fences to mend now, but I'm betting she'll stay."

"Don't forget, the bureau is going to want to know how much she and Paul were aware of what was going on in their shipping room," Rick said. "So she's not off the hook just yet."

"Speaking of the bureau," Mort said, "I spoke with the district attorney and he said you'll have to wait until the trial is over, but there's a good chance you'll be able to get your gun back."

"That's a relief. Made me look like a fool to have to report to my supervisor that it was stolen. Maybe I'll get back a little street cred if I can say it's been recovered." He leaned back against the pillow. "Would you gentlemen mind if I spoke with Mrs. Fletcher privately?"

"Not at all," Seth said. "I'll give you five minutes, and then all visitors must go. You're not a well man yet. But we'll get you there."

"If anyone can, it's you, Doc," Rick said.

Mort and Seth left the room, closing the door behind them.

"Jessica, I've been thinking a lot about this, and I want to get it off my chest."

"What is it, Rick?"

"You were right. And I was wrong. I wasn't straight with you and I feel bad about that. I'm sorry I lied to you, Jessica. Or at least that I wasn't completely truthful."

"You were working on the case," I said. "I should have understood and not pressured you. I'm sorry about that."

"You're being very gracious, but it's I who should have trusted you. What you found out—the information you were able to uncover—will go a long way toward wrapping up this matter for the bureau."

"Thank you, Rick. That's very kind of you to say."

"No thanks are necessary. We need to finish with Lennon-Diversified, and it looks to me as if you've made it possible. Besides, I'd like to get back to being retired."

"And go see the Red Sox play at Fenway Park," I added.

"That, too," he said, laughing. "Maybe you'll join me for a game."

"I'd like that."

Amos lifted his suitcase and placed it in the trunk of his rental car. "Havin' dinner with a couple of old friends in Boston tonight, and I've got a flight out tomorrow first thing. Lookin' forward to gettin' home, and I hear the temperature in Kentucky is cooler than Cabot Cove right now."

"It was great seeing you, Amos," Mort said. "Anytime you miss police work, you're welcome to come up here and be my deputy. I'll be proud to work with you."

"I don't think I'll be missing the action as much as I did before," Amos said. "Miz Fletcher took care of that. I've had enough stimulation to last me twenty or thirty years, I'd say."

We laughed, and I gave him a hug. Seth held the driver's door open and Amos climbed in. "Be seein' you again sometime," he said. "Tell Charlene Sassi thanks for the doughnuts." He patted the box on the passenger seat and drove off, the three of us waving till his car was out of sight.

I sighed. "It was nice having him back for a little while. Now I'll miss him all over again."

We walked slowly toward Seth's car and Mort's cruiser.

"By the way, Mrs. F, I got a note from Denise Lennon about you."

"You did?"

"She wants to know what to do with the fifty-thousand-dollar reward for the person responsible for the arrest of her husband's murderer. She says you turned it down."

"I don't want to be singled out. It was a group effort. We all worked on finding Joseph Lennon's killer."

"I think someone had better accept it," Seth said.

"Now why would you say that?"

"With her husband gone and Mrs. Lennon focusing on teaching her son the business, I doubt we'll have Lennon-Diversified financing the next Independence Day celebration."

"And a good thing that is," I said. "I think the town should appoint Chester Carlisle to chair the committee for the next Fourth of July. He needs something to keep him busy and make him feel important. He had enough to say about this year's event. Let's see if he can do better."

"Good thinking, Mrs. F. Maybe I'll just tell Mrs. Lennon to give the money to the committee. They can bank it and make it last for years."

"I'd like to see Chester's face when Denise Lennon gives the committee the money with no strings attached," I said.

"Speaking of Chester," Mort said, "he

told me he had given Dante a T-shirt for free. He did it as a joke, but it really backfired on him."

"That it did," Seth said.

"What's he going to do with all those T-shirts now?" I asked.

"He says he doesn't want to sell them to anyone in Cabot Cove," Mort replied, "but I heard he put an ad up on eBay." Mort got in his car. He rolled down the window. "Whew! This car got hot fast." He turned on the air conditioner. "Did you know they sentenced that kid that attempted to mug you?"

"I knew it was coming up," Seth said. "What did they give him?"

"He has to go through rehab for a month and then he'll be on probation for five years."

"Sounds fair," Seth said.

"He would have been on his way to prison if you hadn't testified on his behalf."

"Hate to see someone so young being sent to jail. He was genuinely remorseful, and fortunately for all of us, he did no permanent damage."

"You're a good guy, Doc."

"Yes, he is," I said.

"I gotta be on my way," Mort said. "Maureen wants me to pick up some groceries at the market. She's trying out a new recipe she saw on TV." Mort's expression was pained. "But nice to have the town back to normal, huh, folks?"

"Is the town back to normal?" I asked Seth when Mort had gone.

"What's that cryptic comment supposed to mean?"

"You know exactly what I'm talking about, Seth." I took his arm and we walked toward his car. "You were thinking about hiring a company to come in and sell your practice. Is that still your intention?"

"Madam, you will be happy to hear that I canceled that appointment."

"Oh, Seth, I *am* happy. What made you change your mind? I know it wasn't my scolding."

"That might have had a slight influence, but I don't want to give you a big head."

"Thanks for that."

"Actually, it was a number of things."

"And are you going to tell me what they are?"

"Mebbe."

"Seth!"

"All right, woman. You have no patience."

"I know what the first thing was."

"And what's that? You're already stealing my thunder."

"No one could do that. But when you diagnosed Rick Allcott with malaria when everyone else thought it was the flu, I had a feeling that gave you a nice jolt of confidence."

"Much as I hate to admit it, you wouldn't be wrong. Made me think there's some life in the old man yet—and that a lifetime of experience comes in handy."

"It certainly does. What else?"

"You know that day you brought Rick's card to the emergency room?"

"Yes, I remember."

"I told you I had a couple of other patients come in. Well, one of them was Agnes Kalisch."

"Is she all right?"

"Not yet, but she will be. She'd called the office and Harriet told her I was over at the hospital, and she followed me there. Said Dr. Boyle's pills weren't doing her any good, and she wanted me to do the tests I'd proposed."

"I'm so glad she recognized that you were the right doctor for her."

He harrumphed, a bit embarrassed, but I knew he was pleased.

"Can't tell you what the diagnosis is," Seth said. "That would be a breach of patient privacy, but suffice it to say she has what I suspected it might be, and we'll be starting treatment soon."

"You may be protecting her patient confidentiality," I said, "but I met Agnes at the bakery this morning and she was telling everyone who would listen that she has a rare disease that only twelve people in a million get and that Seth Hazlitt is a brilliant doctor."

"You don't say?"

"I do. She even wrote down the name of the disease for me." I fished in my pocket and drew out a slip of paper. "Waldenström's macroglobulinemia."

"That's it, all right."

"It's cancer, isn't it?"

"Of a kind, yes. And it's incurable. But the good thing is it's usually indolent. That means it's slow to progress. Right now, she needs treatment, but once we've gotten over the hump, she could live a long and fruitful life. We'll just have to see."

"She's lucky to have you as her doctor."

"Mebbe."

"And I'm lucky to have you as my friend."

"I agree with that," he said. "And now I have an important question to ask you."

"You do?"

"Yes." He looked at me very seriously and said, "Do you have any of that coffee ice cream left?"

I looked up at the sky as if I were pondering the answer and replied, "If you drive me home, I might be able to find some."

"Well, what are we waiting for?"